DEAD OR ALIVE

DEAD OR ALIVE

Ken McCoy

This first world edition published 2016
in Great Britain and the USA by
SEVERN HOUSE PUBLISHERS LTD of
19 Cedar Road, Sutton, Surrey, England, SM2 5DA.
Trade paperback edition first published
in Great Britain and the USA 2016 by
SEVERN HOUSE PUBLISHERS LTD

British Library Cataloguing in Publication Data
A CIP catalogue record for this title is available from the British Library.

ISBN-13: 978-0-7278-8633-0 (cased)
ISBN-13: 978-1-84751-738-8 (trade paper)
ISBN-13: 978-1-78010-802-5 (e-book)

Typeset by Palimpsest Book Production Ltd.,
Falkirk, Stirlingshire, Scotland.

To Erin, Travis and Noah

ONE

1 March

The Italian's heart rate quickened when he heard them coming. Many a heart would have ground to a dead halt under such circumstances, but not his heart. He was almost certain that he would be dead within minutes but there was sufficient uncertainty to confirm, in his mind anyway, that it would not be suicide. That would be against his Catholic religion and would guarantee him a one-way ticket to Hell. Taking a life is a mortal sin, even if it's your own life. He looked up to heaven and murmured what he hoped would be a final prayer – the Confiteor. He said it in Latin as he thought that might give him an edge when he arrived at the Pearly Gates. Every man needs an edge, even a dead man.

'*Confiteor Deo omnipotenti, beatae Mariae semper Virgini, beato Michaeli Archangelo, beato Ioanni Baptistae . . .*'

His voice was quiet and unheard by the two men approaching him. They were the type of men who had street names – Spud and Sharky. They were both in their forties, medium height and medium build, but they weren't medium men; Sharky was black English, Spud was ginger Irish and they were hitmen of considerable aptitude. Such aptitude was essential in men who worked for Vincent Formosa.

They were to meet the Italian in Adel Woods because the Italian knew the area. He had a cousin who lived nearby and, as boys, they had played together on a disused aqueduct called the Seven Arches. It was at the Seven Arches that he had arranged to hand over the "goods", as he called them. The "goods" comprised of a velvet bag containing half a million pounds worth of diamonds for which he was being paid one hundred thousand in cash. It was raining and the footpath was a mass of leaf mould clinging to their footwear. Spud wasn't happy.

'Jesus, man! This is an arsehole of a place. Couldn't we meet him somewhere a bit more pleasant – like a public shithouse?'

'We's meetin' here because there is never no people around here,' said Sharky.

'I never knew it'd be rainin' or I wouldn't have come.'

'Yes yer would, because Vince told yer ter come.'

'Yer tink I'm scared o' Vince?' said Spud.

'Any man who's not scared o' Vince is a dead man.'

Spud didn't argue because Sharky was right. They trudged on until the arches of the stone bridge across the wooded valley came into view through the trees. At one end stood a man they assumed must be the Italian. He was a small, monochrome man; pale-faced, wearing a long dark raincoat and standing initially under a black homburg hat and then a black and white golf umbrella with a Nike logo. All this fitted the description they had been given. They hadn't been given his name, nor he theirs. Just a form of greeting. He saw them and made no sign of recognition, nor did they. As they got closer the man called out without looking their way.

'Is this bridge safe?'

'It hasn't fallen down in a hundred and seventy four years.'

'Then we must hope it survives for another twelve minutes.'

'We must definitely hope so.'

The Italian turned to look at the two approaching men. Sharky called out to him.

'So, you're the fucking Eyetie are you?'

'Yes. So you're the fucking nigger are you?'

This last exchange wasn't part of the coded greetings which had already been done to their mutual satisfaction. The Italian's words were more offensive than his manner, which was mild. Sharky was offended, but not Spud, who wasn't here to make friends. The man was carrying a large, leather briefcase. He placed it on the stone bridge which, where they stood, was no more than waist-high from the ground. From the briefcase he took out a black velvet bag. Spud and Sharky joined him, one either side.

'Them the sparklers?' asked Spud.

'Diamonds,' said the Italian who looked as if he hadn't smiled in his life. He looked all around to check no one was about, then, using the bridge as a table, he placed a black velvet square on a stone slab and emptied the contents of the bag on to it. Even in the dull, damp light the diamonds glittered. The Italian sheltered them with the umbrella.

'All we know is to count them,' said Sharky. 'We ain't got no eye-glass or nuthin'. If they ain't the right diamonds you is a dead man.'

'Do not fucking insult me, the diamonds are good,' said the Italian. Once again his words were harsh but his voice was quiet. 'You count them, I count the money.'

'I ain't waiting around in this pissin' rain fer you ter count out a hundred grand,' grumbled Spud, placing a Samsonite suitcase beside the diamonds and opening it. It was full of what looked like bundles of fifties, all used notes.

'I have machine to count the money.' The Italian took a money-counter from his case and moved the umbrella to shelter the money, the counter and the jewels. He added, 'You will please hold the umbrella for me.' His voice was faint and barely audible.

'What?'

'You will please hold the umbrella.'

Sharky took the umbrella as the Irishman began counting the diamonds. By the time the Italian had organized himself to start counting the money Spud had already finished. 'Fifty two,' he said to Sharky, 'one for every week of the year.'

'All correct then,' said Sharky, looking around him to check for unwanted witnesses to their dealings.

'There won't be no one around here in this pissin' rain,' Spud said, pouring the diamonds back into the velvet bag.

The Italian's hand was shaking as he was about to feed the first bundle of notes into the machine. He didn't appear to see Spud take a silenced handgun from his pocket with which he shot the man through the back of his head at point-blank range. The Italian's life ended instantly, before he had the chance to switch on the machine, but not without splattering a few of the notes with blood, brain and bone. What neither of them saw was the acute grimace of anticipation on his face just before he died.

The 9mm bullet made a hole the size of a plum as it exited through his forehead before burying itself in a distant tree. Propelled by the force of the bullet, the Italian's body twisted in a brief danse macabre as it collapsed to the ground.

'That was a good shot for you,' said Sharky, looking down at the body of the Italian whose hat had fallen off, revealing a completely bald head. Sharky held the umbrella aloft, sheltering only him, the money and the diamonds, leaving the Italian at the mercy of the elements. He had landed face upwards with his dead eyes defiantly open against the pouring rain which was washing the blood away from his wound.

'Ye'd have missed at that range,' commented Spud.

Taking the piss was a habit they'd got into after each job. It lightened the mood of the moment for them. Ruthless men as they were, they were only human and they liked a bit of light relief now and again. It was a habit common among psychopaths.

'You took your time about that,' said Sharky.

'I knew what I was doin'.'

'You only just managed to get him before he found out most o' them notes aren't made of money. You fuck about too much sometimes. He called me a fuckin' nigger. Did you hear that? The racist bastard. He wants shootin'.'

'You *are* a fuckin' nigger and we *have* shot him,' Spud pointed out.

'I don't care, it's not fuckin' right, I were born in Barnsley, me. How can I be a nigger if I'm born in Barnsley? Me mother were a Methodist and me dad were a West Yorkshire bus driver. How does that make me a nigger?'

'Shurrup, I'm counting.'

The Irishman counted the splattered fifties. He counted nine. 'That's four hundred and fifty. I bet Vince uses some o' these to pay us out. Will this blood clean off?'

'No idea,' said Sharky. 'If he does they'll all be yours. You made the mess when you shot him. You should have been more careful.'

'Jesus, Sharky! If yer not a fuckin' nigger yer an awful fuckin' gobshite!'

'When's us next job?' asked Sharky.

'I dunno. It's my guess it's gonna be a dissy plin job.'

'Who's bein' dissy plinned?'

'How the fuck do I know? None of us knows anybody else in this crew. All I know is we ain't been asked ter do a dissy plin job fer ages.'

'Could be someone's been given a dissy plin job on us.'

'Why would he wanna dissy plin us?'

'Cos we been with him too long. It's the way these boss guys work. The longer ya with 'em, the more ya know.'

'That's why I don't trust nobody in this crew.'

'One more job and I'm on me toes,' said Sharky.

'If this'd been a real hundred grand I'd have been on me toes already – fifty each.'

'Man I doubt if there's two grand in this case.'

'Which means Vince don't trust us,' Spud pointed out.

'Shit!' said Sharky. 'We is high on the list ter be dissy plinned.'

'One more job an' we're out of it as soon as we're paid,' said Spud.

'Correct. We take the money and run. I know a Fiji island where he won't be able ter find his own arse, never mind us. A man can live like a king on twenty dollars a day.'

'I'm wid yer, man.'

'We could take the diamonds and go now,' suggested Sharky.

'Yeah, but what do we know about sellin' diamonds without Vince finding out and trackin' us down?' said Spud. 'No. We take the diamonds to the man then he'll trust us long enough fer the next job. *Then* we disappear. We'll have done him no harm so why would he track us down?'

'Because he's Vincent Formosa,' said Sharky. 'And he is the world's most evil bastard.'

'One more job then,' said Spud. 'I reckon we can risk one more job.' He held out a hand and they agreed the deal over the dead Italian's body which they dragged under the first of the arches, the lowest of them all. It was choked up with long grass and weeds. They wedged the small man under the narrow angle where the arch met the ground and rearranged the grass and weeds over him. It would be a long time before he was found, which meant it would be a long time before a police investigation was mounted. Then they packed up the two cases and left with both money and diamonds just as they had been instructed by Vincent Formosa, who didn't like parting with money if there was an alternative; and murder, to Formosa, was always an acceptable alternative.

TWO

27 April
Nunroyd Secure Psychiatric Clinic, North Yorkshire

'**D**id you have any sympathy for Cyril Seymour-Johnstone?'

'None whatsoever.'

Professor Jane Gilmartin lit a cigarette and stared down at Sep. 'Do you even know what sympathy is?'

'It's in the dictionary between shit and syphilis.'

Sep stared up at her, trying to detect a rewarding smile for his witty answer. There was none so he asked a question of his own.

'Are you allowed to smoke in here?'

'No.'

'So why are you smoking?'

'Because I make the rules for staff and inmates, not for me.'

'Can't I be a patient instead of an inmate?'

'You can be whatever you like, just as long as you behave yourself.'

'I'll be a doctor then, gimme a cigarette.'

'You don't smoke.'

'I was thinking of starting. It'll be good for my health in this place.'

He'd been in the clinic for two weeks, having taken the alternative offered to him by the magistrates. It was either hand himself over to psychiatric professionals in a secure psychiatric unit until he was safe to be let out, or spend a minimum of three months in prison for threatening behaviour and criminal damage. The latter would have meant him serving his whole sentence in a local dispersal prison, probably HM Prison Armley, in the company of men who would all know he was an ex-copper, which is not a good thing to be in any prison. He might well have arrested some of them himself and they might be somewhat aggrieved over the matter and wish to seek retribution. Prisoners were often like that.

This option might have him back out in a month or so if he behaved himself and proved himself to be no danger to the general public – failure to do so would have him incarcerated indefinitely. Many hardened criminals wouldn't have taken such a risk and would have chosen the fixed-term prison option.

He was sharing a room with three other men, all of whom were bi-polar in varying degrees. Sep hadn't been diagnosed as yet but he knew the drill in these places. All he had to do was act as normal as the staff working there and they'd struggle to find anything wrong with him. He'd told them his story without displaying any paranoia or self-pity, just acceptance of a difficult set of circumstances. They'd tested his memory, his cognitive skills, his behavioural profile and his emotional intelligence. He'd passed these tests with flying colours. They didn't tell him this, but he knew by the mounting frustration on their faces caused by him being at least as normal as they were. Today he was in Professor Gilmartin's office for his first assessment, asking her the killer question he'd prepared earlier.

'You don't really know why I was sent here, do you?'

He was to have weekly sessions with psychiatric professionals but Gilmartin's assessment was the important one. She could pronounce him sane and set him free. He actually liked her. She was fiftyish, overweight and plain, but she was likeable. She had a desk equipped with a computer and two monitors, a telephone and various bits of stuff he didn't recognize, but she chose to loom over him as he reclined on a couch looking up at her. She smiled down at him and said nothing, so Sep answered his own question, just as she knew he would.

'I came here because the alternative was three months in the nick. I came here because I was wondering myself if I was a nutcase who deserved everything that was being thrown at me.'

'I know exactly why you came here,' Gilmartin said. 'It's my job to know such things. So, what's the result of your self-assessment?'

'I'm happy to report that I'm not a nutcase and that I'm safe to be let out on the streets.'

'That's your professional opinion as a doctor, is it?'

'It is, despite the fact that you've surrounded me with genuine nutcases and I've got no idea what goes on in their heads, which brings me to my point: if I was one of them I'd know, wouldn't I?'

'Not necessarily.'

'I think it takes one to know one. I think you're keeping me here in the hope that you can turn me into a genuine nutcase and keep me here forever.'

'And why would I do that?'

'To fill up your quota of nutcases, thereby justifying your existence.' She chose not to answer, so Sep continued. 'I tell myself that you've thrown me a challenge and I've accepted it. Of course there is a limit to how long I'll last before I crack.'

'So you think you might crack?'

'You mean I might have another nervous breakdown? Only an insane man could withstand these conditions which are clearly designed to make us sane guys crack, but I won't because I'm ready for you.'

'I could give you medication for it.'

'I wasn't ordered any medication by the court.'

'It might help.'

Sep held out both hands which were as steady as rocks. 'I'm the only one in this place who can do this without shaking, and as far as I can see I'm the only one in this place not on medication. Professor, with respect, you can stick your medication where the monkey shoves his nuts. I don't want to ever rely on medication. I don't want to end up like that guy in *One Flew Over the Cuckoo's Nest*.'

'You mean McMurphy?'

'That's him.'

'And I suppose I'm Nurse Ratched.'

'I hope not. But if I do have another breakdown, I don't want to blame it on my medication – or lack of it. I want to blame it on you.'

THREE

3 March, 6 weeks earlier
7.30 p.m. Allerton Police Station, Leeds

'The BFB's arrived, sir.'
    'Any problems?'
    'Well, he's a bit overexcited.'
'Really?'
'And he's a big bugger, sir.'
'Yes, I do know that, John. OK, I'm coming through.'

Sep pushed his chair back and got to his feet. The detective constable was speaking to him through the partially open door to his boss's office. He opened it wider so the detective inspector could hear the noise of raised voices. Reception was often unruly on a Friday night, but not this early. This noise wasn't the usual late-night drunks, they'd be along later. This noise came from one man – a man of self-importance who didn't want to be there. Despite his loathing of this man of self-importance, Detective Inspector Septimus Black knew it was his job to make sure he was properly dealt with and not unduly roughed up, as sometimes happened to suspected paedophiles, especially one with such a conclusive and sickening weight of evidence against him. The suspect, Cyril Seymour-Johnstone, aka the Big Fat Bastard, was not only a twenty-five-stone man-mountain but he was also a high-profile member of parliament who assumed that his position in society would afford him respectful treatment. But he'd never been in the care of the West Yorkshire Police before.

'Get your fucking hands off me you shower of shitheads or I'll have your jobs, the lot of you!'

'I think he's had a bit to drink, sir.'

'Well spotted, John.'

Sep had no time at all for the BFB, but it was his job to treat him in a manner that would give the man's lawyers no cause whatsoever to question the legality of his arrest. Johnstone himself had been some sort of legal executive before he'd decided that politics was an easier and surer way to acquire the authority that had always desired. He had a large presence and large mouth with which he made a pretence of defending the working class – or the "lower orders" as he called them behind their backs. Of course when referring to them in public they became the "hard-working voters of this fine city." People whose votes were easy to pick up because they didn't grumble much when all his ridiculous shouting on their behalf came to naught, as it invariably did. They felt themselves lucky to have such a high profile character on their side, and failed to see him as an incompetent, pompous, self-serving fool.

'Calm down, Mr Johnstone. They're only doing their jobs.'

'They should be out on the streets chasing real criminals and my name's *Seymour*-Johnstone.'

Sep ignored this because he wasn't in the habit of pandering to pretentious paedophiles.

'We have good reason to believe you've committed many serious crimes, Mr Johnstone.'

'*Seymour*-Johnstone. Are you deaf?'

'Until these crimes are properly investigated we're required to keep you here, charge you, and present you at magistrates' court on Monday morning.'

'Properly investigated my arse! This is political! This'll be in the Sunday fucking papers, blackening my good name and the name of the party, you twat!'

'Using obscene language at a police officer is an offence and will be added to your charges . . . Johnstone.'

The MP had now lost his "Mr" title. He would never get it back.

'This is all to do with cuts in the police force.'

'I don't believe your party has ever been in power.'

'We have influence, you brainless twat! We can sway the vote. I have influence – influence with the Home Office, to which you lot of fucking wankers will have to answer!'

Sep decided to use his seniority to help deal with this obnoxious man. He stepped forward and took the place of one of his officers. 'Let's take him straight through custody to the cells. We'll leave him there for a few hours until he's sobered up *then* we'll charge him.'

'What? Are you saying I'm pissed?'

'Well, Johnstone, you don't appear to be at your sober best,' said Sep, 'but I'm happy to offer you a breathalyser test and a blood-test, if you wish.'

'Fuck you and your breathalyser! It'll be fixed. I know how you bastards work.'

'I'll take that as your refusal to take a breath or blood test, in which case we'll treat you as a hostile and intoxicated prisoner until we consider you sober enough to be charged.'

Johnstone had the sense to realize he was fighting a losing battle. 'Just one twat please,' he sneered. 'The other twats can let go of me.'

'I'll handle him,' said Sep. 'You two stay close.'

'What is it I'm being accused of, twat?'

Sep was now losing his cool, such as it was. 'I think you know what you're accused of. Having sex with under-age children as young as eight. You were caught in the act by my officers and we have statements from several of your victims. Now kindly do as you're told before I kick you in the bollocks!'

But he said it with such inoffensive equanimity that some of the other officers looked at each other, as if checking that they'd heard him correctly.

'That's ridiculous!' Johnstone was shouting. 'All these people are liars!'

'Would you like us to call your solicitor?' asked Sep. 'If you're as innocent as you say you are, a solicitor will have you out of here in a jiffy; otherwise we're keeping you here until Monday morning when you go to magistrate's court.'

'You can't keep me 'til Monday! Twenty-four hours is all you get, you brainless twat! Don't you know your own rules?'

'That's the limit we can keep you without charging you,' said Sep. 'The CPS have already given us the green light to charge you with enough to keep you away from children for the rest of your life.'

Johnstone began to struggle again. Sep, himself no midget, took the MP in a tight headlock and bent him forward so that he was almost off balance and unable to struggle without further hurting himself. But the MP continued to struggle and it took all Sep's considerable strength to hold him. Then Johnstone gave a mighty shudder; his legs collapsed from under him. Sep had no option other than to lower him to the floor where the huge man lay face-up and rigid. His eyes were blinking and he was making gurgling sounds and drooling. He began to twitch and then convulse. Five policemen stared down at him. None of them felt inclined to give this serial child-abuser any help, least of all Sep, whose first aid expertise had never been great. He looked up and asked, 'Anyone know what to do with him? Kiss of life, maybe. Or do we think he's just trying it on?'

'He's having an epileptic fit, sir,' said a uniformed sergeant. 'We need to put him in the recovery position and put a cushion or something under his head to stop him injuring himself.'

'Epileptic fit?' said Sep. 'Oh, bloody great! There's no mention of epilepsy in the report we've got on him.'

'That's definitely what it is, sir. My nephew's epileptic. I've seen him in this state a few times.'

'Right, do your best, sergeant. With him being an MP, we've been ordered to treat him with kid gloves . . . which we have up to now.' He added the last bit as he looked around at the circle of his subordinates and waited for them to nod their agreement, which they all did.

The sergeant and two constables struggled to place Johnstone in the recovery position. Sep took off his coat, folded it up and put it under the MP's head. Johnstone continued to gurgle and convulse.

'If he hasn't come round in five minutes,' said the sergeant, 'we need to call an ambulance. Apart from that there's nothing we can do. He'll probably come round in a couple of minutes, sir.'

Johnstone was now having difficulty breathing. His skin had turned pale. This worried Sep.

'A couple of minutes? Are you sure, sergeant? He's not looking so good.'

'I only know about my nephew, sir.'

Sep bent down and took Johnstone's pulse. 'His heart's racing like mad. Better get the duty doctor here . . . quick!'

Even as he spoke Johnstone gave a great shudder and stopped moving. His body went limp. No noises came from him now. Fearing the worst, Sep checked his pulse again.

'Is he OK, sir?'

Sep shook his head and looked up. 'Not really, sergeant. I think he's dead.'

FOUR

10 March
Allerton Police Station, Leeds

Superintendent Ibbotson was sitting at his desk, his uniform immaculate as usual. Sep was standing opposite him, looking less than immaculate. He was wearing a tweed sports jacket with a pen in the top pocket and a regimental badge in the lapel, grey flannels and an open-neck rugby shirt. It was an outfit that fitted the bill of a man not wanting to look like a plain-clothes copper. The leather patches on his elbows made him look more like a Geography teacher. He'd been summoned there to be brought up-to-date on the investigation regarding the death-in-custody of the MP. That was what he'd been told, but he had good cause to feel pessimistic about the outcome. The superintendent studied him.

'You could do with a haircut. Senior officers have to maintain standards.'

'I know that, sir, but this case I'm working on requires that I'm not known to be a copper.'

'You're not undercover as far as I know.'

'Not officially, sir, but the people I'm currently dealing with don't know that.'

'You're an unorthodox man, Sep. Sometimes this goes against you.'

Sep shrugged. 'I am who I am, sir. It seems to work for me.'

'According to the IPCC investigators your colleagues aren't being very helpful to you.'

'So I believe, sir.'

The superintendent frowned and sat back in his chair, rubbing his mouth with the palm of his hand in the manner of a benevolent doctor trying to diagnose a patient with a mystery illness.

'Any idea why not?'

Sep gave his answer a few seconds' consideration. He knew his boss wouldn't like it, but it was the truth so what the hell?

'The new man who came up from the Met last month is adept at stirring up malcontent.'

'You mean DI Cope?'

'I do, sir. I believe the Met are carrying out a big internal investigation to root out corruption down there. I do hope we haven't imported some of it up here.'

'That's a serious accusation. Do you have anything to substantiate it?'

'Only common sense, sir. For the last week he's been advising my colleagues not to contact me or associate with me or they might find themselves under investigation themselves, which is nonsense, sir.'

'Why would he do that? He barely knows you.'

'My point exactly, sir. The minute he comes up here he begins to stir up trouble for an officer he barely knows. But I know him – or rather I know *of* him from a friend down in the Met who believes Cope applied for a transfer up here the minute he caught wind of their corruption investigation. My friend is of the strong opinion that Cope isn't above a bit of corruption, sir.'

'That's your friend's opinion is it?'

'It is, sir, and I value his opinion quite highly.'

'Do you now?'

'Yes, sir. I mean Cope's a Londoner, born and bred. Why would he want to come up here? Does he have family up here, sir?'

'Not that I know of.'

'No, nor me, but I know he has family down there, sir.'

'As far as I know he's a single man.'

'He wasn't very single down there, sir. He led a very full social life according to my friend. Up here he seems to have cut himself off from everything. He was also a great theatre lover.'

'Leeds has theatres.'

'Only one to match the ones in London, sir, and even then we only get the regional theatre actors, none of your big stars. He likes the big stars does Cope; knows a few of them as well.

He also likes the London nightlife. In Leeds, the nightlife only caters for people under thirty, not middle-aged coppers. He'll be like a fish-out-of-water up here, sir.'

'You've checked on him have you?'

'I keep my eyes and ears open, sir, as you know. To me, him trying to distance himself from the Met's investigation is the only thing that makes sense. My informant also believes he might have followed Vince Formosa up here, sir.'

'Vince Formosa! Oh my God! Now you are in the realms of fantasy. Formosa's been up here five years.'

'And he's been running rings around the police for five years. Not a single arrest. My informant reckons Cope was in Formosa's pocket down there, sir.'

'Anything ever proved?'

'Of course not, sir, which is why he's still a serving police officer.'

'Well, there you go. If the investigators need to question him they'll drag him back down there soon enough.'

'Possibly, sir, or possibly he's working on the out-of-sight-out-of-mind theory. Who knows?'

'Not me that's for sure,' said Ibbotson, 'and in the light of no concrete evidence of your suspicions I have to assume his reason for coming up here was for a change of scenery to God's Own County.'

'I don't know of any Londoners who have that opinion of Yorkshire, sir. The Met looks upon us as provincial plods. It's usually our lot who have ambitions to join the big boys in the Met.'

'Have you by any chance made this suspicion of yours known around the station?'

'I've mentioned it to one or two, sir.'

'Enough for your views to have got all round the station and back to Cope no doubt. No wonder he's got it in for you.' Ibbotson leaned forward on his desk. 'I assume you're aware that the investigation into Cyril Johnson's death is an independent investigation and that the Independent Police Complaints Commission only conduct investigations into incidents that cause the greatest level of public concern – for example, deaths in or following police custody.'

'I'm aware of that, sir.'

'Is it true that you threatened to kick him in the bollocks?'

Sep didn't answer. He was annoyed that his colleagues had blabbed on him to this extent, although he knew who'd put them up to it.

'I'm also aware that his nickname was the BFB . . . the Big Fat Bastard. Are you aware of this DI Black?'

'Yes, I was aware of it but there wasn't much I could do about it, sir. What I wasn't aware of was that he was epileptic. I should have been told this at the beginning of the investigation against him, sir.'

'I'm not sure anybody knew.'

'So, how was I expected to know? It wasn't in the file we had about him.'

Ibbotson shook his head. 'And are you aware that even if the IPCC find you not guilty of any misconduct, the media will be down on us like a ton of bricks, accusing us of protecting our own?'

'I'm aware that I'm about to be made a scapegoat to protect the police's reputation.'

'Not quite, another matter had just arisen that doesn't help your cause.'

'What's that, sir?'

'Your wife has just accused you of assaulting her. She's in St James's hospital right now with facial injuries – injuries she displayed to the whole station when she came in to report the matter earlier today.'

'*What?*' said Sep, shocked.

'She says you assaulted her.'

'I did no such thing. My wife and I are currently separated.'

'I wasn't aware of that.'

'It's not a permanent thing, just a bump in the road as far as I'm concerned. When's this supposed to have happened? She was fine the last time I saw her, which was last night when I dropped my daughter off at home.'

'She's not fine now, and what's more the whole station knows about it. If you need any of them to speak up for you to the IPCC, I'm afraid you're out of luck.'

'I think I'd like to go and see my wife, sir. Find out what this is all about.'

'You are not to go within a mile of her, Black. I order you to stay away from her and find yourself alternative accommodation or you'll be arrested.'

'I already have alternative accommodation.'

'Good.'

Sep hung his head in bewilderment. What the hell was happening here? He looked up as a thought struck him. 'If I assaulted her, shouldn't I be arrested and charged anyway, sir?'

'Yes, you should, but she hasn't pressed charges as yet and I'm holding the matter in abeyance until I decide on the best way to deal with you.'

'I'm thinking you've already decided that, sir.'

'The best way to deal with this is for you to voluntarily resign from the force. That way we can satisfy the media that a man has been punished.'

'Will the media be made aware of Johnstone's crimes, sir?'

'Did you call him Johnstone when all this kicked off?'

'I did, sir. I believe his hyphenated name was just pretentious rubbish. He was just plain Johnstone before he became an MP.'

'I bet that annoyed the hell out of him. Anyway, the media won't be hearing about his crimes from us.'

'If I get the boot I might have a story or two of my own to tell them.'

'In order for you to avoid being prosecuted for his death you will be asked to sign a legal document preventing you from giving such stories to the media. The MP died before he was found guilty of anything. In the eyes of the law, which is us, he died an innocent man.'

'Sounds like I'm being stitched up well and truly, sir.'

'Just for the record, Black, I don't believe a word of this nonsense about Detective Inspector Cope being corrupt.'

'Can I go now, sir?'

'Yes.'

Sep walked through the station watched by a host of frosty eyes. No one spoke to him. Under normal circumstances the IPCC investigation wouldn't have troubled him overmuch given the witnesses who could testify to Johnstone's accidental demise. He paused in his step and spoke as he concentrated his gaze on the exit door, speaking to them all and yet focussing his attention on the door, 'My wife says I beat her up. I'm saying I did no such thing. I have no idea why she said it, but I know it was Cope who set you lot against me.' Still with his eyes on the door he shook his head and added, 'I'm truly amazed he's managed to take you all in so easily. And you call yourselves coppers!'

Without sparing any of them a glance, he picked up his step and left the room. This wife thing had him baffled. Their marriage had had problems; their separation hadn't been a permanent thing – just a couple of weeks or so apart to give each other time and space to think. Sep had harboured hopes of reconciliation, if only for their daughter, Phoebe's, sake. He'd certainly never hit his wife. What the hell was all that about? And he wasn't even allowed to speak to her. And who was looking after Phoebe? She'd presumably be at school right now, due out at half past three. Presumably he wasn't banned from picking her up. Or was he?

He sat in his car within sight of the school gates. It was a distinctive car, a bright red classic 1985 Audi Quattro. Phoebe would spot it straight away and head for it. There was a mass of children and parents blocking her from his vision for a while, then he saw her standing at the gate, looking directly at him. Small for her eleven years and a pretty girl in Sep's eyes, but possibly not in anyone else's. Phoebe was a girl who might well grow into her good looks one day, but that day had yet to arrive. Apart from his mother she was the only female Sep had ever loved, and that included his wife and five sisters.

He raised a hand to acknowledge he'd seen her but she didn't head his way. She crossed the road and got into a late model black BMW which was parked facing him. It set off and passed within a few feet of him; close enough for him to recognize the driver – Detective Inspector Lenny Cope. What the hell was all that about?

Fifteen minutes later he parked outside his marital home. Cope's car was in the drive. Sep opened the front door and went in. He heard Cope shout out, 'Who's there?'

'The owner of this house,' said Sep, coming into the living room. 'What are you doing here?'

'He stays with us sometimes, Daddy,' said Phoebe. Sep noticed there was no affection in her voice. It was cold, almost on the verge of tears.

Cope got to his feet. 'Come to take a swing at me have you, Black? It won't be as easy hitting me as hitting your wife.'

'I imagine it would be a lot easier, but I never touched my wife and you know it.'

'That's not what she says.'

Sep looked at Phoebe. 'When did this happen, darling?'

'You know,' said Phoebe.

'But I don't know. I know that *you* didn't see me hitting Mummy.'

'I was in bed. I heard you though.'

'I don't know who you heard, but it wasn't me.'

'Mummy said it was.'

Sep sighed; he didn't want to have an argument with his daughter. He looked at Cope. 'What's all this about you staying here?'

'I stay here sometimes. I know Rachel told you because that was what your argument was about.'

'I didn't know, and there was no damned argument!' said Sep, angry at this man's lies.

Phoebe spoke up. 'When I came home last night I went straight to bed and I heard you and Mummy arguing.'

'Phoebe, when I dropped you off, I didn't even come in the house. I brought you to the door as I always do, then I drove straight off.'

'You didn't Daddy. I heard you arguing with Mummy.'

'You might have heard *someone* arguing with Mummy, darling, but it wasn't me.'

'Mummy said it was. I heard the door bang and your car drive off so I came downstairs and saw Mummy with her face all bleeding. She asked me to ring for an ambulance. Uncle Lenny got here just before the ambulance arrived.'

Sep looked at Cope and said, 'Did he really? How convenient.'

'I do hope you're not saying I hit her,' said Cope. 'Why on Earth would I do that?'

'I don't know. God moves in mysterious ways and so do creeps like you.'

'Mummy says it was you, Daddy.'

'Well, it wasn't, Phoebe.'

'I think you'd better go before I arrest you,' said Cope.

Sep looked down at his daughter who was weeping silently and he felt a depth of despair he'd never felt before. Events not of his doing were causing him to argue with, even hurt, the person he loved most in the world. Worse still, the person he knew was responsible for all this was standing right in front of him with a smirk on his face; a man he could throw out of this house without breaking sweat, and the temptation to do just that was almost overwhelming, but he knew he mustn't because this smirking man would simply have him arrested and make his life even worse.

'Cope,' he said, 'I know you're as bent as an Arab's dagger which is why you quit The Met and came up here. But now I've got time on my hands I'll catch up with you, mister. Be very sure of that.'

The artificial laughter which was Cope's response was a sound that would ring in Sep's ears for some time to come. It was laughter that needed ramming back down Cope's throat, but not right now. His problem right now was leaving his daughter with this bloody man, but he had no option. Stay, and Cope would have had him arrested and further humiliated in front of Phoebe. So Sep said goodbye to his tearful daughter and went out of the home he'd done so much to create; the home where he'd lived with her since she was born; down the crazy-paving path he'd laid himself and out into the street where he'd taught Phoebe to ride a bicycle. A neighbour across the street waved to him, Sep waved back, got in his car and just sat there, trying to clear his head. In the space of a few hours everything he valued had been taken from him with frightening efficiency. How the hell did he get back from this?

Take a deep breath and try and think clearly, Sep. Was there anything at all he could salvage? Money? Yes, he needed money, proper money, not credit card money that he'd have to pay back with interest. He checked his wallet. Forty-five pounds. The only good thing about this day was that it had happened three days after his salary had been paid in, but it was a joint account – an account also available to his wife. His wife who had dishonestly accused him of assaulting her. Shit! He hadn't checked his account since his salary went in. If she could lie about him assaulting her what else was she capable of?

Sep took out his iPhone, went on to the internet and thence to his bank account, cursing to himself when he saw she'd been in the bank and had drawn out a thousand in cash on each of the previous two days – the maximum allowed without giving them notice. Bloody hell! She'd been planning this! He had just twelve hundred and eighty-two pounds left in the account which he transferred electronically to a rarely-used savings account – an account in his name only. Including the money in his wallet his personal disposable wealth was now thirteen hundred and twenty-seven pounds. How long could he live on that?

At ten o'clock the next morning, Sep was standing in front of Ibbotson's desk once again. This time he had a Police Federation representative with him. The rep was doing the talking.

'I understand the difficult situation Detective Inspector Black is in but I have checked with the IPCC who are not currently planning to take action against him.'

'That will be because the dead man died of an epileptic fit and not strangulation,' added Sep.

The rep glanced at Sep is if to tell him to shut up. Sep got the message. The rep continued: 'If the post-mortem shows the man to have died of natural causes then they have no case against Inspector Black.'

'I know that,' said Ibbotson. 'But I also know that an epileptic fit can be brought on by extreme stress, such as a man holding him in a headlock.'

'The man was struggling, violently. I was using a standard restraint procedure,' said Sep.

'He was also a very large man,' added the rep. 'Restraining him would have required exceptional force.'

'I know all this as well,' said Ibbotson. 'But I also know the difficulty it will place the police in if we take no action at all against the officer who restrained him, and who is also facing a charge of criminal assault against his wife.'

'I haven't been charged yet,' Sep pointed out.

'Charge or no charge, we have to look at the broader picture,' Ibbotson said. 'If the media gets hold of the wife story, they'll make mincemeat of us.'

'Not if we give them the details of Johnstone's crimes against kids,' said Sep, 'and you are overlooking one major advantage in Johnstone being dead.'

'What's that?'

'I imagine there'll be lots of parents out there very relieved that their kids won't have to relive all the horrors they've been through in court – and that's not to mention the kids themselves who'll no longer have the spectre of their abuser still being present in their lives. Complete closure, you might call it – if that's at all possible.'

'I get your point,' said Ibbotson, 'but we have orders from the Home Office to give no details of why, or even *that* he was arrested,' said Ibbotson. 'They're talking about issuing a D Notice to that effect.'

'D Notice? That's only for matters of national security,' said Sep.

'Ours is not to reason why,' said Ibbotson.

'Ours is but to protect the reputation of parliament – at my expense,' Sep countered. 'Imagine the embarrassment in parliament when all the eulogies Johnstone's been getting from his fellow MPs turn out to be for a prolific paedophile . . . and I have information to suggest that a lot of them strongly suspected it, but have said and done nothing.'

The rep intervened: 'I submit that if my client signs your document prohibiting him from talking to the media, he be allowed to resign as normal and leave with full accrued pension and no stain on his employment reputation. Also no charges will be brought against him.'

'I think I can get that agreed,' said Ibbotson, 'but if the charges against Johnstone leak out into the social media this document will be declared null and void.'

'But I've got no control over social media,' protested Sep, 'no one has.'

'There are experts who can trace such leaks back to their source,' said Ibbotson.

'That's rubbish! Anyway, I'm hardly leaving without a stain on my reputation if you want the media to think I've been sacked for Johnstone's death.'

'Sep,' said Ibbotson. 'Think about it. With you being a senior police officer, the assault on your wife could get you two years, and you'd be kicked out anyway.'

'Congratulations!' said Sep. 'You bloody lot have done me up like a kipper.'

FIVE

24 March

The only thing Lee Dench liked about this job was the five grand he was due to pick up for it. Five grand for less than forty minutes work, start to finish. Drive there, pick the kids up, deliver, job done. The pick-up shouldn't be a problem. They should pick themselves up. If they didn't the job was off. Five grand up the spout. Too risky to pick up two struggling kids in broad daylight, especially outside their school, and his boss was a minimalist as far as risk was concerned. Lee didn't like having to wear a woman's wig and a woman's coat, but he knew the only reason he'd been picked for the job was because he was slightly built, like the young woman he was impersonating.

His MO had been worked out for him. There'd be plenty of women and kids milling round. Cars parked all over the place. All he had to do was drive past the two waiting kids, who'd recognize the car, which had false plates to suit the real one. He'd park up a few yards past them. His information was that they'd approach him from behind and get in without any help from him. This is how they'd done it before. Their real nanny never bothered to get out of the car to help them, they were big enough to help themselves. The minute they shut the door he'd press the child-lock button and they were captured.

Greenlees Preparatory School, Harrogate, Yorkshire

Milly Strathmore was in tears as she walked over to where her brother was standing at the school gates. He sighed in exasperation. 'What is it now?'

'George Butterfield's been bullying me.'

'You mean calling you names? You'll have to learn to stick up for yourself.'

'He's been calling me Squinty and getting all the other kids to gang up on me.'

'You won't be squinty for long. You're having your operation in a couple of months.'

Milly said nothing. She wasn't looking forward to her eye operation. They'd been mucking about with her eyes ever since she could remember and she'd been told this was the big one – the big operation that would straighten her eyes for good.

'He pushed me as well. I fell over and dirtied my dress, look,' she showed her older brother a grimy streak down the side of her dress, '. . . and I grazed my knee.'

'What am I supposed to do about it? If I thump him I'll be in trouble – mos' probably expelled this time.'

'I told him you'd bash his head in but he said you couldn't knock the skin off a rice pudding.'

James was ten – two years older than his sister. George Butterfield was big for his nine years – at least as big as James.

'He said that, did he?'

'Yes,' lied Milly, who knew her brother wouldn't let such an insult go unpunished.

James spotted George approaching, swinging his school bag around his head causing the people around him to take evasive action. It was home time. James looked around at the teacher who was on gate duty, ensuring that children who were waiting to be picked up didn't go galloping off on their own. She had her back to James. There were no other teachers around, just a huddle of parents standing by the school door, paying no attention to anything other than themselves. James walked over to George and grabbed his swinging school bag.

'You owe my parents five pounds,' he said. 'If you don't bring five pounds tomorrow I'm gonna knock your teeth down your throat.'

'Why? What have I done?'

'You know.'

'No, I don't.'

'You've been bullying my sister.'

'No I haven't.'

'You've torn her dress and made her leg bleed.'

'So?'

'So we'll have a fight around the back of the reception block at dinnertime tomorrow. Me and you are about the same size. If you don't wanna fight you'd better bring five pounds to pay for our Milly's dress.'

He said it loud enough for George's classmates to hear. George was considered to be a tough guy who would fight anyone. For him not to accept James's challenge would destroy his reputation. But he knew he could never beat James, who had a well-earned reputation as being the best fighter in the school – a reputation that had brought him no end of trouble, including a threat of expulsion. George dropped his eyes under James's threatening gaze and slunk off. James went back to his sister.

'What did he say?'

'Not much, but I might be a fiver better off tomorrow.'

As Laura Graham pulled up at traffic lights, her Picasso was shunted from behind. She swore and looked in the mirror at the car which had hit her. Its driver was holding up his hands in apology. Laura got out, taking care to remove the keys – she'd heard about car thieves using this method to steal cars left with the key in the ignition. The other driver got out. Laura looked around to see if any would-be thief was heading for her car. There wasn't.

'I'm really sorry,' the man said, getting out of his car. 'I'm not used to this car. My foot must have caught the accelerator as I put it on the brake.'

He was middle-aged, a fussy type, annoyingly so. Overly apologetic. A man who didn't use one word where ten would do. Other cars were now moving around them as the man insisted on giving her his insurance details that he had in his glove compartment, but which he couldn't find immediately. Laura looked at her watch.

'Look,' she said, 'I'm picking children up from school and I'll be late.'

'They're here somewhere,' he said. 'Look, this was all my

fault. I'm not used to this car your see. I've just bought it. I'm
fully insured so you've no need to worry about paying for repairs.
It'll just take a minute. I always keep my details in the car. You
never know when you'll need them . . .'

She'd been delayed ten minutes by the time he managed to
give her all his details. The damage was slight and her car perfectly
driveable. She got back in and drove off, not realizing that every
detail he'd given her was false, including his car registration
number.

The two Strathmore children stood at the school gates waiting
for their nanny's car to pick them up. She was normally already
there and waiting for them, but not today. Then a light blue
Picasso cruised past them and pulled up on a yellow line a few
yards away. The teacher on gate duty tut-tutted. All parents had
been told not to do that.

'Is this car for you?' she asked.

'Yes, it's our nanny.'

'You must tell her not to stop on the yellow lines.'

'Yes, Miss,' said James, amused that their nanny was in trouble
with a teacher.

The children ran towards the vehicle, opened the door and
clambered on to the back seats, closing the door behind them
and shouting, 'Hi Laura,' to the driver, then both taking out their
iPhones.

'You're not to stop on the yellow lines,' added James, as he
tapped at the tiny screen, 'or you'll get detention.'

The car was already under way. His sister giggled at this as
she tapped at her own screen. Five minutes later an identical car
parked just across the road and Laura got out. She walked over
to the gate-duty teacher.

'I'm a bit late. Some idiot crashed into me from behind. Milly
and James not out yet?'

The teacher stared at her. Recognizing her as the children's
nanny who, right now, should be driving them home.

'They've . . .' She could hardly get the words out. 'They've
been picked up . . . in . . . er, in your car.'

'What? My car's there.' Laura pointed at it. 'Bit of a dent in
the back but it's my car all right.'

'I know, but another car just like that picked them up a few minutes ago.'

'Well, it wasn't my car.'

'Perhaps their parents have two similar cars.'

'No, their dad's got a black Mercedes and their mother drives a white Audi. I'm the only one who drives the blue Picasso.'

The teacher clasped her hands to her face and stared in shock at the nanny, who was also looking scared.

'Oh my god!'

They said it in unison.

Lee Dench had been driving for several minutes before the children turned their attention from their iPhones to talk to their nanny, whom they'd known all their lives. They were both probably too old for a nanny but Laura had become a family friend and undertook other duties around the house to justify her existence. James looked at Lee's reflection in the driver's mirror.

'You're not Laura.'

'Laura couldn't make it. I'm taking you back instead.'

Lee's limited talents didn't extend to impersonating a woman's voice – certainly not enough to fool a ten-year-old boy.

'You're not a woman, you're a man!' James shouted.

The car stopped at traffic lights. James tried the door, but it was locked. 'We want to get out!' he shouted.

Milly began to cry. James began to punch Lee on the back of his head as he drove away from the lights. Lee pulled in to a side road, stopped the car and turned round in his seat. He had a gun in his hand. He pointed it at Milly but spoke to James.

'Just behave yourselves and you'll come to no harm. Kick up a fuss and I'll put a bullet right through your sister's face. Do you understand, boy?'

Both children slumped back in their seats, white-faced and terrified. Too scared to say anything.

'That's good,' said Lee. 'That's very good.'

SIX

4 April

I t was good weather for the job in hand – dark, miserable, cold, drizzling. People who venture outside in such weather tend to turn their collars up and their faces down rather than check out drivers of passing cars. The Mondeo was a nondescript vehicle. As dark and dirty as the night itself. It had false plates and a quiet petrol engine which didn't attract attention with it being driven responsibly. No screeching of tyres or revving the engine that might alert a passer-by to its existence. It carried two men who both wore dark clothing – in fact boiler suits – but no hoodies or baseball caps that might make people think they were kids up to no good. It was the Irishman who asked, 'What did Vince mean when he said we've got to put on a show? What sort of show?'

Sharky gave the question a few seconds thought. 'One that'll scare the shit out of everyone. Dench won't be on his own. We need people to witness this – witnesses who'll be scared shit-less and put the word about that you don't fuck with Vince Formosa.'

'Shitless witness,' said Spud. 'Poetry that.'

'Retribution must be seen to be done,' Sharky said. 'It's a bit like justice in a way.'

'Who'll be with him?'

'His woman and however many people live in that house which, I believe, is several.'

'His woman? What's she like?'

'Like a whore.'

'We leave her alive, do we?'

'We leave 'em all alive except Dench.'

'So we shoot 'em up a bit, though . . . to make a show of it?'

'We scare 'em, yeah,' Sharky said. 'We're not here to commit mass murder. Our policemen tend to take mass murder very seriously – Human Rights and all that crap. Takin' out a dickhead like Dench is really doin' them a favour.'

'Maybe we should send 'em a bill,' said Spud.

'It'll be my turn to do Dench, by the way. You did the Italian.'

'Are ye sure? I thought you did the Italian,' said Spud.

'No, yer shot him in the back of his head while he was counting the money.

'Agh, dat's right. Silencer job, and you ain't got no silencer for dat wild west revolver o' yours.'

'You can't silence a revolver properly.'

'You and yer Colt forty fuckin' five. D'yer tink yer Billy the fuckin' Kid or someone?'

'Nah, Sundance Kid, me. In fact I think I might change my name to Sundance, wotcha think?'

'I don't tink Sundance was no nigger,' Spud said.

'Ackroyd Street, this is it,' said Sharky. 'Turn left here, number seventeen, it's on the left.'

Spud drove the car down a street of decaying terraced houses. It was an area that had been designated for redevelopment twenty years ago and had since been deteriorating daily. It was a street of largely empty houses; a street no longer on the regular schedule of Leeds City Cleansing Department. Litter was abundant, as was abandoned furniture. The general detritus was animated by feral cats and scavenging rats. A few old cars were parked there, one burnt out, one with its bonnet propped open by a brush handle and one with its wheel hubs sitting on bricks; a full tank of petrol would have doubled the value of any one of them. There was a Toyota Corolla that might have been worth a couple of hundred, had it been taxed. The Irishman peered through the swishing wipers.

'Sharky boy, dis is an awful gobshite of a street. Even I never lived in a street as bad as dis back in Limerick.'

'It's where that Toyota's parked,' Sharky said. 'I think that's Dench's.'

'How do we get in?'

'We're civilized people, we knock.'

Lee Dench was in bed with his prostitute girlfriend, whose name was Christine Prisk but she called herself Chantelle when she was working. Both of them were naked, having just had sex, and were now sharing a joint. Noise was coming from an adjacent room where three men and a woman were watching television amid a fug of cannabis fumes. Chantelle nipped out the last inch of the joint in a bedside ashtray and turned to Lee, asking him, 'When do you get paid the rest of the copper's money?'

'I get it in two stages. A grand when they pick Vince up, which is tomorrer, and another grand after I've given evidence.'

'Fuck, Lee! That's peanuts and it could be months.'

'I know, but they'll put us in a safe house. I also gerra clean slate which is more important ter me. They can't touch me fer nothin'. Shan, I've got over thirty-five grand stashed so we can move ter Spain and start over. I gorra cousin over there who's straight and well in with the locals. He'll set me up with a half share in a car sales business he's gorrin' Malaga.'

'Thirty-five grand?'

'Yeah. Vince might be a twat but I've made real money with him and I've been saving every penny. Why d'yer think we live in this shit'ole squat? It's because I'm not wasting no money on rent, that's why.'

'Thirty-five grand. Where is it?'

'It's in Barclays Bank, proper account and everything. They think I'm a used-car dealer. Which I am – well, now and again, as yer know.'

'You never told me about no thirty-five grand.'

'There's a lorra things I don't tell yer, Shan. Mostly it's fer yer own good. I know too much, that's my problem. I just make me money and say nowt ter nobody. Best way.'

'Yer tell me all sorts o' stuff, Lee. Enough fer me ter grass Vince up meself. If he knew yer were turnin' him in he'd skin yer alive – literally.'

'I know, but I can't start a new life while Vince's still on the loose, Shan. There'll be nowhere safe in the world, never mind Spain, which is only a couple of hours away. I need him and his people banged up. When the courts bang him up they'll clean him out completely. All his bank accounts, his investments, all his property, cars everything. It's the way they do things nowadays. Proceeds o' crime they call it.'

'How d'yer know?'

'My copper told me. They've got details of every last thing he owns, includin' how many of them flash suits he gets from Bond Street, which is fifteen apparently – two grand each. Fifteen suits at two grand each. I've just got that one what I bought from TK Maxx for fifty-two quid, the last time I was up in court.'

'Yer looked flash in that suit, Lee. I reckon it knocked six months off yer sentence.'

'It'll be more than two years in the nick if I get picked up as part of Vince's mob. Takin' kids isn't my fuckin' style at all, Shan.'

'Yer'd not much ter do with it, Lee. All yer did was drive the car.'

'I had ter wear a bloody wig ter look like a woman.'

'There's no law against wearin' a wig.'

'It were me who picked 'em up, disguised as a woman. They'll throw the book at me. My copper's already told me that.'

'Them kids – what's happened to 'em?'

'No idea. The whole thing went tits up when the cops got wind of it.'

'Will he have killed 'em?'

'I think he might have, Shan. It's bad stuff is that – killin' kids. That's why I'm deffo out of it. When they bang Vince up he won't have a penny ter scratch his little Maltese arse with. In this business money's power. Take away Vince's money and he becomes a loser and no one respects a loser – especially a loser who kills kids. Inside the nick he'll be two rungs down the ladder from a dog turd. Lower in the peckin' order than all them twats who take their orders from the wing's main man, who won't never be Vince fuckin' Formosa, not with him killin' them kids. I reckon he'll ask to go on the block and stay there fer his own safety.'

'So, we both go straight? I don't have to shag any holiday-makers or Spaniards?'

'No, only me. From now on we're straight as an arrow, both of us. Man and wife when we get there. We'll get married on a beach in our cozzies while Vince is rottin' in a cell in Wakefield nick.'

'Bloody hell, Lee! This is scary shit.'

'It's the only way, Shan.'

'We'll have ter learn ter speak Spaniard.'

'We'll pick it up before long and there's plenty of English over there, Shan.'

They didn't hear the knock on the front door.

The four in the other room were watching *Britain's Got Talent* where a dog act was impressing Simon Cowell. It was a polite knock, possibly an acquaintance come to call on one of the residents. One of the men in the other room went to answer it. On opening the door a gun was thrust in his face and he was pushed backwards until he backed into the television room.

Spud had a Glock 17, Sharky was holding a sawn-off shotgun which he aimed at the television and pulled the trigger. The 45 inch flat screen disintegrated before the noise had died away. The cannabis haze suddenly cleared from four heads as they all became alert to the mortal danger arriving in their midst. The woman screamed, as did Chantelle in the bedroom.

'Where's Lee fuckin' Dench?' enquired Spud. 'An' I'd like an immediate answer or I'll blow someone's fuckin' head off.'

The screaming woman pointed a shaking finger at the wall, beyond which were Lee and Chantelle, both of them now terrified. Sharky went into the hall and kicked open the bedroom door. He pointed the gun at Lee's head.

'Out of bed, both of you.'

Chantelle tried to maintain her modesty by covering herself with a bedsheet, but Sharky dragged it off her, leaving her as naked as Lee.

She tried to cover herself with her hands. 'Put yer hands on yer head!' Sharky said. They both did as ordered. Lee's body was littered with cheap tattoos, hard to make out, like damp newsprint. Sharky shouted at him. 'Not you, her! Who the fuck wants to see you? Both of yer through there.'

Sharky indicated with his shotgun that they go into the next room. They did as he ordered. Both of them weeping with terror. In the next room Spud had got the occupants lined up against a wall, facing him. Lee and Chantelle were made to join them. Chantelle had a generous body and a mean face which was now distorted with fear. Sharky did all the talking.

'Yer've gotta a snake in the grass among yer. D'yer know that?'

They all shook their heads, including Lee, who had no idea
how they could have possibly found out. His sole contact in the
police wouldn't have given him up. He assumed they were talking
about someone else. Fucking hell! Chantelle! She was the only
one who knew enough to grass on Vince. He glanced sideways
at her, she was sobbing and shivering with terror. Yeah, it's definitely Chantelle. You're dead, girl! What a fucking idiot! Just
when they had their getaway set up. He instinctively moved away
from her.

'Mr Lee fucking Dench,' said Sharky, pointing the shotgun at
Lee's face. 'Why d'yer grass Mr Formosa to the police?'

Lee's eyes sprang open wide with terror. 'I . . . I . . . I . . .
didn't, man,' he sobbed. 'No, not me. I wouldn't grass him up.
Please, yer've gotta believe me, man.' He inclined his head
towards Chantelle. 'She's the one yer after.'

'It wasn't me, it was Lee!' screamed Chantelle. 'I don't know
anything!'

'Yer lyin' bitch!' shouted Lee.

Sharky seemed to give this a moment's thought, then shook
his head, saying, 'Hmm, I'm inclined to believe the bitch,' He
looked at Spud. 'Who d'yer believe, him or the bitch?'

'Not him,' said Spud.

'Anyone want to see what happens to people who grass
Mr Formosa up?' Sharky enquired.

They all just stared at him, not knowing how to react. Lee
collapsed to his knees. Sharky aimed the shotgun at the top his
head and pulled the trigger. Lee's head exploded. Blood and
brains and bone sprayed all over the room. The two women
screamed. Chantelle's scream was choked off as Spud stuck his
handgun in her open mouth and pulled the trigger. The bullet
lodged deep in the wall behind her, along with parts of her brain
and skull. The surviving woman fainted, two of the men vomited.
Sharky looked down at the remains of Lee Dench and remarked,
'Very thin legs for a man.'

'Yours are thinner,' said Spud, retrieving his bullet casing from
the bloody mess on the floor and sticking it in his boiler-suit
pocket. Losing the casing would have meant getting rid of his
precious Glock lest a connection be made.

'What? I ain't got thin legs. My legs is wiry, that's all.'

The woman was just coming round from her faint. Spud said, 'OK, show her your legs, see what she thinks.'

'Bollocks!' said Sharky.

'No, just yer legs.'

Sharky ignored this and turned his attention to the four survivors. 'If y'ever describe us to the police we'll know about it an' someone will come and deal with y'all.'

'An' that includes describin' his thin legs,' added Spud.

No one saw any humour in this, certainly not the men, who were Romanian. Sharky glared at his partner as he loaded another two cartridges into his now empty shotgun. 'What d'yer think? Maybe we should we waste another one?'

The Irishman took his time looking from one to the other, as if making up his mind which one Sharky should kill. The woman fainted again.

'Nah,' decided Spud, after a long moment, 'two's plenty. Like yer said, we're civilized people, not fuckin' animals. I tink they get the message.'

The room was heavily spattered with blood from floor to ceiling. There were two naked bodies on the floor, one man weeping, another man vomiting, and a woman in a dead faint beside the dead bodies. Satisfied with their work, Spud and Sharky strolled from the house in the manner of a couple of insurance salesmen who had just sold the occupant a lucrative life policy. Neighbours, alerted by the shooting, were coming to doors and windows to watch the car being driven sedately away. But they weren't neighbours who would ever be much help to the police. Talking to the coppers had never done any of them any good. They watched but they wouldn't see anything. Half a mile away the two men swapped cars in a large, lock-up garage out of sight of prying street cameras. They took off their boiler suits and stuffed them into plastic bags.

'Why d'yer shoot the whore?' said Sharky, looking in the driver's mirror and wiping blood from his face with a wet wipe.

'I thought we agreed I could do Dench. It was my turn,' Spud told him.

'Jesus, man! Yer've got some sort of crap memory you have. It was my turn. You shot the Italian last month. So, you wasted

her because you thought I went out of turn? That's just fuckin'
childish, that is.'

'Dench might have been telling the truth,' Spud pointed out.
'It might have been her what grassed.'

Sharky gave this a second's thought and shook his head.
'Nah. You were just pissed off because you thought I went out
of turn. I thought she looked quite tasty. Big girl. I thought we
might bring her with us and have some fun before we wasted
her.'

'Agh, we gotta stay professional. She was a fuckin' gypsy
anyway. They all were.'

'Professional? You were making fuckin' jokes about my legs
in there.'

'Yeah, but we showed 'em that we're ruthless bastards as well
as comedians. People find that very scary.'

'You think so? Man, that lot were high on skunk.'

'High, but not out of it,' said Spud, turning the mirror his way
and wiping his own face. 'Dope'll distort and magnify their
memories of what went on, as if it needs any magnifyin'.'

'Jesus Christ!' said Sharky, impressed, 'where'd yer read that?'

'I make it my business ter know stuff about drugs.'

'Could be they don't remember much at all,' said Sharky, 'but
I still think we should have worn masks.'

'Why?' said Spud. 'We ain't gonna be around no more after
this job.'

Sharky grinned. 'True man. We's on our Fiji island livin' like
kings. Anyways, I doubt if any of 'em'll be able to describe us to
the polis. It's hard to take notice when ye doped up and shittin'
yerself. Plus nobody who hears about dis'll want to be on the
wrong side of mad bastard comedians like us. They'll tell the cops
I was a Frenchman and you was an Eskimo.'

'Good point, man. We're real ruthless dudes.' Sharky looked
down at his shoes. 'Do I really need to burn these shoes? They've
got blood on 'em but they're Guccis, which are not cheap. I
should just give 'em a real good clean.'

Spud looked at his own blood-spattered work boots. 'We burn
everything as usual. Yer a fucking eejit fer comin' ter work in
dem shoes. What man in his right mind goes to work in his best
shoes?'

'Jesus, man! You're wearin' bogtrotter boots. These cost me four hundred notes. Surely I can clean a few spots o' blood off.'

'I see a lot more blood than leather. Ye might tink ye've cleaned off all the blood but if any o' dem forensic fellers get their hands on 'em wid their magic fuckin' microscopes, ye'll know different soon enough.'

'Well I think they'll clean up good.'

'Man, we just got us a future lined up and you wanna risk it fer a pair o' fuckin' shoes! Just burn the bastards ye big black gobshite!'

'OK, OK! No need to go all fuckin' racist on me. It's against the law that! You start talkin' like that on our Fiji island and they'll string you up by your Irish bollocks!'

'I'm not a fuckin' racist. I'm an ethnic minority, same as you.'

'An' yer've got no business telling them people I've got thin legs! A man's legs are his own private business!'

They cleaned any possible fingerprints off the Mondeo and removed any possible DNA evidence; then they left in another car, never to visit the garage again. They headed towards the eastbound M62 and towards Hull where they both lived. But not for long.

SEVEN

4 April
11 p.m., Ackroyd Street, Leeds

The whole street had been cordoned off. The house itself was taped off and a plastic canopy had been erected over the front door. The press had arrived, as had TV cameras. Curious neighbours were conspicuous in their absence – none of them wanted their faces to be seen on TV by whoever had done this. None of the house's occupants had called the police. That was left to a neighbour who'd heard sufficient screaming and wailing coming from the house to last her a lifetime, but even then she rang from an untraceable pay-as-you-go mobile and didn't leave her name.

'I think the police had better go to number 17 Ackroyd Street. It all kicked off about an hour ago. I don't know what's gone on there but it's not good. I think they might need an ambulance as well.'

Detective Inspector Lenny Cope had arrived with a detective sergeant after being alerted by the two uniformed officers first on the scene. One of them, a sergeant, stepped up to appraise him of the situation.

'It's like a charnel house in there, sir. Two dead of gunshot wounds, four in a state of shock. There's blood, brains, ears and eyeballs all over the floor.'

Cope winced. 'Great. Is the forensic medical examiner here?'

'She's here with a photographer.'

'She? Is it Jane Duffield?'

'It is, yes sir. And there's a forensic team on their way.'

'I assume no one's contaminated the crime scene?'

'*We* haven't, sir. But the occupants stayed in the house for about an hour before we got the call. Even then it wasn't any of them who called us. We've got them all in cars right now.'

'Do we have names of the deceased yet?'

'A man named Lee Dench and a woman named Christine Prisk who calls herself Chantelle when she's working the streets.'

'Both known to us?'

'They are, sir.'

'And did the four occupants witness this?'

'Well, I assume so, but we can't get a word out of any of them. They're too shocked to talk.'

'Right. We need to take them all in for questioning and we need to do a house-to-house to find out what the neighbours saw.'

'We're already doing that, sir, but there's no one behind most of the doors.'

Cope glanced up and down the dilapidated street. 'Hardly surprising. Anyway, we'd better take a look at the crime scene. Bad, is it?'

'Dench had the top of his head blown off, probably with a shotgun. Most of the mess comes from him. There's bits of him all over the room. The woman was shot once through the mouth with a handgun as far as I can tell.'

'Did you find the casing?'

'Not so far. Despite it being messy it looks like a pro job, so they probably picked up their brass. There's plenty of double O shot around the room but that stuff leaves no forensics behind.'

'And Jane Duffield's in there now is she?'

'Yes.'

'Rather her than me by the sound of it.'

'And me, sir.'

'Has she left anything we can cover our feet with?'

'There's a box of stuff in the entrance hall. She'll want you to cover up completely, sir – and so will you when you see what's in there.'

'Great. I only had fish and chips half an hour ago.'

Ten minutes later the inspector was back outside. His face white under the street lamps. His detective sergeant had gone inside and came straight back out to throw up.

'Sorry about that, sir. I've never seen anything quite like it.'

'Well, it's not something you see every day, even in this job. Anyway there's really nothing in that room that needs my attention right now. It looks like a professional hit so I doubt if they left much behind for us. I should think the four occupants'll fill us in on what happened once they've recovered.'

'I can't say I'm surprised that they're in shock, sir.'

'No, quite. Hang around here for a while – I need to make a couple of calls from the car.'

Cope went back to the car and called the station to appraise his DCI of the situation and to ensure the forensic team knew what they were up against. 'I've got four probable witnesses on their way in, all of them in shock. We need to get them checked out by a doctor before I question them.' When he finished the call he stabbed in another number. It was a brief conversation. A sharp voice, having recognized the caller's number on his screen said, 'Yes or no, do I have anything more to worry about?'

'No.'

EIGHT

'How the hell did Formosa get to know about Dench?'

'I don't know for sure, sir, but I assume Dench's girlfriend knew exactly what he was up to. She told one of the witnesses that she and Dench were planning to leave the country any time soon. A loose tongue like that would soon make its way to Formosa.'

Cope was standing because Detective Superintendent Ibbotson hadn't offered him a seat. 'So the girl opens her mouth and Formosa's hitman puts a bullet in it. Which means she was either screaming or he pushed the gun into her mouth. We really need to catch this man.'

'Yes, sir. According to Jane Duffield her teeth were intact, and there were two hitmen.'

'Descriptions?'

'They vary from witness to witness, sir. The only constant being that they were both white with local accents.'

'And the witnesses are all terrified?'

'Yes they are.'

'So, we can probably discount those descriptions. Did the assailants actually know Dench was about to give evidence against Formosa?'

'One them – the woman – mentioned something about Dench being punished for grassing up Vince Formosa.'

'Would she say that in court?'

'Doubt it, sir. Not after witnessing Dench's head being blown off.'

'Well, her evidence would be tenuous to say the least and I wouldn't give much for her chances when Formosa's found not guilty and back on the streets.'

'We still have our safe house witness, sir.'

'Not for much longer. His evidence alone won't be nearly enough. In support of Dench's evidence we had Formosa bang-to-rights, but he'd be signing his own death warrant if we put him in court. I'll notify the Crime Prosecution Service. They'll drop the case.'

The police had put word out through various underworld connections that an amnesty was available for anyone who could provide help with the recovery of the abducted children. A member of Formosa's gang had responded and had been persuaded to give evidence in court against his old crime boss in exchange for complete freedom from prosecution for a list of crimes he'd committed whilst working for Formosa. Unfortunately this didn't include the abduction. They'd been relying on Dench's evidence for that.

'What about all the circumstantial evidence, sir?

'His brief'll cut through that like a knife through butter. No, it was all good stuff to support what Dench was going to say, but Dench was our main man. Without him we'll have to drop the charges. Mind you, we can tell the bloke in witness protection we're holding him and his statement in abeyance until such time as we nail Formosa again.'

'That's if he'll agree to it.'

'He won't have much choice, Lenny. It does mean we'll have to provide him with another identity and keep him in witness protection until then. Expensive job that.'

Cope dropped his head. 'Bloody hell, sir! What about them poor kids?'

'I know, and you did well, but this is no reflection on you.' Ibbotson looked up and sat back in his seat, elbows on the chair arms, steepling his fingers.

'Tell me, Lenny, are you still shagging Blacky's wife?'

Cope hesitated before saying, 'We're in a relationship, sir.'

'Ah, of course. That's the current jargon for shagging isn't it? I often wish I was in a relationship with Mrs Ibbotson, but all we are is man and wife.'

'I've no intention of ever becoming anyone's husband, sir. Once bitten, twice shy and all that.'

'What shocked me about Blacky,' said Ibbotson, 'was all this stuff about him beating his wife up. I didn't think he was like that. Quite an amiable chap, I thought. He could scare the shit out of a suspect in the interview room, but that was all an act.'

'I don't really know the man, sir, what with us working different shifts all the time I've been here, but she told me he was cruel to her.'

'We brought him in last night, did you know?'

'So I heard, sir. Drunk, was he?'

'Not really. Sober enough to drive, apparently. I spoke to him – I got the impression that he was just angry with the world.'

'I don't think the world's too pleased with him, sir.'

'On a more important matter; I'm expecting Mr Strathmore to come in and ask why we've dropped the charges against Vince Formosa. I want you to sit in with me on that one.'

'Of course, sir.'

'He'll ask if we think his children are still alive and, to be honest, I've got no idea. He's put out a reward of twenty-five thousand pounds for anyone helping in their return.'

'Doesn't seem much sir, considering he's a multi-millionaire.'

'He wanted to offer more but in my experience these huge rewards attract all sorts of chancers and time-wasters. I just hope they're still alive.'

'It could be that Formosa is keeping them alive for some future extortion.'

'Yes, I'd thought of that but, in view of Formosa knowing we have him clearly in our sights for all this, he'll only keep them alive long enough for them to talk to Strathmore on the phone the day before the handover. And don't think the handover will be a simultaneous swap. Not on your life. He'll ask for money first, after which he'll promise to release the kids, only he won't because they'll be dead and never heard of again, and all this time Formosa will be free and gloating because we've got nothing on him. I find this very hard to take, Lenny. I'd like to lift the slimy bastard, take him into the cells and belt the truth out of him.'

'You and me both, sir.'

Ibbotson stared at his DI, remembering Sep's accusation that he was in Formosa's pocket. Then he remembered a time when

Lee Dench grassed up Formosa to Cope and how Cope had Formosa arrested. Hardly the action of a copper who was in Formosa's pay. He cast the thought from his mind as being ridiculous but his stare slightly unnerved Cope.

'Sir?'

'Nothing. I was just day-dreaming about belting the truth out of Formosa.'

NINE

11 April

It was a month since his livelihood and his life in general had been taken from him and, with the weight of the world bearing down on his shoulders, Sep needed a sanctuary. The back room of the Sword and Slingshot was that very place; a personal haven he only ever shared with like souls with whom he occasionally played dominoes and had quiet conversations, but mostly where he read his newspapers and his books. The pub hadn't altered much in the hundred and fifty years of its existence. Its occasional refurbishments had been sympathetic to the pub's original character. There was an open fire, heavy oak furniture, a stone floor, an ancient stained-glass window, a large oil painting of a Yorkshire Dales village and proper beer pumps on the bar – none of your electric stuff. Best of all it was a quiet room with no muzak, no juke box, no television, no one-armed bandit, no dartboard, pool table or games machines; just tables and chairs and the hum of amiable conversation. If Sep had his own way it would still have a vague fug of cigarette smoke even though he didn't smoke himself. Sep was no fan of the nanny state.

But this evening his space had been plagued by youth, noisy youth – four male, three female. Youths had been in before but they'd only conversed with their electronic companions, which was OK with Sep, apart from the slightly annoying beeps. He had a device of his own, one that carried books. He approved of this. He could carry a library of books around without even making his pocket bulge. This was a far more useful device than the tablets and smartphones which could only be detached from their owners by amputation. The other thing he carried was a deep grievance at the world around him; a sense of personal injustice, and this was a heavy burden to bear.

He was sitting at his favourite table, the one under the stained-glass window. It was a heavy, oak table that had been in the pub since the place was built. It bore the scars of pewter tankards being banged down, dominoes shuffled, cigarette burns, scratched initials (a habit now banned by the management) and the dents and bruises inflicted during its tabletop clog-dancing years. It was an honest table that had its life history on display like the gnarled face of an old man who had survived a long, hard life. Maybe that was why Sep loved the table – because it was a survivor, something he was trying his best to be, but it wasn't easy. He looked up at the stained glass window as if for help and guidance. It had a picture of David slaying Goliath with a sword, hence the name of the pub. In the past this had had Sep insisting that David definitely used a slingshot to kill the giant, and this provoked a discussion at the time, a discussion that prompted the landlady to produce a bible which, in the Book of Samuel, mentions both versions. This led to a further discussion about the confusion caused by the bible, a confusion that had created many rival Christian religions. It was such talk that Sep had always found interesting, entertaining and even inspiring – but this juvenile giggling and guffawing bunch was none of those – just annoying.

No doubt students, the lot of them. Probably studying Soviet sociology, or equine psychology, or the tattoos of David Beckham, or some such bollocks. He'd been a student of English; up at Durham at a time when getting a place at such a university was a high achievement and being a student meant being among peers with intelligence and humour and wit, unlike this lot. Proper humour and wit and interesting conversation was seemingly beyond them, probably undeveloped due to electronic gadgets and easy living. Humour was important in Sep's world. It had helped keep him sane in his impossible circumstances, circumstances that might have had a lesser man slitting his throat.

Maybe had he been born fifty years earlier the world would

have suited him better. Fifty years ago no one would have blamed
him for killing that big fat bastard. It would have been covered
up. The BFB's death had left the world a better and safer place,
especially for children. No doubt about that.

But it was just his luck to have been born in a time where the
grinning government man had told the country a blatant lie that
had sent Sep to an Arab war where he'd legally killed men – men
he regretted killing; men far more honourable than the dead BFB,
as Sep had christened him. The BFB's death didn't trouble his
conscience one bit. It was a war that had left his soldier brother
blind and with one arm, not to mention a country destroyed,
along with a hundred thousand lives; a country now at war with
itself. So much for our army's intervention and his brother's
terrible injuries.

It was why Sep didn't vote anymore. Not for anyone. He'd
been brought up to be a socialist like his dad but he soon realized that politicians do too much damage – self-serving bastards
most of them.

He could never vote for the grinning socialist leader, who had
appointed himself a deputy who could barely string two intelligent sentences together. That's what good-looking girls used to
do in his clubbing days; they'd partner up with a plain girl
to make them stand out. His very pretty wife had done the same
– 'twas ever thus, apparently. He'd have been far better off with
her buck-toothed friend who was intelligent and amusing and
decent. You can fix buck-teeth with implants. You can't implant
intelligence and decency.

Sep's favourite political story was that of US president George
Bush Senior whose vice president was Dan Quayle, a man of
questionable intellect. The story was that Quayle was always
accompanied by two FBI men who had orders to shoot him if
anything happened to the president. These and other thoughts
stumbled through Sep's mind as the loud intruders disturbed his
tranquillity. Sep wasn't a political animal, he just despised
bullshit.

So, here he was. The man wrongly accused of killing the BFB
and who had been severely punished for it. He was remembering
a story an old sergeant had told him; a story widely known at
the station. In the early 1960s, as a young constable in Leeds,

the sergeant and a colleague had been called to a local Mecca dance hall to speak to the manager about the various disturbances they were having there. They found him in his office in a compromising situation with three under-age girls. They'd reported the matter to an inspector who had told them to leave it because the manager was a big fundraiser for various charities and a friend of the police. He went on to become a famous TV personality whose paedophile activities would have been nipped-in-the-bud had the sergeant's report been acted upon there and then. Instead he'd cheated justice by dying before his hundreds of vile offences came to light.

These injustices constantly buzzed through Sep's mind, as did all this unfair stuff going on around him, with him getting the blame for it all and yet people moving in higher circles getting away with serious stuff. All these people going around free and respected and yet here he was, a dedicated police officer one day and now a sacked and discredited, unemployed non-citizen who was lucky to have avoided a manslaughter charge, and all because he'd used reasonable force on an epileptic paedophile Member of Parliament.

Rachel, his wife, had left him and had told lies about him beating her, and his daughter believed these lies. To make matters worse, his colleagues had turned their backs on him, and this included a young DC, John Curtis, of whom Sep had high hopes. A truthful word from any one of them would have made a big difference. What was all that about? He knew what it was about. They'd been got at by DI Cope, a copper who'd come up from the Met to avoid being caught up in the bent copper witch-hunt that was going on down there.

Sep had suspected that the Met cop was up to his old tricks up here. Sep had a colleague who had got himself transferred to the Met and who had worked out of the same station as Cope. He'd told Sep that Cope had taken a course in propaganda and he'd really taken to it, to the extent that he was a world expert in spreading rumours. Sep had voiced his doubts about him and the next thing he knew he'd become a victim of Cope's gossip spreading. His colleagues were persuaded to keep their distance from him lest they join him in being associated with the Big Fat Bastard's death. In fact this led to Sep being made a scapegoat for the BFB's death. He was also certain that Cope had somehow persuaded Sep's wife to tell lies about him beating her up. How the hell had he done that? It had been all he could do to keep his rage simmering and not boiling over, which would only get him into deeper trouble.

Today, with all these thoughts spinning round in his head, and all the noise around him, Sep was on a short fuse. He knew it and he knew he mustn't let it get the better of him. Think positive, Sep. OK, what's positive? Maybe women should run countries, that's positive. Bollocks to party politics, all this socialist/capitalist crap – also positive. Just let a good woman run the country like a mother runs her family. He was thinking of his own mother now. Dead when he was twelve. She'd have run the country properly. Not his dad, who was a sweet guy but useless after his mother died. His sisters all had families of their own to look after and Sep didn't want to bother them, so Clive had looked after him. His brother who was now blind and disabled after that stupid fucking war. His brother who was in a home for the disabled because Septimus no longer had the financial wherewithal to look after him. That hurt more than anything.

The only thing his mother ever got wrong was giving him the name Septimus. He'd have much preferred Fred or Joe. Clive wasn't too struck on his name either. He'd been named after Clive Staples Lewis who wrote *The Chronicles of Narnia* – their mother's favourite book.

She meant well, but Septimus wasn't a name you gave a kid growing up in a pit village. However, it did toughen him up. He'd dished out many a thump to kids who'd taken the piss out of his name. Eventually they all called him Sep, which was odd but OK with him.

One of the youths in the room joked that someone they knew had a beard like a lavatory brush. This prompted a hail of screeching laughter totally disproportionate to the joke and Sep felt his fuse fizzing towards the bomb in his brain. His recent circumstances had degraded his self-control somewhat.

'Oh shit!' he muttered. 'Don't lose it. Please do not lose it!'

He knew this was a nothing situation. A situation any reasonable man would get up and walk away from. Just go into another room for a change, away from the racket. But Sep couldn't see why it was he who had to be reasonable all the time. Let someone else be fucking reasonable for a change. Let these noisy sods be reasonable. The noise grew louder, possibly magnified by his anger. He squeezed his eyes shut and heard himself growling. He was a pressure cooker at its limit. He put down his newspaper and got to his feet. He was a hefty man, six-feet-two and sixteen stone of mainly muscle. His size and strength had gone against him at his disciplinary hearing. He could be menacing when he wanted to be, and he wanted to be right now. He walked over to the noisy table, making his presence instantly felt, despite him not saying a word. The laughter subsided and seven pairs of eyes looked up at him. One youth had a patch of hair under his bottom lip. Sep pointed at it.

'What's that?'

He knew what they called such things. He just wanted the youth to set him up for his next line. The youth didn't answer, one of the girls answered for him.

'It's called a soul-patch.'

'On him it looks like an arsehole patch.'

He pointed to a second youth who wore his hair in a ponytail. 'I suppose you call that a ponytail do you?'

By now the menace in his eyes and voice was frightening the group.

'Do you know why it's called a pony-tail?'

No answer.

'Because when you lift it up, you see a horse's arse.'

To Sep this was a better joke than the one that had had them screeching but it didn't raise a flicker from them.

'You're giving me earache. I want you all to leave.'

His rage was suspended on the finest of threads. The youngsters had come here for a good time, not for trouble. One of them put his palms up and said, 'OK, OK, we're leaving.'

They got up to go and had all reached the door when a voice shouted. 'You lot can stay! He can go.'

All eight of them turned to look at Joyce, the landlady, who had heard what was going on. She came from around the bar and, with folded arms, she confronted Sep.

'You might be able to scare these kids but you don't scare me. I was married to a bully like you – kicked him out. I know you used to be a copper and there's a bit of a mystery as to why you left the police in such a hurry, but you can't come in here and tell my customers to leave my pub. If anyone's leaving it's you, and you don't come back. You're barred!'

Sep stared at her with wild eyes. She backed off, thinking she'd been a bit too brave for her own good. He snarled, picked up a chair and smashed it, repeatedly, on the heavy table, adding to its scars. He then hurled the chair at the stained-glass window that had been a major feature of the pub for over a hundred years. It had been salvaged from a chapel that had previously stood on this site since the reign of William III. It was known as Willy's Window but it was there no longer. The chair was now jammed in the window frame, wedged among the broken lead strips that had held the stained glass in position for over three hundred years. Outside, shards of David and Goliath were strewn all over the car park, in hundreds of coloured pieces.

The landlady was back behind the bar now. The youths and their girlfriends ran out of the door. Sep sank to his knees, weeping and hyperventilating and pounding the stone floor with his fists. The landlady picked up the telephone and dialled 999. She asked for both the police and an ambulance.

Sep went outside and sat on a low wall, staring into space. The weather was as foul as his mood, with black and grey clouds stampeding across the sky, driven by heavy gusts of wind. In the distance he could see the mist of descending rain and it wasn't long before the first drops lashed into his face. It didn't occur to him to take shelter. This was no more than he deserved.

A marked police car arrived first with its blues and twos flashing and blaring and, as if to add to his ignominy, he was arrested by two of his erstwhile very junior colleagues; two young constables who had been in awe of him when they had first arrived at the station, such was his reputation back then. It was he who advised them to cuff him.

'I may turn violent. That's why you're arresting me.'

'Yes sir,' said one of them.

Sep didn't correct him in his form of address. The rain was now drenching him and the constables. The young people and the landlady stood in the shelter of a doorway to watch proceedings as Sep was put in the back of the car just as the ambulance was arriving. It was waved away by one of the constables.

'You should have let them take me to hospital,' said Sep, 'with one of you in the ambulance and one of you following in the car.'

'Are you injured, sir?'

'I'm mentally disturbed and need treatment that I can't get at the station.'

'We can take you to St James's if you like.'

'It's OK. Just take me to the station and get me the duty doctor.'

TEN

27 April
Nunroyd Secure Psychiatric Clinic, North Yorkshire

'You killed a man,' said Professor Gilmartin.

Sep shook his head. 'No, I didn't.'

'Explain that to me.'

'For a start, that man accidentally dying in police custody is not the reason I'm in here. Had he not been epileptic, I'd still be a detective inspector with the West Yorkshire police.'

'Had he not been a suspected paedophile would he still be alive?'

'Who knows? The CPS found I had no case to answer and here you are, still banging on about it. The coroner's verdict was "sudden unexplained death in epilepsy".'

'Tell me about him.'

'He was sexually abusing children. The evidence we'd collected was cast-iron, not to mention sickening. To me he wasn't a human being; he was an enormous, filthy pig with a foul mind and chins down to his belly button.'

'So, you're glad he's dead.'

'It was a result, no doubt about that. His death's made the lives of a lot of good people much easier.'

'I assume you mean the victims?'

'Yeah, and their parents. He did a lot of lasting damage did Johnstone. Dying is probably the only decent thing he's ever done in his life. I'm just pissed off that I'm carrying the can for it. His death attracted a lot of publicity and the IPCC needed a scapegoat to show that the police can't get away with a death in custody without someone being punished. They also took great care to cover up why he'd been arrested. I'm guessing you thought it was a driving offence – driving under the influence or some such thing.'

The look on her face told him he'd hit the mark.

'I'm right, aren't I?'

'You see yourself as a scapegoat, do you?' she said.

'Of course I'm a scapegoat.'

'What about the incident in the pub?' she asked him.

'Well, I'll give you that one. That was possibly my own fault but there were mitigating circumstances. You see, to handle my getting the sack and my wife shacking up with Detective Inspector Cope, and my daughter not wanting to know me, and my colleagues turning on me, etcetera, etcetera, I needed a comfortable place to go that wasn't the tatty bedsit I'm living in right now.'

'You mean everyone turned against you for no reason?'

'No truthful reason. My wife, from whom I was already separated, claimed I'd assaulted her, which wasn't true, but it didn't stop her reporting it to the police – or to my colleagues, as they're otherwise known. It was her word against mine and she had the cuts and bruises to back her story up.'

'Which she didn't get from you?'

'No. I think she got someone to thump her so she could have some bruises. Don't ask me why.'

'She might just have fallen.'

'They weren't those type of bruises. There wasn't enough evidence to charge me, but enough for my colleagues to turn their backs on me . . . my daughter as well. Under any other circumstance my colleagues would have closed ranks around me when I was accused of killing the paedophile, but not one of them lifted a finger to help me, even people I thought were my friends.'

'Wife-beaters don't get much sympathy.'

'Wife-beaters don't deserve any sympathy. That room in the pub was my bolt-hole, if you like. That room helped me cope after everyone abandoned me.'

'Everyone?'

'Pretty much, with the exception of my brother who's blind and disabled. My sisters never had much time for either me or our Clive, plus they all live too far away. My dad's eighty-eight and in a nursing home, my wife and daughter don't want to know me, and my friends outside the job have all gone to ground. I'm a forty-seven-year-old has-been. I mean, who wants to be friends with a killer? All I had was a room in a pub. Actually, I made a few friends in that room. You deny me my room, you take away those friends, and that includes a lady called Winnie O'Toole who seemed to have taken to me.'

'Have you taken to her?'

He gave this some thought. 'Very much so. She's an old customer of mine. I arrested her three times. Once for drugs offences, once for prostitution and once for ABH – she stabbed a punter who got rough with her.'

'She sounds a real charmer.'

Sep grinned. 'She is, actually, but *you* might find her a challenge. Winnie's not what I regard as a natural born criminal, she was just . . . I don't know, born into the wrong circumstances, broken home, fell into bad company, but she has a real spark about her. Winnie's the only woman I've ever known who smokes a pipe. She's an intelligent woman, she makes me laugh and she could have that gold watch off your wrist without you knowing it was missing until you wanted to check that my hour's up.'

Gilmartin instinctively looked down at her watch, then looked up to see Sep still grinning her, as if to say, *Gotcha!*

'Has she been to visit you here?'

Sep shook his head. 'No. I don't suppose she will. We're not lovers or anything. She's trying to turn her life around, whereas I don't seem to have one to turn around.'

'Will you try and make things up with your wife?'

'No, I can't forgive what she did to me, nor can I understand it. Anyway, she's found another man – one of my so-called colleagues. Not a man I'd trust, even though I don't know him all that well.' He omitted to tell her that he thought this copper might be behind a lot that had gone wrong with his life, and not just him losing his wife to the man.

'You hardly know him but you don't trust him?'

'Well he did take my wife from me. He's one of these good-looking, smarmy types.'

'Not ugly like you then?'

Sep smiled at her. 'Something wrong with your eyesight, prof?'

She smiled back. 'Has your wife leaving you for a good-looking smarmy type offended your handsome male ego?'

'I'm heartbroken about my daughter believing all her mother's lies about me and turning her back on me. I've tried to explain my side of the story but she doesn't want to know.'

'You haven't explained why you went wild in the pub. Smashing a very valuable window.'

'Ah, yes. I really regret that. I liked that window. What happened was a gang of really annoying kids came in and started braying like a bunch of hyenas.'

'Upsetting your equilibrium.'

'If you like. OK, I overreacted. I lost it and shouted at them.'

'You scared the life out of them.'

'I know. I'm a big bloke, I can do that, but I was never going to touch any of them. I've never in my life attacked anyone in anger. Being able to scare people is a handy thing in a copper. Some villains need a good scaring.'

'Do they really?'

'Yes, they really do. Then the landlady barred me from the pub. She was quite right to do so, but she was taking away from me the only place that was helping me hold my life together.'

'Which is why you lost it?'

'Yes it is. Every man has his breaking point and that was mine. I'd sooner have broken my own leg than break that window. My leg'll mend but that window won't. When I get out of here I'll have to find a new place.'

She looked at her notes. 'I did wonder how you managed to rise to the rank of detective inspector in the space of seven years. You left the army in May 2004 at the age of thirty-seven, which is when you joined the police force. You've been a detective inspector since the age of forty-four.'

'Sounds about right.'

'In your psych evaluation before you joined CID, it says you had periods when you were bordering on bipolar.'

'I had my ups and downs, yeah, mainly due to what happened to my brother in Iraq.'

'Yes, I know about your brother.'

'Does it say that I love my brother?'

'No it doesn't.'

'Maybe you should make a note of that.'

'OK.' She turned over a page. 'It also says that you have a unique talent for sensing guilt in a suspect and that they're often so amazed at what you appear to know about their involvement in the crime that they confess.'

Sep nodded. 'It's all part of the vibe I was talking about. It's a question of using what knowledge you have to its best advantage and mix it up with a few potent lies that you know will really throw the suspect. It's possible to question a suspect in a way that makes them admit to things without realizing it. Some police interviewers do it. I just take it to a different level.' He grinned. 'The villains think I'm some sort of mind reader.'

'It's why you made detective inspector *despite* your psych evaluation.'

'Is it? I didn't know that.'

'According to this they made a balanced judgement and promoted you.'

'Then they made an unbalanced judgement and sacked me.'

She went to sit behind her desk, looked at her computer monitor and tapped away on the keyboard, talking to him as she did so. 'Would you say you're having your ups and downs again?'

'Obviously, but not for no reason. It was never for no reason. Outside agencies always caused my ups and downs.'

She looked at her watch, Sep took the hint. 'Time's up, eh?'

'Not quite.'

'Well,' he said, 'you've left no stone unturned so, what's my psychiatric condition? Does everything I've just told you add up to me being a nutcase, or a man who's got things figured out?'

'I'll let you know in a month.'

She stopped what she was doing and studied him, waiting for his reaction, but he held himself in check and said, 'I do hope you're not going to ask your people to step up their offensive against me, to get me to crack before my time is up.'

'They don't have an offensive against you.'

'So what am I doing here? Do you honestly think you can make me better than I already am?'

'I want to see if you can maintain your level of sanity.'

'This is not a good place for a sane man to be, especially a sane man being treated as an insane man, so if I don't maintain my sanity you only have yourself to blame.'

'I can live with that.'

'Can you?' he said, annoyed now. 'Maybe you should stick me on the Broomhill Ward with the advanced nutters who piss themselves and shout at the wall and bang their chairs on the floor all day long.'

'Yes I understand you've been in there. There was a complaint from one of the patients – Mr Cordingley.'

'Don't know him.'

'Well he knows you – you threatened him.'

'What? Oh him – of course I didn't threaten him. This old bloke kept dancing about in front of me trying to block my way. I wanted to go through there to get to the so-called library. You know, that room with all the comics and Rupert Bear books.'

'What did you say to him?'

'If you must know I said if you don't get out of my way, I'll put a frog in your colostomy bag.'

ELEVEN

12 April

Peter Strathmore was sitting opposite DI Cope and Detective Superintendent Ibbotson. Strathmore was thirty-five years old and looked many years older. He had the pale, drawn features of a spiritually defeated man who hadn't slept for many nights. His voice was hoarse and without strength as he spoke to the policemen.

'I want you give me a straight answer. Do you think Formosa's killed my children?'

'We honestly don't know, Mr Strathmore,' said Ibbotson.

'But you know it was Formosa who took them.'

'Sadly, with the death of our main witness we have no proof of who took them, which is why we can't charge Formosa.'

'Look cut the crap! You know it was Formosa, just as you know it was Formosa who killed the witness.'

'We've no idea how Formosa could have found out about the witness,' said Cope, 'or how he found out we were about to arrest him. Because of the children we were playing it very carefully. We didn't want to scare him into doing anything rash.'

'You mean like killing my children?'

'We, er, we suspect the witness might have inadvertently given himself away,' said the superintendent.

'Shouldn't he have been in a safe house or something?'

'He was due to be moved into a safe house today as a matter of fact.'

'What about the other witness?'

'The other witness's evidence wouldn't have been enough to convict him.'

'Does this other witness know where my children are?'

'I'm afraid not. Nor did the witness who was killed.'

Strathmore hung his head and began to cry. His shoulders heaved with great sobs. He looked up at the policemen and said, 'Jesus Christ! We all know who took them and yet we can't do a thing about it. If ever I get my hands on Formosa I'll kill him, you know that, don't you? He'll tell me what happened to them, then I'll kill him and hand myself over to you.'

Strathmore was a big man. Originally a bricklayer who had built a house-building company up from nothing. He had huge hands that would throttle the truth out of Formosa if he could get them around his neck.

'That probably wouldn't be wise,' said Cope, 'but we couldn't blame you.'

'All this for a piece of poxy land. If I'd owned the land myself I'd have given him it but my partners thought it best to call you lot in.'

'I understand the land is worth over four million and Formosa wanted you to sell it for half a million.'

'He wanted it to look like a standard business deal, so as not to arouse suspicion. Hard thing to steal is land.'

'Did he actually tell you he'd taken your children?' Ibbotson asked.

Strathmore shook his head. 'No, all he ever did was to ask me if anything valuable was missing from my life. If so, that thing might well be restored to me once the deal was signed. At the time I didn't know what he was talking about. He'd just made the stupid offer and I'd just turned it down.'

'Did he say this in front of witnesses?' asked Cope.

'No, just me. Then he left. Ten minutes later my wife rang to say the kids had gone missing. I was so worried I actually didn't associate what Formosa had said to me with them going missing until later that evening.'

'But you didn't tell us – why?' asked Ibbotson. 'We were already on the case.'

'I wasn't thinking straight. I just wanted them back. I rang him up and asked him what he'd done with them. He acted as though he knew nothing about it but he said he might be able to help if I went round to see him, but I mustn't say anything to you lot.

'I told my wife and she told me to do exactly as he asked, so I did. I went round to meet him. All I wanted was to get my kids back.'

'Where did you meet him?'

'Oh, in a pub car park.'

'Which pub?'

'The Wellington out on Wetherby Road. He didn't get out of his car and I was surrounded by three heavies with him otherwise I'd have dragged him out of the car and throttled the truth out of him. He said he might be able to help me because he has influence with people who kidnap children, but I must help him first by selling him the land for half a million. I told him I had three partners and he told me to get them to agree.'

'But they wouldn't,' said Ibbotson, who already knew the story.

'No, they wouldn't. They told you lot without asking me, the lousy bastards! If my kids are dead it's their fault!'

'We're working on the assumption that your children are still alive,' Ibbotson said. 'He might well be holding on to them for some future blackmail attempt. You're a wealthy man and your children are his key to your money.'

Strathmore looked at him with a gleam of hope behind his tears. 'Do you think so?'

'It's a possibility.'

'Well, do you think I might be able to do a deal with him?'

The policemen looked at each other. Ibbotson didn't think the children were still alive and neither thought Formosa would go along with such a risky deal even if they were. Superintendent Ibbotson shook his head and said, 'I'm afraid we couldn't approve such a thing.'

'I'm not asking for your fucking approval!' said Strathmore.

TWELVE

13 April

Vince Formosa was of Maltese extraction. He was a small, squat man in his late forties. He had fallen into bad company in Manchester as a youth, ending up running the gang he had joined as a thirteen-year-old who had a sub-human capacity for violence. At the age of eighteen he had skedaddled to London as the police were looking at him for a murder. Luckily for him the two witnesses to this crime had both died in suspicious circumstances. In future years many people who threatened Formosa's freedom died in suspicious circumstances. It was this sort of luck that had kept him out of police clutches for so long. In Vince Formosa's world a man made his own luck.

In London he'd prospered under the name of Vic Robinson until things got too hot for him, which was when he moved up to Leeds in Yorkshire, once again operating under his real name. A Met officer, who had been in his pay in London, had recently followed him up to Leeds in anticipation of the Met's corruption investigation. He was still in his pay.

He now kept a low profile. His existence was known by the police and villains but his actual whereabouts wasn't; few people knew the location of his domicile or his headquarters. He'd relied heavily on a fearsome reputation which kept away challenges from all underworld competition, plus his reputation made the police very wary of him. He ran a very tight and ruthless ship and right now he had some tidying up to do. He had two men whose work was good but whose tongues were not one hundred per cent reliable, and reliability, to Vince, had to always be one hundred per cent. They were both standing in front of him, awaiting payment for their latest job. Vince looked up at them and smiled. His office was a basement in the centre of Leeds. He had four offices scattered around the city. No one but he knew the location of all four. In the next room were another two men who were both one hundred per cent reliable. He had four such pairs of men. None of these pairs knew of the existence of the others. Additional men, such as out-of-towners Sharky and Spud, were recruited on an ad hoc basis. There was another level below this basement in which there was a furnace room which had originally heated the four-storey block above. In more recent years this had been replaced by a modern gas heating system, but the old furnace still remained, connected to the original chimney but not to the heating system. The block was owned by Vince Formosa.

'You did an excellent job,' Vince told Spud and Sharky. 'You probably wasted one more than was necessary, but no matter. She was a cheap whore and her death rubbed the message in a bit deeper. People out there will know better than to cross me in future.'

'No fear of that, Mister Formosa.'

Vince opened a drawer in his desk. The two men assumed he was taking out their money – five grand each. Instead he brought out a 9mm automatic handgun, into which was screwed a silencer. He pointed it in their general direction.

'However,' he said, 'I'm not too happy with the one of you who's planning to do a runner.'

He sounded as if he was criticising them for some minor transgression, but Spud and Sharky both knew that there was no such thing as a minor transgression in Vincent's world. They both froze, each assuming it was the other who had let something slip. Vince aimed his gun at Spud whose heart skipped a beat just before his boss shot him clean through it. Dead on his feet, Spud's legs ceased to support him and he collapsed to the floor without taking his dead eyes off Vince. Sharky frowned and looked down at the Irishman. Spud had been an arsehole at times, but he was the nearest Sharky had to a friend. As he looked down, a shudder of realization ripped through his body. He looked up at Vince who was now pointing the gun at him and explaining the situation in a matter-of-fact voice.

'Actually, it's both of you, but I didn't want you panicking and making yourself a moving target.'

Sharky was about to do just that when Vince shot him through the heart as well. He was also dead before he hit the floor. Vince rose from his chair and peered over his desk at the two bodies. He gave a nod of self-congratulation. The second pop of the gun acted as a signal for the men in the next room to come in. Vince put the gun back in the drawer and got to his feet. He then looked down at the rug under the two dead men and tutted in exasperation. It was stained with blood. Not too much, because dead hearts don't pump blood, but the slightest drop of incriminating blood had no place in his office.

'You'd think they'd have had the decency not to bleed on my rug. Better burn it as well – and get me another one. Something with a nice cheerful pattern . . . and remember . . . this only happens to men who disobey my rules. I must be always obeyed to the letter.' He noticed the Colt in a holster strapped to Sharky's leg in wild-west style. 'I'll have that gun and his gun belt.'

The two men nodded and did his bidding, then they dragged the bodies out to take them down the stone steps to the furnace room below. In ten minutes all trace of Spud and Sharky would be reduced to ashes, as were all connections between Vince Formosa and the deaths of Lee Dench and Chantelle.

THIRTEEN

'How was I to know he wears a colostomy bag?'
Professor Gilmartin walked away from Sep and sat down behind her desk. 'Well, he does.'

'OK. I'll apologize to him and tell him he's got nothing to worry about. His colostomy bag will be forever frog-free.'

Gilmartin nodded, then said, 'There's more than Rupert Bear in the library, surely.'

'They're the only decent books in there,' said Sep. 'The Rupert stories are written in prose as well as rhyme, so you can take your pick.'

'Tell me what you like.'

'The Lottery, best idea anyone ever had.'

'Lottery?'

'Yeah. It gives people hope of great riches. Yeah, I know it's a zillion to one shot but it's real and it's the best two quid's worth in town – and half of that goes to charity.' He looked at her and asked, 'OK, what does that make me?'

'A dreamer.'

'Yeah, I'll go with that.'

'I meant whose books do you like?'

'James Joyce.'

She shook her head, 'I might have known.'

'Mind you, I think you have to read him while you're drunk which is what he was when he wrote *Ulysses*. I also studied him at university.'

'Ah, that's right. You have an English degree.'

'I eventually got my Master's, which is a necessity when reading Joyce, although an Irish degree might be more useful.'

'So *Ulysses* makes immediate sense to you?'

'Absolutely. Read it from cover to cover in my pub before I was banned. The more I drank, the more sense he made.'

'Do you hate everything that doesn't make immediate sense?'

'Hate's a strong word.'

'Tell me what you hate.'

'I hate being told lies.'

'Lies, eh?'

She cast him a challenging glance and asked, 'OK, where does Rupert the Bear live and what do they call his best pal, the badger?'

'What?'

'I've asked you a couple of basic questions about Rupert the Bear. If you're such an expert you'll be able to tell me.'

'I've forgotten.'

'He lives in Nutwood, the badger's name is Bill and you don't know anything about Rupert the Bear.'

'I said I don't like *being told* lies, not telling them. Telling them's a necessary evil we need to get us through life. I hate Rupert the bloody Bear. My dad wanted to call me Rupert, but my mother won the day with Septimus.'

'If you don't like your name, change it.'

'What? Change Septimus Ruddigore Black?'

'Ruddigore? Good grief!'

'That's right. Ruddigore's a Gilbert and Sullivan opera thing – personally I preferred Gilbert O'Sullivan.'

He emphasised the O.

'I'm forced to agree with you.'

'To change my name would be going against my mother's wishes. I once asked her why she'd called me Septimus. She said, and I can pretty much quote her verbatim: "Because you're my seventh child, and Septimus means seven in some language or other. It's because it's a proper name that'll make people remember you. Make you stand out. No one would remember Joe Black . . . or Fred Black like your dad, but you tell 'em your name's Septimus Black and they'll sit up and take notice. You could be the prime minister with a name like Septimus Black. Why? Do you not like it?"'

'I told her I wasn't too struck on it. She told me my dad wanted to call me Rupert.' He smiled to himself. 'If there was an answer designed to stop me moaning about my name that was it. I have five sisters, the youngest is fifteen years older than me, and thirteen years older than our Clive. So by the time I was up and running my sisters were mostly up and married. Clive and I had always been close but I scarcely knew my sisters. They all behaved like distant aunts.'

She looked at his file. 'It says here you served in Three Commando Brigade in Iraq and were awarded an MM plus a mention in dispatches. Was that after you got your MA?'

'Yeah, I left uni and joined the army. I'm officially Septimus Ruddigore Black MM, MA – not many of us about.'

'Why Ruddigore?'

Sep smiled. He always saw the humour in his full name. 'My parents went down to London for their honeymoon and consummated their marriage in the Savoy Theatre in the Strand during a production of *Ruddigore*. They conceived me into the bargain.'

'In the theatre? That must have been a bit awkward.'

'Well, it would have been had that story been true. It's actually something I made up to explain the name. My mother thought it chimed well with Septimus. Mum and Dad were middle-aged when I was conceived.'

'Were you an officer in the army?'

'No, if I'd been an officer it'd have been an MC they gave me. I joined as a common soldier and ended up an even more common sergeant.'

'It also says you come from a mining family.'

'You didn't ask me how I won my medal.'

'If I had would you have told me?'

'No . . . I don't remember much about it myself – and don't read anything into that. A man's mind and memory often switch off to allow him to do stupid and dangerous stuff, especially in war.'

'I know that. So, tell me about coming from a mining family.'

'Yes I broke that tradition. A month before she died my mother told me that I should never go near a pit, never mind down one. I can remember her words to this day:

"It's a dangerous and unnatural world, son, where men only work to pick up a wage on Friday and for no other reason. There's no job satisfaction down a pit, just muck and sweat and an early death. Our men all work together and live together and drink together. It's called a community and once you get stuck in a community you have the devil's own job getting out. I don't want you to be stuck here, son. When you get a job it'll be one you enjoy doing or my name's not Agnes Black".'

'So you got a Master's in English then joined the army. Why?'

'Why not? My alternative was to be a teacher or something. Can you see me being a teacher?'

She shrugged, saying, 'Did you enjoy your job as a copper?'

'I did, yes. I think I'm suited to it. The army's a young man's game.'

'You looked upon it as a game did you?'

'I enjoyed it up to a point, yes.'

'That point being?'

'Having to kill people. That's not an enjoyable part of the job.'

She paused to ponder this, then asked, 'And do you enjoy being called Septimus?'

'I loved the person who gave it to me, which is all that counts in a name.'

'And no one poked fun at your name?'

'I just thumped anyone who did. Oops! Admitted to being violent. Done it again. Hoist with my own petard! Bit of Shakespeare that – *Macbeth* I believe – and petard is a french word for a fart.'

'It's from *Hamlet*,' she said, 'so much for your Master's – and a petard is a kind of siege bomb used for blasting a hole in a wall.'

'Madam, I will have you know that petard is a French word for a loud discharge of intestinal gas . . . as well as a word for that siege bomb of yours and, as for that boring bugger Shakespeare, he wrote the same play thirty seven times then he switched things around a bit, gave people different names and gave the plays different titles just to fool us. If he was around now he'd be writing for *Coronation Street*. So, am I going to need one of your petards to get out of this joint?'

'Mr Black, you've just covered the Lottery, colostomy bags, Rupert Bear, James Joyce, Shakespeare and whether or not a petard is a siege bomb or a fart – and now you want me to pronounce you sane.'

'Could an insane man talk intelligently about such diverse subjects without losing the thread?' countered Sep.

She opened her mouth to respond to his argument then thought better of it. 'Look,' she said, 'I can't release you without notifying the court and they might decide to have you do the remainder of your prison sentence in jail. If I keep you here for another month I can guarantee that won't happen. So, all you have to do is hold your act together for another four weeks. Or you could buy a lottery ticket and try to buy yourself out.'

'Do you have any other wise words to get me back on the road to normality?'

'From where you are now, it's a hard road.'

'Dead or alive,' sang Sep.

'Pardon?'

'Nothing. You just reminded me of an old blues song of that name.'

'Woody Guthrie,' said Gilmartin.

FOURTEEN

14 May

Sep had lost a lot in his life but he'd kept his car – a classic Audi Quattro, bought and paid for and in pretty good condition. He was sitting in it outside the Sword and Slingshot the day after he'd been discharged from the Nunroyd Clinic with written confirmation of his sanity. In fact he had it in his pocket when he saw Winnie approaching. She was a creature of habit and always turned up at around seven. Sep gave a short blast of his horn. She looked up and waved, indicating that he come across and join her in the pub. Then her wave turned into a flap of the hand when she realized this wouldn't be possible. She made her way over to his car got in and sat beside him, asking, 'Have you escaped from the loony bin?'

He took his discharge letter from his pocket and handed it to her. 'Nope, I got an honourable discharge yesterday. Written proof that I'm officially no longer a loony. How many people have written proof of that?'

Winnie took out her pipe and proceeded to load it up with tobacco from a pouch. 'Not me,' she said, 'mind you, with me it's my insanity that keeps me going. Does this mean you're a free man?'

'More or less. Free to do what, I'm not too sure.'

Winnie lit her pipe and blew out a perfect smoke-ring. Sep buzzed down the window to let it out.

'Take me for a drive,' she said. 'I know some stuff that might interest you. Jesus, Sep! You really are some scruffy sod! Does it ever occur to you to go to a barber?'

'Why do women keep telling me that?'

'Because you look like Ben Gunn.'

'Ben who?'

'Him from *Treasure Island*. He hadn't seen a barber for years. I used to quite fancy you.'

He almost said he felt the same way about her, but he didn't want to drop his guard – the guard that kept a distance between him and any other person who might let him down and hurt him. He looked at her until she said, 'What?'

'Oh, nothing.'

Winnie was about ten years younger than Sep and unusually pretty for a woman who had led such a dissolute life. She had natural, dark-red hair that hung about her shoulders in a wild way that might look unattractive on another woman, but it somehow suited Winnie who had a beautiful smile, great teeth and a gypsy look about her. Sep had often wondered if she had Romany ancestry. He hadn't asked because that would have shown him to be interested in her, which he was. He drove along the Harrogate Road through the outer suburbs of Leeds.

'There's a pub in Harewood,' he said. 'It should be fairly empty on a Monday.'

'Does it have any stained glass windows?'

'It might have. It's a fairly ancient place.'

'We'd better hope they don't know about you.'

'What's the talk in the Sword and Slingshot about me?'

'Those noisy kids still come in – pain in the arse. Loud as

hell. I think Joyce regrets interfering when you scared them away.'

'Would she let me back in, then?'

'Ooh, now you're asking. She's having that window repaired with it being a major feature of the pub. It's costing an arm and a leg according to her.'

'Is she? Great. Maybe if I paid for the damage.'

'What? You've got money have you?'

'Some.'

He tapped his steering wheel. 'And I could sell this tomorrow for fifteen grand. A lot more if I was prepared to wait for the right buyer. In fact, the way I am for money it might well come to that. Sell this and buy me an old banger for a few hundred; something I can leave outside my hovel without fear of it being nicked. I've been renting a garage to keep this in, so I'll be making money and saving money. The problem is . . .' His voice tailed off.

'The problem is what?'

'Oh, I'm probably being ridiculous, but driving round in this gives me some self-respect – a commodity which is in short supply right now.'

'You're not being ridiculous.'

They were still discussing this when they arrived at the Harewood Arms.

'Ah, they've got outside seats. I can have a smoke as we talk.'

'OK, I'll get the beer in . . . pint?'

Winnie sat down at an empty table. 'What else?'

Sep went inside and brought them both pints of Sam Smith's bitter. 'So,' he said, sitting opposite her, putting her pint in front of her, 'what's this stuff that might interest me?'

She looked around to see if anyone could overhear her. No one else was occupying the outside seats. 'Well, it's stuff that might get my throat slit if word gets out that I'm passing this on to an ex-copper. In fact I might get my throat slit if a certain person finds out what I know.'

'Is this something that might be of interest to me? Because if not you should keep it to yourself.'

'Really?' said Winnie, nodding her head and sucking on her pipe in the manner of some wise old *éminence grise*. 'Let me tell you, my boy, a story about Socrates.'

'Socrates? Are we talking about the Greek philosopher or the Brazilian mid-fielder?'

'Foolish boy. This is an ancient story – about 400 BC. A student came up to Socrates one day and told him there was a rumour going around that concerned him.

"Will it be of any interest to me?" Socrates asked.'

"Not sure," said the student.'

"Will it enhance my life?"

"Doubt it."

"Is it true?"

"I've got no idea, it's just a rumour."

"So," said Socrates. "You come to me with a rumour that might not be of any interest to me, it will not enhance my life and yet you don't even know if this rumour is true. I suggest you go away and take this ridiculous rumour with you . . ."'

'And?' said Sep.

'And that's why Socrates never found out that Plato was shagging his wife.' Winnie blew a series of three smoke rings as if to underscore the end of her story.

'Wise words, oh master,' said Sep, 'but I happen to know already about the copper who's shagging my wife – as you so poetically put it.'

Winnie spoke in a whisper, despite there being no one within earshot. 'That copper's working for Vince Formosa.'

Sep gave this time to sink in as he watched a double-decker bus passing by on its way to Harrogate.

'How the hell would you know that?'

'Because I've seen them together. I know what they both look like and I've seen them both together. That how I know.'

'I hope there's more to it than that.'

'Well, I happen to know Vince Formosa's car. He's got one of them new Bentleys – a black one. On the streets it stands out like the bollocks on a starving dog. It hasn't got blacked-out windows because he's wise to that. The police see a car with blacked-out windows and they see a car carrying someone who doesn't want to be seen, which is why such cars are very likely to be stopped, and Vince doesn't like belong stopped by anyone, least of all the police.

'I mean, everybody knows whose car it is. He's got a man

who drives him around. Big feller called Jez who used to be a boxer. Anyway this car comes past and I see Vince in the back. He looked straight at me. No mistaking who he was – he's got eyes like a shithouse rat.'

'Winnie! Do your best to be ladylike.'

'Sorry. He looked at me but he didn't see me, if you know what I mean. To him I was just some tart touting for business.'

'Were you dressed like tart?'

'No, I was dressed like this. Can I get on with what I'm trying to tell you?'

'Sorry, carry on.'

'Thank you. Anyway his car stops about fifty yards beyond me and Jez gets out and starts walking away, aimless like – as if he's been told to make himself scarce but not to go far. I'm a bit curious so I just hang around on a corner as if I'm looking for punters – which I wasn't by the way,' she added, hastily. 'Never worked the streets, ever.'

'That's none of my business anymore,' said Sep. 'Although I always thought you were better than that.'

'Really? Oh, that's very nice, thank you.'

Sep shrugged away her thanks and said, 'I assume there's more to this story.'

'Oh yes, a lot more. After a couple of minutes another car turns up and parks behind Vince's Bentley. That copper gets out of it and gets into Vince's car.'

'You mean DI Cope?'

'I do. When you were a DI did you ever have any secret meetings like that with big time villains?'

'None that my bosses didn't know about. In fact I can't think of a single one.'

'Well, this was in the back of Vince Formosa's Bentley and they were there for nearly half an hour. I turned away three punters. Could have made a few quid.'

'If you hadn't given it up.'

'Oh yes, I've definitely given it up. Anyway, after about half an hour this copper gets out, chats to Vince through the car window for a few seconds then Vince sticks his mitt out of the window for Cope to shake, like a couple of good buddies.

Cope gets back in his own car, Jez appears from nowhere and they both drive off.'

'And Formosa was definitely in the car?'

'Definitely. I wouldn't put you wrong on something like that, Sep. I saw it coming down the street, I knew it was his car and sure enough there he was in the back.'

'And he saw you but he wouldn't recognize you again?'

'No. He glanced at me for one second and I had a dark wig on. I often wear a wig on the streets. My hair's got a mind of its own. I look like a fucking gypsy half the time.'

'I quite like your gypsy hair. Would Cope know who you are?'

'You like my hair? What else do you like about me, Sep?'

'I quite like your colouring.'

'You mean my tandoori tan?'

'I mean your light-brown complexion. Where does it come from?'

Winnie smiled. 'Not absolutely sure. I know my father was a man called Patrick O'Toole, full-blown Irish, born in Galway and my mother was a bit of a mixture. My grandmother on her side was a brown-skinned woman from Wigan, but she died when my mother was very young and no one really knew of her origins. As for my grandfather he could have been anyone by all accounts. My father was a racecourse bookie whose work took him all over England, including York where he met my mother, who was a real beauty by all accounts. He left her when the York race-meeting ended. I came along nine months after that and my mother died when I was born. They tracked my dad down, with him being well-known in the racing fraternity, but he was also well-known to the police and was locked up for fraud or some such thing. So I ended up in a children's home.'

'So, you had a bad start. Did you ever track your father down?'

'Never tried . . .' She hesitated for a while, just looking at him.

'What?' Sep said.

'Well there is one thing you should know about me, though – and it's probably why I took a shine to you.'

'Why's that?'

'It's because you killed Cyril Johnstone.'

It was Sep's turn to hesitate now. He stared at her, completely bemused. 'You took a shine to me because I killed Johnstone?'

'Yes.'

'Well at the risk of taking the shine off our relationship, Winnie, I didn't kill him. He died of an epileptic fit. I had no idea he was epileptic.'

'I heard he was struggling with you when he had his fit.'

'As it happens, yes he was, but I didn't do anything to kill him. How did you know that?'

'I talk to people who talk to the police.'

'Yes, the police did me no favours on that – mainly Cope's doing. He found out I didn't trust him and spread a lot of poison around the station about me.'

'I'm guessing it's why you had to leave,' Winnie said.

'It was. So why did you take this . . . shine to me?'

'Because Cyril Johnstone sexually assaulted me when I was in a home.'

Sep's face froze for a few seconds when he heard this. Winnie added, 'That's why you arrested him isn't it?'

'His arrest had nothing to do with you, Winnie.'

'I didn't mean me personally. I meant because he was a kiddie-fiddler.' She studied Sep's face, but he gave nothing away.

'I was twelve years old,' she said, 'and I was scared to death of him. He used to visit the home now and again with him being the patron of a children's charity.'

'Northern Orphans,' said Sep. 'I always thought it was a daft name. Very few of the kids were actually orphans – just kids who weren't wanted.'

'Well that was me. One day he took me into a room where we were alone and took my knickers down and . . .'

Sep put a hand up to stop her. 'Whoa, whoa! You don't have to go on. I know all about what he did to young girls . . . and boys for that matter.'

'Sep, you don't know! I was twelve years old, and skinny as a rake. Can you imagine how terrifying it was being raped by a filthy giant like him? He was ten times as big as me. I thought I was going to die.'

Sep shuddered at the image it conjured. 'I can't imagine it, no.'

'So I'm right about why he was arrested?'

'Yes you are.'

She gave a huge, satisfied smile, saying, 'It wasn't just once, he did it to me a lot – every time he came to the home. I dreaded seeing his car turn up.'

'Did you ever tell anyone?'

'Oh yes, we had a matron, I told her, but she just said I was lucky to be living there and that Mr Johnstone was a very kind and important man and that I was a dirty girl with a dirty mind and I mustn't tell such terrible lies about him. So I kept my mouth shut. He did it to other kids and they said nothing either. You know, it hung over me all my life. It's the injustice of it . . . that someone can get away with stuff like that and then lie about it and everyone believes him not you, because you're just a kid. When I heard he was dead it was like a big weight had been lifted off me. I was dying to know why he'd been arrested. I knew it wouldn't be a driving offence like they said it was.'

'We had him bang to rights,' said Scp. 'He'd have got fifteen years minimum had he lived and he knew it.'

'I'm really glad he knew it. It's a pity they can't tarnish his memory like they did with Savile.'

'Jimmy Savile wasn't a member of the establishment,' said Sep. 'Rumour has it that one of our former prime ministers was up to no good with kids, but MI5 went to great lengths to cover that up. I wasn't going to let that happen to Johnstone. He knew his game was over, believe me. He got his comeuppance and he knew it.'

'That's good,' said Winnie. 'I know it cost you your job but it made a big difference to my life and it would have made a big difference to a lot of people's lives who he assaulted. It's a pity they can't know *why* he was in police custody.'

'Well I can't tell them or I'll be in breach of an agreement that might land me in jail, but there's nothing to stop you going to the papers. Could you track down anyone else who he assaulted?'

'Doubt it. Most of them won't want to drag it all up again.'

'I could give you a few names of people who *would* have gone to court against him had he lived,' Sep told her. 'If any of them rings a bell I could point you in their direction.'

'It sounds to me as if you want this story told as much as I do,' said Winnie.

'Well, I think the story about me being sacked for being the cause of his death will come out at some time. The papers'll certainly make a meal of a story like that. But if your story gets there first it'll do me no harm.'

Winnie grinned. 'Septimus, that's good enough for me. Let me hear a few names.'

Sep took a couple of minutes reciting names he'd committed to memory some months previously. Winnie knew two of them and those two might know others. He promised to give her their addresses, on one condition.

'My name does not come up when you talk to the papers. In fact, if you're asked if you got the information about Johnstone from the police, you say no, they're just kids whose names you remember.'

'Not a problem. I'll tell them it's none of their business.'

'So, back to why we're here,' said Sep. 'Would Cope know who you are?'

'No, and he certainly won't know I know who *he* is.'

'Then I can't see any reason why Formosa might have an issue with you.'

'An issue? You mean he'll have no reason to have me topped?'

'No reason at all.'

'Jesus! I can't believe such a crook is allowed to exist in this day and age. This is Leeds in the twenty-first century, not Chicago in the 1930s.'

'Villains have a bad habit of adjusting to fit the age and place they live in,' said Sep. 'In Chicago in the 1930s they mainly dealt in booze, nowadays it's mainly drugs. Luckily in this country we've got strict gun laws so our gun crime has always been massively lower than it would be if everyone could buy guns.'

'There's a few I'd have shot if I'd been able to get my hands on a gun,' she said.

'You and thousands of others . . . anything else?'

'Yes, there is.' Winnie brushed away a strand of dark hair from her eyes. 'Look,' she said nervously, 'Formosa doesn't know I know this, and he never must.'

Sep put his hand on top of hers. 'Whatever it is, he won't get it from me. The odds are that I can't do anything with it. Everyone down at the station thinks I'm a murdering wife-beater who's just come out of a nuthouse. What's this other thing?'

'It's to do with a girl I knew called Christine. She was killed by Vince's heavies when they went to kill her boyfriend for grassing on Vince for that kidnapping job.'

'The Strathmore children?'

'Yeah, poor little beggars. They've been gone a while now. I think Lee Dench was involved. He was Christine's boyfriend.'

'Don't know much about him. How long ago was this?'

'A few weeks ago,' said Winnie. 'The word on the street is that Formosa's behind it. What do you think?'

'I don't know. I haven't actually had my ear to the ground recently.'

'I think he's probably killed them.'

'Doubt it. He won't kill them before he gets his hands on the money. This happened when I was banged up in the nuthouse. Good job I had an alibi or my colleagues would have fingered me for that as well.'

'What? Oh, yeah. Anyway, I used to keep an eye on Christine – or Chantelle as she called herself, when she was on the streets.'

'I thought you never worked the streets.'

'I didn't, but I knew Christine. She kind of looked up to me. She wanted me to get her into Henrietta's but she was always lower end of the market was Christine. Tattoos and piercings and stuff. Never a good look in a high-class establishment. *And* she was a real coke-head, never in her right mind from sniffin' charlie. It's OK in small doses, that stuff, but no one ever takes it in small doses.'

'Did you ever use it?'

'Yeah, there's little I haven't done. I used charlie, acid, weed and everything, but I kicked it all when I felt it getting a hold of me. It's dulls the mind and I hated not being in control of me – I'm all I've got. Anyway, I put myself in a private rehab place out in the country, which wasn't cheap. A grand a week for six weeks – and don't ask me where I got the money from.'

'None of my business, anyway I'm impressed – that makes you very special in my eyes.'

'Really?' Winnie smiled. 'Thank you.'

'So, what's the connection with Cope?'

She hesitated before saying, 'Lee grassed Vincent up to Cope – Christine told me.'

'Good God!' said Sep. 'Talk about the kiss of death!'

Winnie nodded. 'See what I mean about this being dangerous stuff?'

Sep's brow corrugated, deep in thought. 'Then Cope used the information Dench gave him to get Formosa arrested. But why would he do that if he's in Formosa's pay?'

'You think I'm giving you dodgy information?'

'Oh no – quite the opposite. I'm guessing that Cope told Formosa first, and Formosa *told* him to pass the information on to the police.'

'Why would he do that?'

'To cement Cope's reputation with the police. He knew that all he had to do to get himself off was to kill Dench.'

'*All* he had to do? I'd say it's quite a lot.'

'Not for someone like Formosa. Having people killed is just business. Cope will have had tabs on Dench's whereabouts. Formosa gives the order and the job's done, just another piece of business to him. I always figured Cope to be staying clear of London while they had their purge of police corruption down there. What you told me about Cope and Formosa ties in with what I already suspect. Formosa moved up from the Smoke about five years ago. It's my information that Cope was tied in with him back then. In fact, I mentioned it to one or two people, which was what set Cope against me.'

'To the extent that he started bad-mouthing you to the other cops?'

'Yeah, and me being suspicious of him would really worry Formosa. He needed Cope to be squeaky-clean in the eyes of the police force. A senior police officer in his pay would be a massive asset, and Cope turning Formosa in would kill any suspicion that Cope was anything other than a straight cop doing his best to fight crime. Certainly not a cop in Formosa's pocket.'

'That's all very devious.'

'Well, deviants tend to be devious. It also made Cope the blue-eyed boy with the police,' Sep said, 'even though they had to drop the charge against Formosa, with Dench being dead.'

'Still, it was a risky thing for Formosa to do.'

'It was, but it was a risk worth taking to Formosa. Dench was a dead man the minute he opened his mouth to Cope. Formosa will have been laughing his socks off at getting one over on the cops. He's got too much clout has that bloke. He really needs bringing down. No sooner had I opened my big mouth with my suspicions about him and Cope and my whole world collapsed around me. I lost my job and my family. This Formosa guy's a dangerous man to cross.'

'Tell me about it,' said Winnie. 'The only people who can connect all the dots on this were Lee and Christine who are both dead.'

'Yeah, well, that just about sums it all up,' agreed Sep. He's not a man who leaves loose ends isn't Formosa, and his pet copper's living with my wife – and my daughter. I'm not happy about that, Winnie, not happy at all.'

'Blimey, Sep. You can't tell your wife this.'

'I know that. It seems to me that the only way to get him out of my house is for the police to have good reason to arrest one of their own.'

'Which they don't like doing.'

'They didn't mind stuffing me for something I didn't do.'

Winnie got to her feet and took out her purse to pay for more drinks. Sep looked at her, curiously. 'Tell me to mind my own business if you like, but now you're going straight, where do you get your, er . . . your wherewithal?'

'I, er, I do some bar work plus a bit of buying and selling. You know, sell cheap, buy cheaper. I could get you a classy Tommy Hilfiger top for a tenner. That's cost price, that is.'

'Genuine or counterfeit?'

'Would you know the difference?'

'I would if all the stitching came out in two days.'

'Not in these it wouldn't. I get my supplies from Naples, or at least my supplier gets them from there and brings them into this country using means that don't concern me. Over there he's in a position to pick and choose which batch he buys – and he knows what to look for.'

'Naples, eh? That's where the Camorra hang out. Is your man connected?'

'No, he's a bloke whose clothing business went down the drain because of dirt-cheap Asian imports made by women and children earning two pence an hour. Pretty much like all the garment industries around here. I've got regular customers who have market stalls and they're more than happy to pay cash for the good stuff.'

'So this stuff's all fake and probably smuggled into Naples from India and China and made by fakers.'

'Bangladesh actually. There are good fakers and bad fakers and my man knows all the good ones who pay much better money to their workers for a much better product – I mean as good as the real thing – the only thing that's fake is the label. He even goes over to Bangladesh now and again to give them the benefit of his expertise.'

'I don't suppose he gives the Customs and Excise the benefit of his expertise – that could be a problem for you.'

She glared at him. 'OK, Mr Perfect, so I dabble in the black economy to keep me off the dole. Your problem isn't me, it's Cope, who's as bent as a nine bob note.'

FIFTEEN

The sign above the door said "Peter James Hair Solutions". Hair Solutions? What the hell was all that about? Did this mean that Peter James wasn't an actual barber? What solution would he come to regarding Sep's hair? Through the window he saw two men sitting in barber's chairs, so maybe he was reading too much into the name. He went in and, before he sat down to read the customary newspaper, he asked, 'Is this an actual barbers?'

'Of course it is, sir. What else would we be?'

'It's that thing about hair solutions. What exactly does that mean?'

'It means that if your hair's a problem, we solve that problem.'

'Well my hair's a problem because it's too long and I'd like you to solve that problem by cutting it.'

'That's what we do, sir.'

'So you're just a barber, nothing more.'

'What more is there, sir?'

'I'm sorry, my brain's obviously not behaving itself today – perhaps it's overheated with all the hair around it.'

'Well, I can certainly remedy that, sir. This chair's free, if I could take your coat?'

Septimus sat in the chair and stared at himself in the mirror and he wasn't impressed by what he saw – a middle-aged man who wasn't growing old gracefully. His hair was greying rapidly. His eyes were tired, his skin pale and his teeth needed whitening. Maybe after this haircut he should go to one of those tanning places, then have his teeth whitened. He'd look more presentable then. This set him wondering. Were there any advantages to not looking presentable?

The barber put a cloth around his neck and tucked it into his collar, talking constantly.

'Finished work early sir, or are you having the day off?' He had a Scottish accent – an accent that set Sep's brain whirring. An idea was forming.

'I'm retired.'

'Ah, early retirement, eh? Must be nice to be able to do that. I've got another twenty years before I can put my feet up. So, what do you have planned for today, sir?'

'I was thinking of becoming a Trappist monk today.'

'Really, sir. And what does that involve?'

'A lot of silence.'

He'd purposely come to a different barber who wouldn't know who he was. In fact, this was the first time he'd been to a barber in several months. His greying hair, which he had usually kept cropped close to his head, was down over his ears. No particular reason, he just hadn't got round to having it cut. He'd been combing it back, in an attempt to keep himself looking reasonably respectable. What he didn't realize was that this uncharacteristically long hair had done him no favours with his subordinates, who had surprised him by turning against him in his hour of need. They regarded it as all part and parcel of his personality change – the change that had had him hitting his wife, and possibly being responsible for the death of Cyril Johnstone. Of

course Cope had spotted this and had mentioned it to increase
the animosity the troops had for Sep. He was a man trained in
such things.

Sep was thinking about what Winnie had told him about Vince
Formosa having Lee Dench killed because he'd grassed him up
to the police and that she was certain that Dench's contact was
DI Cope, the very man who'd taken his wife from him. He and
his wife had never really got on, and her telling such a damaging
lie about him meant he was well rid of her, except that she would
probably keep the house, although he was wondering how she'd
keep up with the mortgage because he had no money to give her.
He barely had enough money to get by on. He didn't consider
the dole to be an option yet. That would be conceding defeat.

His idea was almost fully formed, but it was an idea that
required him to keep the tonsorial tangle around which the now
silent barber's scissors were hovering. It was an idea that might
mark the first step on his *Hard Road* back. It might be a mad
idea, but a mad idea is better than no idea at all. The words to
the song, *Dead or Alive* weren't far from his thoughts, especially
the "hard road" bit.

'Would it break your vow of silence to tell me how you want
it, sir?'

'One moment please. I'm thinking.'

It was the man's accent which had provided the finishing touch
to Sep's idea – an idea which didn't involve him having a haircut.
In the past he would have asked for a number three which should
have left it three eighths of an inch long all over, but as he stared
he saw a much more useful image staring back at him. He saw
himself with his beard and his hair much longer and straggly
and, in his mind, he heard himself speaking with a certain
Glaswegian accent which he'd perfected while working up in
Scotland in his early days on the force. Then he thought of a
way he could use this masquerade to its greatest effect. The
audacity of his plan had him smiling and shaking his head. He
removed the cloth from around his neck and stood up.

'Changed my mind,' he said.

'About becoming a Trappist monk, sir?'

'Not quite.'

Sep took a couple of pound coins from his pocket and gave

them to the barber. 'Thank you for your trouble. When I really need my hair cut I'll be sure to come here.'

Back in his flat he examined his image in the mirror above his dressing table, one of the six pieces of furniture in his room. His plan was building up into something significant.

'See you, Jimmy,' he said to his reflection. 'See you, Jimmy Lennon.'

As a detective constable he'd known a Scottish villain called Jimmy Lennon, whose voice he could imitate perfectly, or so Sep thought, certainly good enough to pass as a Glaswegian who'd spent many years in England. Jimmy was roughly the same height and age as Sep, although there the resemblance ended. Jimmy was by nature a scruffy individual.

Sep ruffled his hair into a state of disarray and took another look. 'See you, when you was up in Barlinnie doin' a two stretch fer knockin' seven shades o' shite out of a guy who was tryin' te do the same te you.'

Jimmy Lennon had indeed done time in Barlinnie prison for such a crime. He had a habit of moving away from any town whose police knew him well enough to arrest him, so he'd moved down to Yorkshire on his release and had come very quickly to Sep's attention. Sep had used Jimmy as an informer but was unable to help him when he was picked up for burglary and banged up in Armley jail for eighteen months.

True to form Jimmy had upped and left Leeds soon after his release. A year later he sent a letter to a friend in Leeds with instructions to show it to Sep. Jimmy was now a bank security guard in a small town in Nebraska, USA. Despite being arrested by him, Jimmy had always considered Sep to be a good guy. He just wanted Sep to know he'd at last turned his life around, as Sep had often tried to persuade him. It was information that Sep had kept to himself at Jimmy's request. How Jimmy, with his criminal record, had got a green card was one of life's mysteries, but the Jimmy Lennons of this world were adept at overcoming such problems.

Sep was planning to borrow Jimmy's identity. He would become a Scottish ne'er-do-well, down on his luck; a hard man who could look after himself; a man who would fit easily into the West Yorkshire underworld as a copper's nark. His plan was to somehow make contact with DI Cope and become his informer, just as the real Jimmy had been his own informer many years ago. This way, he could use his position as Cope's trusted informer to drop the bent cop in shit deep enough to drown him. It would be simply a question of spotting the main chance when it came along – and main chances always come along. As he gazed at the mirror, he could scarcely keep the grin off his face as he imagined the many scenarios that would come his way and send Cope down.

Then he wiped the smile off his face and told his reflection, 'Don't get ahead of yourself, Septimus.' He was quoting his mother. 'It's a great plan but it's bloody dangerous. Cope's in Formosa's pocket. Do the job properly, think it all through. Keep on your toes. No slip-ups.'

Then he smiled again and said, respectfully, 'Yes, mother.'

The first problem would be how to make contact with Cope. To facilitate this, he'd need help in the form of an introduction or someone who moved in Cope's circles, or someone who knew what circles Cope moved in. It would have to be someone he trusted implicitly. Only one name sprang to his mind. Winnie O'Toole.

He and Cope had always worked different shifts and he'd barely said half a dozen words to the man, so he wasn't too worried about being recognized; not with his unkempt beard and hair and his thick Glasgow accent. The most time he'd spent talking to Cope was back in his house when Phoebe was there. His hair had been long then but neatly combed and much more respectable than it looked right now, and his mode of attire had been quite smart. His main disguise would be his beard. He hadn't shaved since the incident in the Sword and Slingshot, which was many weeks ago. Maybe he could dye his hair a few shades greyer. That, plus his accent, plus his general scruffiness, should do the trick. No one in the station would recognize him, never mind Cope.

If Cope checked him out Sep knew enough about Jimmy's past to match himself up with most police checks. The right age, type, accent and build. Perhaps moving digs might be a good idea. Sep moves out of here and disappears; Jimmy Lennon moves in elsewhere. He'd done undercover work before and knew the dangers. UC work they called it. UC work was dangerous because criminals tended to kill undercover cops if they were discovered. Using a different accent was usually a no no – the slightest slip of an accent would arouse suspicion – but he wouldn't be living a full time undercover life in the company of criminals, so he reckoned he could wing the accent bit. Winnie would need to know what he was doing and he knew he could trust her. She could fill him in with enough information to make him plausible and useful as a copper's informer. He allowed himself a smile. He had no idea where this outrageous idea might lead but at least it was leading to somewhere, and somewhere had to be better than nowhere. What he needed now was a plan of action.

What he didn't know was that a strange form of serendipity would present him with an initial plan in the form of a distressed young lady called Gabriela who was, at that very moment, planning to escape from her imprisonment in a Leeds brothel.

SIXTEEN

16 May

Gabriela Ciobanu was eighteen; she was pretty and could speak reasonably good English, something she hadn't mentioned to her captors who had only spoken Romanian to her. When she arrived in England she had been handed over to a group of Romanians who were headed by an Englishman called Whitey who had thought she didn't understand a word of English. In Romania she had answered an advertisement in the *Bucharest Daily News* for young women who wanted to train to become nurses in the United Kingdom. The airfare would be paid and accommodation found. Becoming a nurse in England was her dream job. It sounded too good to be true, which of course it was. Her accommodation turned out to be a brothel where she was imprisoned and forced to work as a prostitute to pay off her air fare and other ongoing costs. It was a debt she had no hope of ever repaying.

She had stayed there, along with nine other girls, for three nightmare months, never once being allowed out of the house. It had two outside doors, both of which were only opened from the inside by a key pad. No one from the street could enter the house without being allowed in by one of Whitey's men, or Whitey himself. The code was changed on a regular basis and Gabriela had heard one of the men asking what the new code was. Neither of the men knew their conversation was being overheard by an English speaking girl. As far as they knew none of the girls could speak English, but it was how Gabriela learned the door code – one, nine, six, nine. She had worked out how to open her room door by prising the mortise lock away from the door jamb with a steel bar she'd removed from her ancient bed frame. Up until then it had been of little use, only allowing her access to the landing outside her room. She hadn't dared venture downstairs lest she be caught and punished.

Armed with the outside door code she left her room at two in the morning, crept down two flights of stairs, opened and closed the door very quietly and walked out into the garden wearing only her night dress and with bare feet. She was a little dismayed to find the gate wouldn't open but it was a low gate which she climbed over easily. Once in the street she had no idea where she was or where she was going. All was quiet, which was good. She wanted to get away from this terrible house where she was made to have sex with vile men; many of them drunk and some quite violent. She decided to go to her left. At first she ran, barefoot, with tears streaming, darting into gateways and doorways whenever she saw anyone. Fifteen minutes later it was this surreptitious behaviour that alerted Winnie to the fact that here was a young woman in trouble.

Winnie was in her van, on her way home from a city centre club where she worked behind the bar. She'd caught a glimpse of Gabriela in her headlights and had slowed down when the girl darted into a shop doorway. Winnie pulled up alongside her and wound down the passenger window.

'Are you OK, love?'

Gabriela looked at her. She was glad it was a woman and not

some dirty man but she didn't say anything. Winnie got out and walked over to her.

'Bloody hell, love! You must be freezing.' She took her coat off and hung it around Gabriela's shoulders. 'Can I give you a lift anywhere?'

Gabriela burst into tears. Winnie gave her a hug and took her over to the van. 'Look, just sit in there. I've got the heater on. At least get yourself warm and I'll see if I can help. My name's Winnie, by the way, what's yours?'

'Gabriela.'

There was enough accent in her voice to tell Winnie she wasn't a local girl. Gabriela got in the van and Winnie climbed into the driver's seat.

'Right, I'll take you wherever you want to go providing it's in Leeds.'

'I don't know what Leeds is.'

'You don't know what Leeds is? It's where you are, love. Bloody hell! Where are you from?'

'Romania.'

'And what are you doing wandering the streets at this time in your night clothes and with nothing on your feet?'

'I have escaped from bad men who make me do bad things and keep me locked up in a horrible house.'

'Oh, shit! I think I know where you're coming from. Have they had you on the game?'

'I don't understand you.'

'Have they been making you have sex with men?'

Gabriela said nothing.

'It's OK, you don't have to answer that, love. Do you want me to take you to the police?'

'Will your police want me to face the bad men in court?'

'I imagine so.'

The terrified look on Gabriela's face was enough for Winnie to say, 'OK, no police – look, do you want to come home with me? I live on my own so you won't have any mucky men to bother you. Tomorrow we can sort out what to do with you. And I've got loads of clothes that'll fit you – stuff that won't fit me anymore but I can't bring myself to chuck away.'

'Thank you,' said Gabriela. 'You are good person.'

'I think I might be just what you need. There's been times when I've needed people and never found anyone, so it's a pleasure to be able to help you.'

'I have no money and no passport. They took it away from me.'

'They're just bits of paper, love. You're a European citizen so you've as much right to social services help as anyone.'

'I'm scared of those men and I don't want to make trouble for them. If they find me, they kill me.'

'I won't do anything without you agreeing to it, love.'

Winnie started up the van and drove off. As she drove she sensed Gabriela staring at her. She turned and looked at the distressed girl, saying, 'What's up, love?'

'Nothing, I just . . .'

'Just what?'

'Why do you keep calling me "love"?' Gabriela asked her.

'I call you love because this is Yorkshire and it's what we call people up here. If you were from Nottingham they'd call you duck.' Then a thought struck her that had her laughing out loud. 'Bloody hell, Gabby! You think I'm a lesbian!'

'No, I . . . I am just wondering that is all.'

'You wondered if I wanted you to be my lover?'

'I do not know why you help me.'

'Bloody hell! I bet you thought you were out of the frying pan into the fire!'

'Which is this frying pan?'

'Never mind, love. And no, I'm not a lesbian. You'll have a bed to yourself tonight. I'll straighten you out tomorrow.'

'You will straighten me out?'

'Like I said, never mind.'

Winnie's house had three bedrooms. She had friends who came and went; friends who needed a bed for a night or more. Friends who moved around in dark places and who trusted Winnie with their secrets. Some of these secrets had outlived their owners and it was these secrets she intended passing on to Sep.

Gabriela slept fitfully that night, occasionally calling out in her sleep. Winnie was a light sleeper who was woken up by each of these outbursts. At nine the next morning she tapped on Gabriela's door and opened it.

'You sleep all right?'

'Yes, thank you, but I keep waking up thinking I am back in that horrible house.'

'I know, I heard you.'

'Oh, I'm sorry if I keep you awake.'

'Gabby . . . do you mind if I call you Gabby?'

'Not at all. My friends at home called me Gabby, but my mother did not like it.'

'Mother's tend not to like nicknames. My real name's Winifred which is a bit of a mouthful.'

'Like Gabriela.'

'No, Gabriela's a beautiful name. Anyway, I want to talk to you about this house you were kept in. I'd like to find out exactly where it is.'

Gabriela became frightened. 'Please, I do not want to go back there. They will know I am missing and they will be looking for me.'

'You don't have to go there. We can search for the house on my computer.'

'Can we? I was never very good with computers. My young brother, he is the computer one in our family.'

Winnie sat on the edge of her bed. 'Tell me about your family and where they live.'

'We live in a beautiful town called Vatra Dornia in the Carpathian mountains in the north of Romania. It is a ski resort and my father works there.'

'What? Is he a ski instructor?'

'No, no. He works the ski lift and does any other jobs they require him to do. He is a good man. My mother works some-times in a baker shop in the town so we have plenty of bread and cakes to eat.'

'Lucky you.'

'I was going to go to medical school in Romania when I saw an advertisement in the newspaper asking for young women to go to England to train as nurses.'

'Which is how you ended up here . . . bastards!'

Winnie listened with mounting disgust at the story Gabriela told of the vile men who brought her and three others to Leeds in the back of a van and hustled them into the house at the dead of night. All of them were made to strip and were raped by their captors before being imprisoned in rooms in a large terraced house.

'Did you get any of their names?'

'In the time I was there the Romanian names I remember are Dragos, Stefan, Grigos and Cezar. All of them are very bad men. There was one Englishman who I think was the boss. He was called Whitey.'

They talked for half an hour until Winnie thought she knew all she needed to know about this unfortunate young woman, then she took her to her own room and opened her wardrobe at the bottom of which was a large drawer packed with various garments.

'I'm not saying they're the height of fashion but they're all wearable and clean and too small for me.'

Gabriel smiled broadly. 'This is very good. I haven't been dressed in any proper clothes since three months when I come to the house.'

'Yeah, I can imagine. There's a few pairs of jeans that should be OK, and some tops. I think you can make yourself look presentable.'

'Presentable? You say words I do not understand.'

'It means you'll look good, pretty, attractive. There's a bathroom if you want a bath and I've got stacks of make-up. I think you should stay here for a few days until those men stop looking for you. It'll give me a chance to figure out what to do to help you.'

SEVENTEEN

I f Sep's plan were to succeed he needed to be a hard man to track down, and his car would be a dead giveaway. His bright red Audi Quattro was known to most coppers from his station especially to Cope. If Cope saw his car his plan would be in tatters. If Cope saw his ragged, penniless informer in any car, his plan would be in tatters – unless the car wasn't registered in his name – not only not in his name but in Jimmy Lennon's name. How the hell did he get around that? Buy a car but not tax or insure it? That would be a ruse with a limited life. Public transport? Possibly, but a bit inconvenient for a man with his mission in life. There would be occasions when he needed to get to places quickly, without waiting half an hour at a bus stop. Plus he might need to get to places in the middle of the night when the buses weren't running.

Sep advertised his car in the paper and sold it within two days for 15,250 pounds. He then spent a thousand of this on a bicycle. It was no ordinary bike, it had a carbon frame made to fit his height, and twenty speed gearing. He paid for mudguards to be fitted to avoid him being sprayed in wet weather, and decent lights for his night-time riding. It was the best bike he'd ever ridden. It was light and comfortable and went up hills as if it were motorised. To make it thief-proof he had it fitted with a concealed computer tracking device and he bought a top-of-the-range chain and lock. Sep was delighted with his purchase, especially as the exercise would do him no harm at all. His first port-of-call was the Sword and Slingshot.

The window space was still boarded up. He went in the front door and smiled at Joyce who was staring at him from behind the bar. He held up a hand to forestall her diatribe.

'It's me, Sep Black.'

'Bloody hell! You've let yourself go.'

They were welcome words to Sep. Joyce knew him quite well. 'I've had a difficult few weeks. It's OK. I've not come back as a customer. I've come to make good the damage I did.'

'Have you now?'

'Yes. I heard you were getting Willie's window repaired and I thought I'd offer to pay for it.'

'The insurance company's paying for it.'

'Oh . . . for all of it?'

'No, just for a replacement window – but the replacement this pub needs is the original window.'

'I agree.'

'You do?'

'Of course I do. I loved that window. Worst thing I ever did was break it.'

'What, worse than killing that MP?'

'I didn't kill him, Joyce.' Sep said it sharply. He was fed up of being accused of this. 'He had an epileptic fit. But even if I had killed him it wouldn't have been as bad as breaking Willie's window. His life wasn't as valuable as that window.'

'That makes me wonder why he was arrested. Was it kiddie-fiddling?'

'What makes you say that?'

'Stuff I've heard – it was, wasn't it?'

'You'll find out one day.'

'But not from you?'

'No.'

Joyce said, 'The insurance company'll pay seven-fifty for a replacement stained-glass window out of a catalogue, but it won't be anything like the original.'

'*Was* it completely original?' Sep asked. 'I once heard it had been smashed and repaired before.'

'Yeah, about a hundred years ago, and whoever repaired it did a brilliant job.'

'And how much would it cost for a brilliant job now?'

'I've had a quote from a chap in York who's worked on the Minster windows. He's supposed to be the best around. He reckons it'll take him and a lad two weeks and five hundred in materials.'

'How much altogether?'

'Fifteen hundred.'

'OK. Suppose I give you fifteen hundred cash and you can keep the insurance money to make up for the trouble I've caused you.'

'Is that legal?'

'It's fair.'

He took an envelope from his pocket which he knew contained two thousand pounds in fifties – a sum he'd hoped would more than cover the damage. He counted out fifteen hundred and gave it to her.

She took it, saying, 'I hope this has cured you of being such a curmudgeonly old bugger. Are you still picking arguments with people?'

Sep thought back to the barber. 'Well I had a few questions for a barber who said his job was hair solutions.'

'You could do certainly do with a hair solution.'

'It's my new look.'

'If you ever want to come back in this pub you'll have to see the hair solution man.'

He grinned. 'Joyce, you have yourself a deal.'

His new abode was in Middleton, on the south side of the River Aire and four miles away from his former Septimus Black abode. It was by no means luxurious but it was a proper flat with its own bathroom and separate kitchen. He even had a lockable shed for his bike. He had kitted himself out with a wardrobe bought from a charity shop, which he further distressed by dragging each garment through the dirt in a local park, causing them to become suitably stained and torn. He then bought a light-grey hair dye from a supermarket and made a botched attempt to colour it. The end result was to his satisfaction. Jimmy Lennon was indeed a mess to look at.

The fact that he was able to pay a five-hundred pound bond and a month's rent in advance, all in cash, dispelled any doubts the landlord had about Scotsman Jimmy Lennon's dishevelled appearance and almost impenetrable accent.

He'd let Winnie in on his proposed subterfuge and had tested his disguise on her by sitting next to her in a pub she often used. She glanced at him and was about to get up and walk away when he spoke to her in his new accent.

'Too guid te sit next te me, eh hen?'

Not wishing to be thought of as a snob she sat back down and lied to him. 'Maybe if you made an effort to clean yourself up a bit.'

'Agh, ye've changed fer the worse since since I last knew ye, Winnie O'Toole.'

'I don't know you.'

'Agh, yes ye do.' He leaned over to her and whispered, 'I used to be called Sep Black.'

'What?'

She stared at him, keenly. He grinned at her and put a finger to his lips. 'Shhh. Just trying out my new disguise. Do you recognize me now?'

'Maybe your voice . . . yeah, maybe it's you.'

'Of course it's me.'

'Bloody hell, Sep! It's a hell of a disguise . . . why, though?'

He explained his plan to an increasingly dumbfounded Winnie. Then, reverting to his Jimmy Lennon accent he said, 'What d'ye think?'

'I think you're a lunatic.'

'Well, that's mebbe what it'll take te get ma life back on track. An' I need to know if ye can help me in ma dealings wi' Cope.'

'What if I say I can't help?'

'Then I'll find someone who can.'

'Someone else you can trust with a thing as risky as this? Who might that be?'

'OK. I'm prob'ly on ma own if ye cannae help.'

'Sep, you know I'll do what I can.'

Winnie told him she had solid information about a pimp who was really a white slave trader called Whitey.

'Never heard of him.'

'No, neither had I. He must be fairly new to this area. Prostitution's one thing but that sort of nonsense needs wiping out before it takes a hold on this town.'

'I agree,' said Sep.

He also agreed that her information would put Whitey and his gang away for many years. It was information for which Cope would pay good money, and it was information that would get him into Cope's good books as a trusted informer.

'This is guid stuff, Winnie.'

'I'm a good girl, Sep, but you're still a lunatic.'

All Sep had to do now was make contact with the bent, wife-stealing bastard, and Winnie reckoned she could help him with that.

'I dinnae want ye getting personally involved in any o' this, Winnie.'

'Do I look that stupid, Sep? All I want is a cut of the action for stuff I tell you.'

He was happy with Winnie's help but uncomfortable with her almost overpowering eagerness to please him. He didn't want her to place herself in any danger, or was it that he didn't want her to get any wrong ideas about their relationship? Maybe he should lie to her and tell her he wanted his wife back. Or maybe not, lest his source of information dried up. Shit! Why can't life be simple?

*   *   *

The next day

'All I know is where I saw Cope talkin' to Denchy.'

Winnie was talking to Sep in the King's Arms. He wasn't tonsorially ready to make his return to the Sword and Slingshot just yet, nor would he be until his mission to bring Cope to justice had been accomplished.

'At the time,' she said, 'I didn't know for absolute certain he was a copper, it's just that I have a nose for that sort of thing. After Cope left I asked Denchy if he was a copper. He said he wasn't but Chantelle was with him and I could tell by the look on her face that I'd hit the nail on the head. Shit-scared she was. I told 'em I wouldn't go blabbing about it even if he was a copper but Denchy just said he was a bloke he did a bit of work for on his cars. I left it at that but Cope didn't look like no car bloke to me, he had plod written all over him. It was when I saw him with Formosa that the penny dropped that he was a bent cop. Then when Denchy and Chantelle were killed I put two and two together, which is when I told you about Denchy bein' a copper's nark. After I saw him with Denchy, and *before* I saw him with Formosa, I saw him with your missus in a pub.'

'You never told me.'

'What's to tell? You already knew your missus had run off with him and I didn't see him with Formosa until after you'd been lifted for wrecking the pub.'

'Fair enough. So where did you see him and Dench meet up?'

'Horse and Trumpet in town.'

'Do you know if Cope goes in there a lot?'

'I've seen him in there a few times on a lunchtime for his pie and a pint.'

'And do you go in there a lot?'

'Couple of times a week on a lunchtime to do a bit of business – honest business mind.'

'Selling cheap and buying cheaper?'

'You've got it. That bike of yours. How much did you pay for it?'

'It cost me about a thousand.'

'You've gorra be kidding! I could have got you one of them for two hundred, and that's with a bit of bunce in it for me.'

'You might have got me a fake made-in-China copy that would

have had me killed the first time I tried to brake in traffic. Don't make me nervous of you, Winnie. I need to be as straight as I can be, with what I'm doing.'

'Fair point. So, when do you turn into Jimmy Lennon?'

Sep's long hair was hidden under a woollen hat. His beard was now approaching bushy. He stroked it, thoughtfully, like some wise old man, which made Winnie grin.

'I'm going to trim this beard a bit and let my hair out from under.' He then spoke in his Glasgow accent. 'Aye, and right now is when I become a guy frae oot the Gorbals, by the way.'

Winnie's grin widened. She whispered. 'Is this you from now on?'

'Aye, this is the public me. An' there's a favour I'd like.'

'What is it?'

'The next time yer in the Horse and Trumpet and ye see Cope, would ye gimme a bell?'

'I will.'

'And when I arrive would ye call oot ma name so that Cope can hear it. Somethin' like, "What the fuck ye doin' in here Jimmy Lennon, yer Scotch twat?"'

'Well, I might clean it up a bit, but, yeah, I can handle that.'

For the next few minutes he roughly outlined the conversation he and Winnie would have. A conversation that would be over-heard by Cope. A conversation that would be of interest to the detective inspector.

'Sounds like a fine plan,' said Winnie.

'Does yer man normally stand at the bar or does he sit doon?'

'Stands at the bar, always. Coppers always stand at the bar. I bet you did when you were working the pubs.'

'Good, then I'll be right beside him, at which point yer'll take yer leave. I dinnae want him to associate ye with me too much – if at all. Might do ye no harm te wear a wig or somethin'. I might have a bad word to say about ye after ye've gone.'

'It won't be the first bad word that's been said about me.'

'It might take a wee while fer him te accept me as a nark but if nothin' else I know how coppers think and he won't want to miss out on a grass who might have good information.'

'And I have just the thing for you.'

'Ye have details about this Whitey guy?'

'Yes.'

He looked at her and took her hand. 'Aye, well I'm thankful for this, lassie. But after that ye'll not be seen in the pub with Cope . . . ever. It's me who's the grass, not you.'

'I'll do what I can . . . Jimmy. This stuff I have for you might need a bit of further investigating before you present it to Cope, but that's what you do, isn't it?'

'Aye, it's what I do, right enough.'

She leaned over and whispered, 'The accent's quite good and you mustn't *give* this information away free or he'll suss you out very quickly . . .' she grinned and added in a Scottish accent, 'by the way.'

'Correct. It'll be good tae earn a dishonest living at that bastard's expense. Right, let's hear more about this white slave racket ye have for me.'

'Well, it's to do with a young woman I have living with me . . .' began Winnie. 'She's a Romanian girl who's just escaped from Whitey's brothel and she's scared to death. I found her a couple of nights ago at two o'clock in the morning on Harehills Road in her nightie and nothing else. It was freezing. I brought her home with me.'

'She'd been forced into prostitution?' guessed Sep.

'Exactly. She was brought over under false pretences thinking she was going to train as a nurse . . .'

EIGHTEEN

24 May

Sep was out cycling when Winnie rang him three days later. Unknown to him, she'd been in the Horse and Trumpet every lunchtime for three days running in the hope of spotting Cope. Sep had spent two hours of each of those days on his bike. Not having ridden a bike since he was a boy he needed the regain the expertise and fitness required by a cyclist pedalling his machine through traffic. He was happy that he'd got the job cracked. He stopped by the side of the road, pulled out his mobile and smiled when he saw the name on the screen.

'Winnie,' he said.

'I'm in the Horse and Trumpet and our friend has just come in.'

'I assume he can't hear you.'

'I hope not. I'm in the Ladies.'

'Can anyone else hear you?'

'No, I'm on my own.'

'Good. I'm out on my bike. I'll be there in fifteen minutes.'

'I'll get you a pint ready.'

'No you won't. You don't know I'm coming.'

'Of course. Sorry.'

With his bicycle secured to a street lamp he entered the Horse and Trumpet with his trousers still tucked in his socks. He'd ridden there without a hat on and the wind had made a fine job of ruffling his long, wild hair into an even more untidy mess. His beard had been trimmed to a more manageable length, but by his own hand so it was by no means neat. He wore an old, torn and dirty sweater he'd kept in his saddlebag for such an emergency. Winnie caught his eye when he came in and redirected his gaze to the bar where Cope was standing in front of a half-drunk pint, eating a beef sandwich. As Sep headed towards him she called out.

'Is that you, Scotch Jimmy, yer drunken old pisspot?'

Sep turned and pretended not to recognize her. Cope turned as well. Sep shrugged and went to stand beside Cope, who moved a couple of feet along the bar from this unsavoury old tramp. Winnie got to her feet and brought her drink to the bar, positioning herself between Sep and Cope.

'D'yer not remember me, Jimmy?'

'Oh aye, I do so. How're ye keepin'?'

'I'm keeping fine. How are you? Last I heard of you'd gone back to Glasgow.'

'Aye, that right enough. Ended up in fuckin' Barlinnie. Two years for skelpin' a guy. Hey, I couldnae skadge a ciggie off ye could I?'

'Course you can.' She took out her cigarettes and said, 'Can I get you a pint?'

'Aye, why not? I'm a wee bit pissed fer some reason, but I don't suppose another pint'll do me harm.'

She signalled the barman to pull Jimmy a pint, aware of Cope's interest out of the corner of her eye.

'So, Jimmy, what yer doing down here?'

'Och, I thought I'd come back and sniff around. See what's happenin' yer know.'

'Anything of interest?'

'As a matter o' fact there's a lot of interestin' stuff goin' on . . . as well as a lot of slimy stuff that makes me ashamed ter be a member o' the criminal fraternity.'

'Such as?'

'I'm talkin' about them foreign guys bringin' lassies over, drugging 'em up tae the eyeballs an' locking 'em in brothels never te see the light o' fuckin' day and paying 'em no money. That's terrible that is. I'd round the bastards up and hang the lot o' them by their testicles. I mean a hoor needs tae earn a decent livin' like anyone else. Are you still on the game, by the way?'

'Not any more, Jimmy.'

'Shame that.'

'Why's it a shame? You could never afford me.'

'Aye, true enough.'

'Anyway, I was just going. Thought I'd say hello.'

'Aye, hello yersel'. Guid te meet ye.'

Winnie left the pub. Sep picked up his pint, took a huge swig and grinned at Cope. 'I've not a fuckin' clue who she is, by the way.'

'You seemed to know she was a prostitute.'

'Och – that was just an easy guess. Women do that tae me, y'know. Come up an' speak tae me, buy me drinks. There must be somethin' about me that's attractive. I reckon it's ma resemblance te George Clooney.'

'Yes, I can see that.'

'And I can assume ye takin' the piss,' said Sep.

'You assume correctly.'

'By the way, if yer a copper I was also takin' the piss when I told her I was a criminal. I wouldnae tell a proper friend o' mine anything like that.'

'What makes you think I'm a copper?'

'I'm not sayin' y'are.'

'I imagine if I was a copper you'd have plenty of information to sell me, especially about these foreign pimps you hate so much.'

'Och aye. I'd grass them bastards up right enough – fer the right price, of course. I'm no grass, never have been, but them bastards needs banging up. I did two years fer nuthin' compared to them slimy bastards.'

'Assault, was it?'

'I thought it was a fair fight until it turns out that the other guy's a town councillor, and a man beyond reproach accordin' tae his honour the fuckin' judge. I took a few blows mesel' but I laid him out wi' a stoatin' left hook. Broke three knuckles.'

He showed Cope his left fist, displaying three misshapen knuckles which he'd broken in a fight two years previously. Cope lowered his voice and said, 'How much would you call the right price?'

'What?'

'Let me get you another drink, Jimmy. We'll take them to that table over there and talk business.' He nodded towards an empty table by the window.

Sep pretended to be non-plussed, but went over to the table anyway. Cope brought him another pint.

'Look, mister,' Sep said. 'I'm a bit pissed right now. I've maybe given ye the wrong impression.'

'I don't think so, Jimmy.'

'Are ye the polis, then?'

Cope hesitated then said, 'I am, yes – and I'm even keener than you to get those slimy foreign bastards off the streets. So I'll pay good money for good information.'

'How good?'

'Depends on the information. Up to five hundred for info that leads to a conviction.'

'A monkey? Jeez, man, that's some wad!'

'If you put me on to anyone major it could be a grand. For filling me in with odd bits of information from time to time, it's never less than fifty quid. You don't have to do anything other than tell me what you know. People, places, jobs, times, stuff like that. We don't even have to meet. You can phone me with the info and I'll pay money directly into your account.'

'Account? Ye mean bank account? Do I look like a guy wi' a bank account?'

'Ah, perhaps not. In that case we would have to meet at discreet places. Definitely not here.'

Sep nodded, still maintaining the look of bewilderment on his face, as if he wasn't sure of anything.

'Look,' said Cope. 'Do you know the Adelphi on Hunslet Road?'

'I do.'

'Why don't I meet you there at noon on Friday?'

'What for?'

'To discuss this when you're sober.'

'Oh, right.'

'So you'll be there on Friday?'

'Friday, aye. What time?'

'Noon . . . twelve o'clock. The Adelphi on Hunslet Road.'

'Adelphi,' repeated Sep. 'Twelve o'clock noon on Friday.'

'If you're not there I'll know you're not interested in earning good money,' said Cope. 'Either that or you've forgotten what we've been talking about. Do you want me to write it down and stick it in your pocket?'

'What? No, I'll remember. I'm not an eejit.'

Cope wasn't convinced but he got to his feet and said goodbye.

'See ye Friday,' said Sep.

'Let's hope so.'

Sep watched him go and grinned from under his mop of straggly hair. He finished his second pint and rang Winnie's mobile.

'I'm meeting the guy on Friday tae talk business.'

'Thought you might. You put on a good show while I was there.'

NINETEEN

1 June

Winnie switched on her laptop. She was watched by her guest, Gabriela Ciobanu, who had been with her for over a week without opening up about her captivity. Winnie thought she'd been patient with her for long enough.

'Gabby,' she said, 'if I'm to help you I need to find out where this house is. I've spoken to someone about you and he's going to help.'

'Oh dear. I do not like people knowing about me.'

'He's a good man – he used to be a policeman.'

'Oh dear.'

'Gabby, you're such a wuss I sometimes wonder how you plucked up the courage to run away from that place.'

'What is a wuss?'

'Oh, someone who's frightened of their own shadow.'

'I am frightened of many things,' said Gabriela. 'This man who used to be a policeman. Why is he not a policeman anymore?'

'He, er . . . he retired,' said Winnie without looking up from the laptop. She went into Google Maps. 'Have you seen this before?' she asked Gabriela.

'Erm, yes. My brother showed me London streets before I came here. I was very impressed.'

'Well I'm bringing up Leeds streets . . . here we are.'

She clicked into Street View, zoomed into the area where she had found Gabriela and pointed to the exact spot. 'This is where I found you and I think you'd been coming from this direction.' She ran a finger along a road. 'How long had you been out when I found you?'

'Oh, I don't know. Maybe ten . . . fifteen minutes.'

'Fifteen minutes. Had you come far?'

'I do not know. I start running but then I slow down because with my bare feet it is painful.'

'I'm guessing about half a mile tops. Do you remember seeing any street names?'

'No . . . but I see a church. A big church.'

'What did they call it?'

'I do not know.'

'Right there are a few churches around there, you can have a look at them.' She brought the little yellow man on to Harehills Road opposite St Augustine's Church.

'That is it!' said Gabriel. 'That is the church. I was coming up a small road and it is right in front of me on the other side of a big road.'

'Coming up a small road? Could it be this road?'

Winnie rotated the image so they were on Lascelles Terrace, facing the church.

'Well, this is daytime. I saw it only in night time but that is what I saw,' said Gabriela. 'But this is the road.' Her face crumpled as she remembered how distressed she'd been when she saw the church. Winnie spoke quickly to take her new friend's mind off her distress.

'So, to see the church you must have come up this side road from Roundhay Road, which is another main road.'

'Did I?'

'Yep.' Winnie clicked her position down to the bottom of the road. 'Here's Roundhay Road, so did you turn right or left up Lascelles Terrace?'

'I turned to my right. It is at the opposite side of the road from which I am walking.'

'So you turned right, therefore we turn left to retrace your steps, and you must have walked uphill on Roundhay Road, not downhill.'

'Er, yes, it was uphill.'

'How far?'

'Quite a long way I think. Yes. First I come down the road where the bad house is and I turn to my, er, to my left up this road.'

'This road being Roundhay Road?'

'I suppose it must.'

'Good, now we're getting somewhere. Right, we're going to move down Roundhay Road and the road with the bad house should be on the right.'

'Yes, I understand that.'

Winnie sent the picture travelling down the road, stopping at all the roads leading off from the right. Gabriel kept shaking her head, then she remembered, 'There is stone wall at the end of this road, with a gate that was open. I remember because I hide inside the garden while a car came past up this Roundhay Road.'

'OK, that's good. That's very good.'

Two roads down, Winnie swung the picture round to reveal a curved stone wall on a corner, with an open gate. Gabriel squealed, 'This is it! That is the road. Oh my god!'

'Spencer Place,' said Winnie. 'Right, we're going to move up Spencer Place and take a look at each house. What side of the street is it on?'

'Erm, it was on the left when I came out so it will now be on the right.'

'How far up?'

'I do not know. Quite a way, I think.'

Winnie moved the picture up the street, looking at each house on the right until Gabriela gave a cry and put her hand over her mouth. 'Oh dear, I think that is it,' she said. 'Could you erm, turn the view round please?'

Winnie moved the picture round 180 degrees until it was showing a mosque at the other side of the street.

'That is it!' Gabriel cried. 'I remember this building. Please turn it back round to the house.'

Winnie did as instructed and brought up a picture of large terraced house set back from the road in a poorly tended, long garden. Gabriel stabbed her finger on the screen. 'It is this house. I remember the gate. I cannot open it so I have to climb over it. It is definitely that one.' She pointed to a window on the top floor. 'That is my room. You cannot see from here but it has bars on the windows. I can see the garden and the gate from my room.'

'Definitely?'

'For sure. That is all I have to look at for three months.'

Winnie stared at the picture for a full minute, memorizing every detail. There was no house number anywhere, and when she got there it needed to be the right house.

'OK,' she said, at length. 'I'm going to have a walk up that street and take a good look at the house. I need to get a proper address. It's all right, you can stay here.'

'Oh please be careful, Winnie. I am lost without you.'

'Before I go, Gabby, I need to tell the man who will help us that I've found out where the house is. Do I have your permission to tell him?'

'Oh dear. I don't know. I'm so frightened of those terrible men.' Gabriela's face had taken on a look of sheer terror.

'Don't worry, love. The more people you have on your side the less frightened you'll be.'

Gabriela took a few seconds to collect herself. 'All right, I am a wuss. You must tell him.'

'Good girl. I'll tell him and I'll leave you his number.'

'Just in case you don't come back, you mean?'

'For your peace of mind, Gabby, just while I'm gone. I'll definitely be back, unless I'm struck by lightning or something.'

TWENTY

'First I need to know they're still using the house,' said Sep, when Winnie phoned him from her van with this latest development. 'With Gabriela having escaped, they might be worried she's gone to the police.'

'If she'd gone to the police, the house would have been raided by now, surely?' Winnie asked. She'd decided not to tell him that she was on her way to the house right now – he'd no doubt give her a valid argument.

'Possibly,' said Sep, 'if she'd managed to get to the police straight away.'

'Not with the Gabriela I know,' said Winnie. 'She's scared to death of authority.'

'No, but the pimps won't be certain of anything. How long since she escaped?'

'Couple of weeks now.'

'That long? I imagine they'd move their girls to another house the second they knew Gabby was missing and move them back once they thought they were safe – which should be about now. They'll have a selected bunch of clients who use the girls and who know where the house is. Move the girls away for too long, you lose money. The one thing you can rely on with pimps is that they're greedy and stupid.'

'So, you think they'll move the girls back fairly quickly.'

'I do, but before I tell Cope about this I'd like to keep an eye on the comings and goings at the house. I don't want the raid to be a false alarm.'

'I've just had a nasty thought,' said Winnie. 'Do you think Cope is mixed up with these people? Keeping the cops off their backs?'

'Dunno. When I speak to him I'll tell him about a gang operating a brothel in Spencer Place. If the gang are still in the house now, but clear off soon after I tell him about them, we can assume he's mixed up with them. Personally, I doubt it. Wouldn't be worth his while. Formosa's big time, these guys are low-life scrotes. All the same, we need to be very careful in checking them out properly. Think things through without going rushing in.'

Winnie was feeling guilty at not telling Sep she was on her way to the house right now. But what the hell? What harm could it do? She was only going for an eyeball to ascertain the address. She drove past the house and parked a hundred yards away, then walked back down the footpath with a plan in mind – a plan that had just occurred to her. It would have been better had she given her plan more thought, but Winnie had always been a child of impulse.

TWENTY-ONE

Dragos Macedonski was looking through the window of the room vacated by Gabriela. He was a huge, solid man – six-feet-six and two hundred and fifty pounds. After her disappearance, the girls had been moved to another house for ten days as a precaution. But the other house was far too small for the girls to be entertaining clients so, with no visits from the police, Whitey had now brought them all back. As a precaution he had men working in shifts to keep a lookout for anyone in the road outside acting suspiciously. Dragos had now seen something that caught his attention. A woman had walked up the road, stopped at the gate, and looked at the house for around ten seconds before moving on. A few minutes later she had walked back down the road and stopped again. She didn't look like police, but with this plain-clothes lot you never can tell. Whitey was downstairs. Dragos rang him on his mobile.

'Woman has stopped at the gate twice in the last few minutes. She is there now. No, she is opening the gate and coming up the footpath. She is carrying something . . . a book.'

Whitey went to the door and opened it. Winnie was just a few paces away. She gave him what she hoped was a beatific smile.

'Hello, sir. My name is Maria. I'm not here to sell you anything, I simply wondered if I could interest you in a bible reading. In these difficult times people find a reading from the gospel according St John to be most uplifting.'

Whitey stepped down and grabbed her by her coat, dragging her into the house. 'You an't no fucking bible-basher, lady. Not with all that make-up on your mush!' His accent was southern, London maybe; his face was mean and unshaven with a thick moustache and dark eyes; his hair was dark, thick and combed straight back; his lips were full and formed a permanent sneer. She guessed him to be Whitey, the boss.

'I am,' protested Winnie. 'If you're not interested, that's OK.'

He took the bible from her. 'All right, give me a quotation and tell me exactly where it comes from. You know, like St Paul chapter fifteen, verse nine and all that stuff. All you bible bashers can do that. Should know a hundred quotations, just give me one.'

Winnie racked her brains for a quotation. 'Let he who is without sin cast the first stone,' she said.

'Everybody knows that one,' he sneered. 'Where's that from?'

'Er, I'm not sure.'

'Then tell me one I haven't heard before and tell me where it's from.'

'Look, sir, I'm sorry to have troubled you. I'll be on my way.'

'You're not going anywhere until I find out who you are. Why have you been snooping round outside? You're the law, ain't yer?'

'What?'

'You're a copper come snooping round.'

'No, I'm not. I'm just a bit new at this, which is why I don't know the bible as well as I should.'

Dragos had come downstairs and was standing behind his boss, who handed him the bible. 'Take this and take her down to the cellar and lock her in until I find out who she is and what to do with her. While she's in there, strip her naked and see if she has any police identification on her. Bring her clothes out with you. Naked people always find it difficult to escape.'

Winnie drew her fist back and punched Whitey as hard as she could on the end of his nose. He slapped her to the floor then put his hand to his face to stem the flow of blood. He snarled at Dragos. 'When you've got her stripped give her a good fucking. Teach her a lesson.'

Dragos gave a yellow-toothed grin and said, 'Yes, boss.'

Winnie struggled with all her might as the big Romanian dragged her down the cellar steps. Whitey called out for another of his men, 'Grigos!'

A man appeared from one of the downstairs rooms. Another Romanian, younger and not quite as big as Dragos. 'Yes, boss?'

'Get up to the top room and take over from Dragos. I think we've got snoopers interested in us. Snoopers we can do without. I'm not expecting any punters today, so if anyone at all stops at the gate and looks down the path I want to know immediately. I want to know who they are and what they want. It is possible they have some connection with the missing girl.'

Loud, distressed screaming was now coming from the cellar. Grigos looked questioningly at his boss who ignored the noise and waved him up the stairs.

Dragos bent Winnie's arm up her back and dragged her down the cellar steps. She knew what was in store for her – this monster who smelled like a pig. At the bottom of the steps he opened a door on the right and pushed her in. She turned to face him, shivering with fear.

'Please don't do what he said. I don't think he meant it.'

Dragos undid his belt and sneered, 'When Whitey says something, he always means it. Now strip you fucking bitch!'

Winnie made no move. Dragos took out a gun and stuck it in her mouth and snarled, 'Do as you're told or I'll fuck your dead body!'

Winnie took off her top, kicked off her shoes and slipped out of her jeans. He took them and searched the pockets, finding only a mobile phone and a wallet containing thirty pounds and a few cards. Nothing to identify her as a policewoman.

'Winifred,' he read from one of the cards.

He smiled at her, unzipped his fly and brought out the biggest penis Winnie had ever seen.

'Do you like what you see, Winifred?' he said, lasciviously.

'I see a pig's dick – attached to a filthy pig.'

She managed to say it dismissively. Since Cyril Johnstone, she'd had sex with many men but it had always been for love or money and on her terms. It had never been forced on her. She was beginning to think she wouldn't live through this, so why should she be submissive? She looked at him defiantly and said, 'You're going to kill me anyway and I don't want to be around when a filthy pig like you rapes me!'

He reached out and grabbed her bra, ripping it off. Then he knocked her to the floor and did the same with her panties. She rolled over on her side, facing away from him.

'Just don't expect me to help in any way you stinking pig! Is there no bathroom in this house?'

Dragos pulled her on to her back and slapped her into semi-consciousness then he forced himself inside her. She came round as he was thrusting inside her and trying to kiss her. She bit his tongue as hard as she could but, to Dragos, this only added to the passion of his moment.

He finished, withdrew from her and got to his feet, about to pull his jeans up, then he had a thought. He turned around and urinated on her, splashing her naked body with his vile liquid. He laughed as he did it. 'There you go, bitch! You now got Dragos inside and out.'

Had Winnie got any shoes on, she'd be kicking herself. She was locked in a cellar, naked, freezing, stinking of man pee and violated by that vile brute. Why the hell had she tried the bible scam on these low-life pimps? Because she'd left the bible in the van, that's why. It was a scam she'd worked a dozen times. She'd follow people home from various churches, knock on their doors and offer to give them a free bible reading. More often than not she'd be invited in and, before she left, she'd just happen to mention how her main occupation was raising money for an orphanage in Kenya. In fact it was a genuine charity, with a most persuasive and heart-rending leaflet which would fall out from between the pages of the bible, giving her an excuse to tell them what it was all about. Quite often she'd leave with a sizeable cash donation. It was an amazingly simple scam, bordering on honest because she never actually asked for money, it was given freely, often forced on her. To salve her conscience she sent the charity ten percent of her takings which, she told herself, was more than some charities passed on to the people in need.

No thought whatsoever had gone into this version of her scam which had only occurred to her when she noticed the bible in the van. And she'd called Sep a lunatic for his plan!

She was frightened of what was going to happen to her. They could hardly set her free after what they'd just done to her and she wasn't some dumb foreign girl, alone and friendless in a strange land. If they freed her she could do them no end of harm, unless . . . unless Gabriela rang Sep, which is what she'd do.

It was a glimmer of hope, but what would Sep do? The best thing he could do would be to tell Cope to send armed police in. Smash the door down and rush in mob-handed, shouting and banging like they do on the telly. Shit no! Sep wouldn't risk that until he'd checked the place out for himself. He'd need to be a hundred per cent certain of his facts. He wouldn't want to blow the neat deception he had going with Cope. *Bloody hell, Sep! Come and get me!*

Gabriela left it three hours before she rang Sep.

'Mr Lennon?'

'Er, yes.'

'My name is Gabriela. Do you know who I am?'

'Ah, yes, I believe I do. You're living with Winnie.'

'That is me, yes. Winnie has gone off to the house where the bad men are. Do you know what I talk about?'

'Yes, I do.'

'She tell me she is going to get the correct address. We found the house by Google on the computer.'

'Oh, Google Earth. Yeah, I see.'

'But she has not returned. She tell me she will be back in one hour but she is gone three hours and she has not returned. I am most worried.'

'OK Gabriela, I'll be round there in twenty minutes. Hopefully Winnie will be back by then.'

'I hope so, Mr Lennon.'

Sep looked at himself in the mirror and hoped this young foreign girl wouldn't be shocked by his appearance. Maybe he should warn her? Ah, what the hell! Let her find out the hard way.

'Have you tried to ring her?'

'I do not have her number.'

'OK, I'll ring her now.'

Gabriela didn't immediately open the door to his knock. Sep approved of this. She needed to be cautious under these circumstances.

'Please, who are you?' she asked, through the door.

'It's Mr Lennon.'

The door opened wide. She didn't seem taken aback by his appearance but he felt the need to explain. 'Sorry about my scruffy appearance, there is a good reason for it.'

'That is OK, I am sorry to ask who you are, but I am afraid of those men.'

'I take it Winnie isn't back yet?'

'No, she is not and I am most worried about her.'

'Hmm, can you show me this house on Google Maps?'

'I know the name of the street so perhaps you can find it and I will show you the house.'

'That's fine.'

Within a few minutes he was looking at the house that was now possibly holding Winnie prisoner, only he didn't know that for certain.

'This is definitely the house you were kept in?'

'Yes it is.'

His thoughts were now the same as Winnie's thoughts. He needed to be a hundred per cent sure that a police raid on this house would be a success, otherwise he'd jeopardise his relationship with Cope. But if Winnie was in there, she'd need help. Gabriela was looking at him as he tossed things over in his mind.

'Will you go to help her?'

'I really need to know just what she's done. Did she tell you what she had planned?'

'She only told me she was going to look at the house to get its proper address.'

'Yeah, she'd want that to give to me. Why the hell hasn't she come back?'

'Did you phone her?' asked Gabriela.

'I did, but there was no reply.'

'Would she have known who was ringing?'

Sep thought back to Winnie changing his caller identification to Jimmy. 'Yeah, she'll have known who it was.'

'Then this is most worrying.'

'I agree.'

'Are you going to find her?'

'I am.'

Five minutes later he was on his bike, heading towards Spencer Place. He now had a pretty good idea of the actual location of the house. He pedalled up the street, looking to his right all the time. A hundred yards past the house he saw Winnie's van. Riding up to it he saw she wasn't in it.

'Bloody hell, Winnie! What have you done?'

What he didn't see was a man sitting in another large van facing his way, looking at him curiously. Sep rode back down to the house and stopped the bike outside the gate. The man sat up, more curious than ever now.

Sep remained in his saddle and looked across at the house to see if there was any sign of life within. His plan now was to knock on the door of the adjacent neighbour's house and ask if his friend Joe Robinson lived there. He'd say he wasn't sure if it was this house or the one next door. More often than not, if the house next door was being used as a brothel the person he was speaking to would tell him so in no uncertain terms, especially if it was a woman. She might give him more information than he'd bargained for. At that point he'd take a gamble and call in Cope and his troops. It was pretty much all he could do for Winnie.

Sep got off his bike and stood it up with a pedal resting on the kerb, still looking at the house. He wasn't aware of the man who came up behind him and knocked him unconscious with a heavy, cast-iron priest – a tool used by fishermen to render their catch dead. Within a minute the man had brought his van up alongside Sep and hauled him in through the side door, with no one in the empty street any wiser. He phoned for assistance, drove the van around to the back street, parked outside the back gate where Stefan was waiting to help him carry Sep into the house and then into the cellar to join Winnie.

Sep was just coming round when he was dumped on the cold cellar floor. Winnie greeted his arrival with very mixed feelings. She was glad she was no longer alone, embarrassed about being naked with Sep, and worried that her only means of rescue was now locked up with her. There was a small window near the ceiling, giving just enough light to see by. Sep sat up and waited for his head to clear. There was blood matted in his hair. He blinked at Winnie who was trying to cover her nakedness with her hands and arms. He checked his coat for his mobile, which had gone. Normally he would carry a wallet but not when he was Jimmy Lennon – and he thanked himself for that. He struggled out of his coat and handed it to her. She took it without a word and put it on. It was just long to cover her embarrassment. Sep shook his head slowly, anything faster would have given him even more pain.

'Sorry,' he said. 'I came to check the place out. How I ended up in here, God only knows.'

'I knocked on the door,' said Winnie. 'Told this man I was some sort of bible-basher. He didn't believe me.'

'Did you actually think this plan through?'

'Not at any length,' said Winnie. 'It came to me, a sort of inspiration, you might call it.'

'Winnie, I might call it a lot of things, but I don't think inspiration's one of them.'

Sep looked at her. Even in this half-light, dressed only in his coat she looked good, but bruised.

'They hurt you?' he asked.

'Yes.'

'Badly?'

'I was raped.'

'Bastards! Will you be OK?'

'I think so.'

'I'm not surprised the scam didn't work,' he said.

'It was a scam that used to work for me.'

'Not against these sort of people.'

'OK, don't rub it in. That thought's already crossed my mind.'

'And you called *me* a lunatic! Winnie, it would never have worked with people like this. Anyway, who are they? I assume you spoke to them.'

'I saw one at the door and one who brought me down here. He stripped me, then he . . .' she hesitated, then said, 'It brought it all back to me.'

'You mean Johnstone?'

'Yeah. In a way this was worse. I thought he might kill me.'

Sep had interviewed rape victims before, but only in the presence of a woman officer. It was hard to know what to say. He settled for: 'Are you OK?' It seemed inadequate the instant it came out of his mouth. 'Sorry, of course you're not OK.'

'Sep, it was awful. He made me feel worthless, as if my feelings didn't matter. As if I didn't matter. After he finished, he peed on me.'

Sep cringed with disgust. 'Jesus!'

'He treated me like a toilet. I'm not sure I've got any self-respect left.'

'That's what rape's about. It's sickening. It's not about sex, it's about power.'

'It's something I might struggle to get over while ever he's in this world.'

'I'm really sorry, Winnie.'

Sep looked around the cellar. It had whitewashed walls that had seen better days, a dusty concrete floor and a plaster ceiling that was crumbling in many places. The only window was quite tiny, much too tiny for him to crawl out of. Maybe nine inches wide by twelve inches high. It didn't open and the glass was reinforced with wire mesh. He looked at Winnie who was quite small and he visually measured her against the window. She read his thoughts and tried to collect her own.

'I've thought of that as well, but we'd have to smash all the glass with our hands and leave nothing sticking out or it would rip me to shreds, plus I'm fairly sure even I wouldn't fit through it. Maybe ten years ago, but not now.'

Sep nodded his agreement and said, 'We couldn't even get the glass out without proper tools.'

He got to his feet and took a closer look to see if it might be possible to take out the window complete with frame, but it looked to be too well-embedded into the wall. He then punched at the ceiling that was only six inches above his head. He was showered with plaster, leaving his face and clothes caked in white dust. He stood there, looking at Winnie, and tried to make light of their situation.

'My mother said there'd be days like this.'

It raised a faint smile from her. He brushed the plaster dust off with his hands and took a look at what he'd done. He tugged away at the plaster lathes that were nailed to nine inch deep joists that supported floor boards. Given a couple of hours, a hammer and chisel, he reckoned he could break through the floor above him. He listened to see if he heard footsteps above, but there was nothing. It made no difference. He'd make too much of a noise, even if the room above was unoccupied. Then he went over to the door. It was a typical cellar door, built for service not for style – ledged and braced. He kicked at one of the vertical timbers. It didn't move. He knew that once he'd kicked one of them free he could easily kick away a couple more. The one he was kicking now seemed to be giving. He stepped back to give it one almighty kick when the lock rattled and the door opened. Light flooded in behind Dragos, who was pointing a gun at Sep. He took in the situation at a glance and gave Sep a crocodile smile.

'Take off your shoes and socks,' he ordered. 'If you wanna kick the door down you do it with bare feet, but I will hear you and I kill you when you come up the steps. Who the fuck are you, anyway, and why were you snooping around?'

'I wasn't snooping, I was looking for my friend here.'

'She your ladyfriend, eh?'

'Yes,' said Sep.

'She's my ladyfriend now. She let me fuck her.'

He laughed out loud at his own joke. Sep, reluctantly took off his shoes and socks and handed them to the Romanian who said, 'You be quiet down here. You are disturbing the girls who are going about their work.'

'You mean the under-age girls you forced into becoming prostitutes!'

It was an outburst Winnie would regret. Dragos swung the gun in her direction. 'I think maybe you know where our missing girl is. I will tell this to the boss.'

'I hate you, you filthy bastard,' she hissed.

Dragos sneered at her and slapped her face, knocking her to the floor. 'Who cares what you think, bitch?'

He left and locked the door behind him. Winnie rubbed her face and looked up at Sep. 'Sorry about that. They'll know we're tied in with Gabriela now.'

He helped her to her feet, saying, 'Gabriela mentioned underage girls, did she?'

'She did – mainly from India or some such place. The real young ones weren't Europeans, apparently.'

'Smuggled in illegally more than likely.'

'What do you think they'll do to us, Sep?'

Sep looked at her but didn't answer. She didn't want to know what he thought. Winnie knew better than to ask again.

TWENTY-TWO

Vincent Formosa sat back in his chair and looked up at Cope who had just come into the room. Formosa had four places of work and one domicile. None of his employees knew the whereabouts of more than one of his places of work and none of them knew where he lived. Formosa existed on the verge of paranoia about his own safety. Prison would be bad for him, worse than for most. Nowadays, the law had a habit of stripping criminals of their illegally acquired wealth. He did have wealth that had been legally acquired through investments, but not if he had to explain where he got the money from in the first place.

'Ah, Detective Inspector Cope. Thank you for coming.'

Cope stiffened. He didn't like Formosa using his police rank in this place. He would have much preferred to be called Lenny. It made him less of an alien.

'I've had to do a little tidying up. Sharky and Spud are no longer with us. In fact they're no longer anywhere.'

'I see,' said Cope.

'Do you approve of this?'

'I was never comfortable with them knowing who I was. They were a mouthy pair, never took this work seriously.'

'Yes, well you're one of the reasons I had to get rid of them. They were quite efficient in their work, but a loose remark could have jeopardized your position with us, which is why I'm concerned about you screwing the copper's wife.'

'Well he's an ex-copper now. I needed him out of the way because he had this suspicion about me. Nothing he could ever put his finger on, but I think a lot of the local plods don't trust us London lot.'

'So, now he's out of the way, why are you staying with her?'

'Well, she knows a lot of copper's wives who exchange useful gossip, so she's handy to have on my side and she's good in bed.'

'Good in bed being the main reason. So long as you never exchange any loose gossip with her.'

'Vince, I spent four years doing undercover work. I know when to keep my mouth shut. She knows I set her husband up. She helped me do it, to get rid of him.'

'I gather she had you give her a good beating so she could blame it on him.'

'Yeah, she took it well – game girl in many ways. She thought she'd married beneath her, and when she met me, with my sophisticated ways and personal charm, she decided to ditch him for me. I think when I do ditch her there'll be hell on earth and I'm not quite ready for that.'

'I'll tell you when you're ready. It could be that she comes in handy at some stage. Not sure how.'

Cope sat down without being asked and leaned on Formosa's desk. 'What are we doing about the kids?' he asked.

'Do you have any ideas?'

'Well, we either get rid of them or we use them for blackmail. What other options are there?'

'We cannot hand them back alive,' said Formosa. 'However, their parents will want proof that they're still alive, so we'll have to hold them for a while longer. But kidnapping is so much easier when you don't have to hand hostages over.'

'How much might they be worth?'

'Two million.'

'Hmm, well, it's my case so I could keep a handle on things from the police side.'

'Obviously. If it's a successful job you get ten per cent – two hundred grand. I trust you hide this money away surreptitiously.'

'I have investments that the police can't trace to me. I live frugally off my police salary. Mrs Black has the impression that I'm very tight with money.'

'You must keep it that way. OK, we need to make contact again. I assume the Strathmore's phones are tapped by the police?'

'Yes, and everything will be recorded and analysed.'

Formosa drummed his fingers on his desk. 'OK,' he said. 'We will make a demand with an untraceable mobile. Allow them to speak to their children for a few seconds then tell them this is a once-only offer. They pay up or the children die.'

'So, all we have to do is figure out a safe way to pick up the money.'

'This is no problem. I will have the money paid into a numbered Lichtenstein account. Within seconds of the money arriving in the account it will be transferred to other accounts all over the world. The Lichtenstein account will be closed and the money will be untraceable. As a further precaution they will be warned that we will know if the money is being tracked and if it is, the children will be killed.'

'*Will* we know?'

Formosa shrugged. Cope knew not to press him, saying, 'I'm impressed. I also have an overseas numbered account into which I'd like to have my money paid.'

'As long as your account is secure, this is not a problem.'

TWENTY-THREE

Sep was mooching around the cellar, examining the floor and walls in the fading light. He kicked, gently, at a dusty pile that had been swept into a corner, and frowned when his bare toe hit something hard. Bending down he found a piece of brick buried under the dust, maybe a quarter of a whole brick. He studied it and nodded as if to say this was what he'd been looking for.

'What is it?' asked Winnie.

'Just a piece of brick.'

'Oh,' she said, then added, 'Sep, do you think we should be saying our prayers or something?'

'If you know any.'

'Do you know any?' she asked.

'I do, actually. Born and bred a Catholic, me. Lapsed, unfortunately.'

'Are you going to unlapse yourself?'

'It might not be a bad idea.'

'Talking of ideas,' said Winnie, 'I'm sure I saw a nail sticking out of the wall somewhere. Have you noticed it?'

He pointed at the wall. 'There's one there, why?'

In front of him at head height was a nail, sticking two inches out of the wall. He figured it to be four inches long in total, probably there to hang things on, as was often the case in cellars.

'Could you get it out, please?' Winnie asked.

'Why?'

'Just an idea,' she said, 'humour me.'

Taking hold of it between his thumb and forefinger, Sep tried to loosen it. The nail had been hammered into the mortar joint between bricks. The ancient mortar gave way easily. He pulled the nail out and gave it to Winnie. It was what a joiner would call a four-inch-oval. Winnie went over to where he'd found it and stuck it back in the hole it had made, just one inch in. Sep looked on as, using the quarter brick, Winnie hammered the projecting three inches of the nail back against the wall and pulled it out again. It was now L shaped. She then put the other end in and did the same.

'What're you doing, Winnie?'

'Making myself a picklock.'

'You can pick locks?'

'I can. Most basic locks anyway and the mortise lock on this door's as basic as they come. No one puts expensive locks on cellar doors.'

'Were you a burglar at some stage?'

'No, but I've known a few who've taught me the tricks of the trade.'

Winnie knelt down in front of the lock and inserted the nail with one bent end facing upwards. Using the projecting bent end as a tiny handle she moved it back and forwards fractionally until she felt the nail was pressing against the lever inside the lock, then she pressed on the tiny handle and twisted it anti-clockwise; the lock clicked open. She turned to Sep, 'Mickey Mouse lock. If I'd have thought of this earlier you'd still be wearing shoes.'

They stepped out into a narrow passageway, also illuminated by a small window. It was as bare as the cellar they'd just left. To their right was another door, presumably leading to another underground room and to their left was a flight of stone steps leading up to a door which would, hopefully, take them into the house. Sep went up the steps and listened at the door. He tried to open it but it was locked. He came back down.

'I don't think there's anyone behind the door. Can you open it?'

'I'll give it a try.'

He watched as she went up the steps and inserted her picklock into the keyhole. After a minute of trying he saw her shake her head and take the nail out. She inserted it once more and tried again, still with no luck. She came back down.

'It's a much more complicated lock. I'm guessing someone needed the main cellar door to be secure.'

There was the sound of feet moving above them. Sep went to the other room door and tried it. It was open. He signalled for Winnie to come and join him, whispering to her.

'We'll hide in here. Can you lock the other door?'

'Yeah, then what?'

'Give me the brick.'

She took it from the pocket of his jacket which she was now wearing and handed it to him. 'What're you gonna do, Sep?'

'I'm gonna play it by ear. Someone's bound to come down before long.'

Using the picklock, Winnie locked the door she'd just opened and then joined Sep. They stood there in nervous silence for twenty minutes, after which their hearts picked up speed at the sound of the door at the top of the steps being unlocked. Winnie was grasping his arm.

'I'm scared, Sep,' she whispered.

'Just stay behind me. If you get a chance to run out of this place, take it. Don't worry about me.'

He closed the door of their new room quietly and stood behind it as they listened to heavy feet coming down the stone steps. The footsteps stopped. The lock to their recently vacated prison rattled. Sep was picturing exactly where the man was. Right now he'd be opening the door with his back to the passage. In one quick movement Sep opened his door, stepped out, and slammed the brick down on the back of Dragos's head.

The huge Romanian fell to the floor and rolled over, stunned but not completely unconscious. He still had hold of his gun which he aimed at Sep. Sep dived to one side then kicked out at Dragos's gun arm as the weapon fired. A bullet hit the wall behind Sep and ricocheted twice. The gun flew from Dragos's hand and landed in the passageway. Winnie picked it up and pointed it, with shaking hand, in the direction of Dragos who was roaring with rage and clambering to his feet. From where he was on the floor, and with his bare foot, Sep kicked the big Romanian in the throat, sending him back to the floor.

'I've got his gun,' called out Winnie.

Sep fell on top of the Romanian who was much the bigger man, huge and strong and writhing about, trying to shake Sep off, catching him with an elbow and then with a fist to his stomach.

Sep rolled away, winded. Winnie stepped forward, holding the gun in two shaking hands, pointing it down at Dragos's head and shouting.

'Leave him or I'll shoot you!'

Dragos, lying on his back, looked up at her wavering hands and gave a fierce grin. 'You wouldn't fucking dare!'

'Oh, yes I would! This is for pissing on me. You really hurt my feelings.'

Winnie changed her aim to his groin. His eyes widened in horror, now deeply regretting what he'd done to her. Sep was still trying to catch his breath when she pulled the trigger. The bullet found its tender target, ricocheted off the concrete floor beneath Dragos, and more or less retraced its painful path, going straight through the ceiling after making the return journey through the Romanian's manhood. Blood was soaking his trousers and shirt.

'Well, he won't be boasting about that thing anymore,' she said, looking at Sep, who didn't quite know what she was talking about. He was still gasping for breath. Dragos tried to sit up and let out a feral howl of agony. The shock and intense pain quickly got the better of him and he fell back, unconscious. Winnie stood over him, gun in hand, her sense of worthlessness at being raped now completely purged in the most poetic fashion. She looked at Sep.

'Is he still alive?'

She didn't sound as if she cared overmuch.

'I think so.' Sep leaned over Dragos, trying to assess his injury in the dim light of the cellar. 'My God, Winnie! You certainly paid him back for what he did to you.' Then he added, 'I think they'll have heard this shooting upstairs.' He took the gun from Winnie and added, 'So we'd best brace ourselves.'

Loud noises came from upstairs. Men shouting. The main cellar door banged open. Many feet racing down the stone steps. Two hearts thudding in the cellar.

TWENTY-FOUR

Sep slammed the door shut and told Winnie to stand with her back to the brick wall adjacent to the door. Then he pointed the gun at the door and called out, 'Your man's down. I've got his gun. The first men through that door will die before you get me.'

He heard angry voices in reply, but his head hadn't completely cleared from his initial concussion, and his fight with Dragos had made him further disoriented. Winnie was shouting at him but he didn't hear her. His mind was concentrated on what was about to happen to them. Would they come out of this dead or alive? He was wondering if he should send a couple of rounds straight through the door to show them he meant business. He checked the magazine. The gun was a Glock 17. It had fifteen rounds left. He slammed it back in and shouted.

'I've got fifteen rounds in here. I can take all you bastards with fifteen rounds!'

Winnie was screaming at him. 'Sep, it's the fucking police!'

'What?'

'Listen to them!'

The men outside were shouting 'Armed police!'

'What?' shouted Sep.

'We are opening the door. Put down your weapon and stand back or you will be shot!'

Sep shook his head to clear it and called out, 'Who's in charge?'

'Why do you need to know that?' Winnie asked.

'It could be them pimpy bastards tricking me because I've got a gun,' said Sep.

'Oh . . . right,' said Winnie, upset at such a possibility.

'I need te know you are who ye say y'are,' called out Sep, aka Jimmy Lennon. 'Who's in charge out there? Gimme the guy's name.'

There was a brief hesitation then a voice said, 'Detective Inspector Cope.'

Sep smiled at Winnie. 'Guid answer,' he called back. 'The doors no locked, kick it open and I'll throw ma gun out.'

The door was kicked open, Sep threw out his gun. Four police officers came in, all in black, with helmets and visors and bullet-proof vests. Two carried Heckler and Koch MP5s, the others carried semi-automatic handguns. They screamed at Sep and Winnie.

'On the floor, face down, hands behind your heads. NOW!'

Face down suited Sep. He knew a few of the lads in the West Yorkshire Police Armed Response Unit and he was hoping none of them recognized him. This might be a severe test of his new persona. One of them bent over Dragos. Winnie shouted out. 'He's the bad guy. He's one of the pimps! We've been locked up in here. We have nothing to do with them!'

'Get an ambulance,' said one officer, then to Sep he asked, 'Who did this to him?'

Sep decided to answer a question with a question, maintaining his Scottish accent. This had Winnie admiring his presence of mind. He was still Jimmy Lennon to the police.

'Where's yer man Cope?' he asked.

'Why?'

'Just bring him doon here. He knows me well enough and can vouch fer me, and I can vouch fer the lady.'

'Who are you?'

'Just tell DI Cope ye have Jimmy, his big, scruffy Scotch pal doon in the cellar.'

Two of the officers left. A few minutes later Sep, still face down on the floor, noticed a pair of highly polished shoes standing next to him. Cope spoke.

'Bloody hell! I should have known you'd have something to do with this.'

'It was me who shot him,' said Winnie. 'He raped me when I first arrived then when Jimmy got into a fight, he lost his gun so I shot him in the bollocks.'

'Who are you?' said Cope, not recognizing her.

'Winnie O'Toole. If I smell bad it's because he peed on me after he raped me. When a man does all that to you it's too tempting not to shoot him in the bollocks when the chance arises.'

'He was getting the better of me,' said Sep. 'If Winnie hadn't shot the filthy bastard, we'd have been done for right enough.'

'I'll be interested to know what the CPS make of this,' remarked Cope.

'I gather ye were called by Gabriela,' Sep said.

'We were indeed. There was no need for you to get so involved.'

'I'm the reason he became involved,' said Winnie. 'They had me locked in here and Jimmy came looking for me.'

'Yes, Gabriela told me some of the story.'

Cope instructed the two remaining officers to go upstairs and assist their colleagues. 'Get the medics down here as soon as they arrive. I'll deal with these two,' he added.

Now on their own, Sep and Winnie got to their feet. Cope was saying. 'Well if this is the quality of information you have for me I think we can do business, Jimmy.'

'How much do I get for this?' Sep asked him.

'I think your payment should be me talking the CPS out of prosecuting Winnie for shooting him – possibly killing him. He's not looking too good.'

'He raped her,' said Sep, 'and she ends up wi' a gun, and him on the floor. What do the CPS expect?'

'Well, I certainly think his raping days are over,' commented Cope.

Winnie voiced her only concern. 'They took my clothes and my wallet and mobile,' she said. 'I'd like them back please.'

'They're prob'ly wimmie shoes and socks,' said Sep. 'They've also got my mobile and about fifty quid.'

Cope looked at Winnie in Sep's coat, which was barely protecting her modesty, then he went back up the cellar steps, calling out that a woman's clothes and a man's shoes and socks and two mobiles should be about somewhere. His brief absence gave Sep time to collect his thoughts and remember he was still acting out a subterfuge. He murmured to Winnie, 'Let me do the talking. You're supposed to be in shock.'

'Supposed to be? I *am* in bloody shock. Will I get done for shooting him?'

'Hopefully not.'

Cope returned and said, 'I would think the information will be worth five hundred to a thousand, once we have a conviction.'

'That could be months,' protested Sep. 'An' this is a dangerous game, by the way.'

'It's the way we work.'

'Hows aboot five hundred now and five hundred later?'

'It doesn't work like that.'

Sep knew it did. 'Fair enough,' he said. 'Once you have yer conviction and ye pay me ma full grand, that's when I gi' ye ma next lead.'

Cope thought about this. 'OK, you give me another lead and I'll see about the five hundred. Do you still have a mobile number I can get you on?'

'I don't know. Did ye find it? It's a red one.'

'If it's here we'll get it for you.'

'That and fifty quid they took.'

Sep had two mobiles. One for everyday use and a special red one for rare occasions such as this. It was a little-used phone but he remembered the number, which he gave to Cope. 'OK,' he said, 'we'll talk aboot money then. In the meantime, we'd rather not be caught up wi' these pimpy bastards. I assume we're free te go wi' no further involvement.'

A uniformed policeman appeared with a bundle of clothes, Sep's shoes, the two mobiles and Winnie's wallet.

'I'm still missing fifty quid,' said Sep, playing his Jimmy Lennon role for all it was worth. 'I cannae afford te lose fifty quid.'

'You nearly lost your life,' said Cope.

'Aye, there is that.'

'I'd better accompany you outside.'

'Both of us?' said Sep.

'Yes, but I can't guarantee she's out of the woods. If she was raped she needs to come to the station to be examined.'

Sep waited until the other policeman had left before he said, 'I don't think Winnie wants to get involved in a court case with these people.'

'Correct,' confirmed Winnie.

Cope looked down at the unconscious man. 'If he dies he won't have to answer a rape charge, which just leaves us with how he died.' He now looked at Winnie.

'She gave me this lead,' said Sep, 'and she's a victim. If she gets convicted of anythin' I'm out of our arrangement.'

'I'll see what can be done,' said Cope, 'but I can't guarantee anything.'

Once outside, Sep put an arm around Winnie who was shaking with delayed shock. Sep looked round for his bike.

'Bloody hell! Someone's stolen my bike.'

'It could be one of that lot.'

'Doubt it. Anyway, not to worry, there's a GPS tracker on it.'

'You put a tracker on your bike?'

'It's an expensive bike. I got to really like it. Have you not noticed how fit I've been lately?'

But she was in no mood for his attempt at humour. 'Could you drive me home? I'm feeling a bit fragile.'

'No problem.'

'Sep.'

'Yeah?'

'They didn't give me my knickers back. W . . . why didn't they give me my knickers back?'

Sep just squeezed her a bit harder. He thought the police might have hung on to them for some intrusive DNA reasons but it would do no good to tell her that. They'd taken nothing from him that might produce his DNA – of which the police would have a record. He checked his face for wounds that might have left blood behind. He had a sore head and sore ribs but nothing more. He suspected Cope didn't want the identity of this scruffy Scotsman too widely known. Sep was his informant, no one else's. He grinned to himself. His bogus self was being protected by the very man it was meant to damage.

'Gabriela will be pleased to see you,' he remarked as he drove them to her home.

'I'm guessing you left her the copper's number,' murmured Winnie, still not herself.

'I left her Cope's card, just telling her this was the copper who'd be helping us out. I think she must have taken it upon herself not to wait for me to get back. He must have gone straight round to your house, identified the brothel on the computer and organized an armed response team. All that takes time. I bet she rang Cope the second I left your house. Women, eh? They don't trust you to do anything right.'

This raised a slight smile from Winnie. 'Yeah,' she said, then added, 'You came for me though, didn't you, Sep?'

'Yes I did, but I was a bit clumsy.'

'Thanks for coming for me – and we might even have got out on our own. You'd won the fight and I had the gun.'

'Winnie, I was struggling, but you had the gun all right.'

'If he hadn't raped me, I wouldn't have shot him quite so quickly,' she said.

'I think what he did to you directed the bullet to its target.'

'That's exactly right. After all he'd done to me I couldn't stop myself shooting him where I did.'

'I imagine there are plenty of rape victims who'll be cheering you to high heaven if they ever get to hear of this.'

'I do hope no one does.' she said. 'I've never liked hurting people but I certainly feel better for shooting his tackle off. Tit-for-tat, really. He took my self-respect from me, I took something similar from him.'

Sep looked at her, quizzically, 'What's that you said to him? *You really hurt my feelings?* Bit of an understatement wasn't it?'

'I meant it to be. I didn't want him to have the satisfaction of knowing just how much damage he'd done to me.'

'Why not?'

'Because he had no right to know. In his eyes I went way over the top with my revenge. In shooting off his bollocks I took away the power he'd had over me. In other words I got a result, and that's what I wanted. Anyway, right now I want a shower,' she said. 'I smell like a Gents lavatory.'

'How would you know what a Gents lavatory smells like?'

'Cleaning men's bogs was once part of my community service. It made me glad I'm a woman. I wouldn't want to spend any private time in one of those places.'

'Ah, but did it make you change your ways?'

'You tell me. I was doing it for causing actual bodily harm to a man who was assaulting me. I put him in hospital.'

'Seems a bit harsh if he was assaulting you.'

'The magistrates didn't think he was assaulting me. They assumed I'd propositioned him – me being what I am. Mind you, his wife believed me and kicked him out, which was a bit of result, I suppose. She was a wealthy woman and he was a useless tosser who ended up living in a cardboard box down by the station. This world can be an unjust place, so you need a result now and again.'

Sep grinned, 'I'll try and stay on the right side of you.'

'It's a good side to be.'

Winnie was coming round, which was pretty impressive. Most people, hard men included, would have been troubled for weeks after such an ordeal; many of them would have needed counselling. He wasn't feeling too chipper himself.

But he was really getting to like Winnie O'Toole.

TWENTY-FIVE

2 June

'It's quite an organization, sir, and it's unravelling by the minute.'

It was the next day and Cope was in Detective Superintendent Ibbotson's office. Whitey and six Romanians were in the cells; Dragos was under guard in intensive care in St James's hospital. The brothel was still being searched by the police. Nine girls had been taken first to hospital and then to a secure hostel. Secure for their own protection, as the human trafficking gang of which Whitey was a part, wasn't restricted to Leeds, but to many towns in West Yorkshire. Computers found in Whitey's brothel had given up details of many more brothels in that area and over a hundred police officers were carrying out synchronised raids on eight of them – raids which would result in the arrest of sixty-three men and the freeing of seventy-two trafficked women. Cope was taking the credit for all of this, to his superintendent's irritation.

'This informer of yours, is he costing us much?'

'I've promised him a thousand, sir. Five hundred now, five hundred when we get convictions. He's also claiming the pimps stole fifty quid off him, which I suppose I'll have to give him.'

Cope saw no reason to be anything other than honest about how much he was giving his informers. It was too easy for someone to check up on this.

'Give him his grand today. We want him on our side, information like this is pure gold. I understand he's Scottish is he?'

'He is, sir. I pulled an old sheet on him. He used to live in Leeds but moved up to Glasgow. Ended up in Barlinnie jail for an assault so he came back down here.'

'Yeah, that's what they do. Stay in one place for too long and the coppers get to know your face and pull you for the slightest thing.'

'They have a hard life these villains, sir. I'm amazed they haven't got a union.'

'What's his name?'

'Am I compelled to tell you that, sir?'

'Not if you choose not to, but to look on the black side, if anything happens to you we not only lose a valued officer but a valued nark.'

'So long as it's understood he's my man and no one else's sir.'

'That goes without saying.'

'His name's Jimmy Lennon.'

Ibbotson nodded, thoughtfully. 'Scottish . . . big feller, is he?'

'Yes he is. Big and scruffy.'

'Sounds like someone I once came across. Small time nuisance, mainly due to drink if I remember rightly.'

'That's him, sir. He does take a drink, and small time does describe him, but his type gets to know things, and he's a canny man, to quote him, sir.'

'Why would he get mixed up with the Romanians?'

'I think they took his woman, sir. Bit of a looker. What she sees in him, God only knows.'

'I wonder if he might be any help to us on the Strathmore case. Would he fraternize with any of Formosa's lot?'

'I think it's a question of would they fraternize with him, sir. He is a bit unsavoury.'

Ibbotson sat back in his seat and laced his fingers over his generous stomach. 'I wonder if he might be tempted by the prospect of big money for a good result.'

'It's worth a shot, sir. How much shall I say?'

'Well, I could authorize up to ten grand but it would have to be strictly PBR.'

'Payment by results? I think the amount might tempt him, but not the method of payment.'

'Tell him a grand up front.'

'So, you want me to give him two grand now?'

'Yes, I'll authorize it. If it works out it'll be money well spent.'

Cope disguised his feelings of elation with a look of concern. How best should he play this? He couldn't see Jimmy Lennon being of any use to the police, but it would make DI Cope a very valuable person to have on your side – if you were Vincent Formosa.

'I'll do my best, sir. If Lennon knows anything at all he'll give it to me – and maybe I can persuade him to sober up if he wants to earn ten grand in readies.'

'You do that, Lenny. By the way, the Dragos man died, did you know that?'

'I didn't sir. I need to cover up the truth of his death if my informant is to be of any use to me.'

'Were there any witnesses to the shooting, apart from Lennon and the woman?'

'No, sir.'

'Then he was accidentally shot whilst in a confrontation with them. I'll tell the CPS that Lennon and the woman were working undercover for us and neither were armed. It should be enough to have them back off.'

TWENTY-SIX

3 June

'Jesus, Sep! For a handsome feller yer look an awful fucking shambles.'

'Winifred O'Toole, I don't think swearing becomes you.'

'I don't swear much.'

'You do, actually. Just listen to yourself, in general conversation saying I look a "fucking shambles".'

'You just swore yourself.'

'I was quoting you – that's allowed; probably not in polite company, but between friends it is.'

'OK, but me just saying you look an awful shambles doesn't tell the whole story.'

They were drinking coffee in the kitchen of Sep's flat in Middleton. Winnie had driven her van there to keep an appointment made on the day of the brothel raid, two days previously.'

'How's Gabriela?' Sep asked.

'She's hoping to go back home to Romania without having to give evidence.'

'Yeah, I mentioned that to Cope. The law should have enough evidence without having to subject her to a court ordeal.'

'So, she should be OK?'

'I would imagine so. Cope's doing what he can to keep me onside. He gave me a grand yesterday for the info you gave me, plus another grand for me to help him with the Strathmore kidnapping case.'

'Two grand? You are in his good books.'

He took an envelope from his pocket and gave it to her, saying, 'Like I said, it was your info so it's yours.'

She took it and looked inside. It was stuffed with fifty pounds notes.

'How much is this?'

'Two grand.'

'Shouldn't it be fifty-fifty?' she asked him.

'It will be in future, but in future you won't be getting personally involved in anything. It would have panned out just as well if you'd just rung me up with the info you had and left it at that. There was no need at all for you to put yourself in danger – or me for that matter.'

'Point taken. I'm going to give half of this to Gabriela. Money always eases things and she has a lot of stuff that needs easing.'

'She's lucky she found you.'

He stared at her, wondering if he should tell her that Dragos was dead. Some people find taking a human life a severe shock to the system no matter what the circumstances, or how evil the life. On balance he decided she needed to know.

'Winnie, there's something you should know about Dragos.'

She looked at his face and read it like a book. 'He's dead?'

Sep nodded, Winnie frowned.

'Oh, so I killed him, did I?'

'Yes.'

'I killed someone.'

'Winnie, you killed a violent animal which had no right to live. The world is a better place without him.'

She cast her mind back to the vile acts he'd committed on her body and decided, 'Yes, I think I'm glad . . . is that awful?'

'Nope, it's very human.'

'Will I get into trouble?'

'Oh no, it's being put down to a struggle between me and him and the gun – his gun, discharging during the struggle while he was holding it.'

'Bloody hell!' she said, 'The police have their own sweet way of covering things up.'

'Luckily for you,' said Sep. A thought struck him. 'Talking of guns, Winnie, you have a knack of being able to acquire things.'

'I have.'

'Well, I wonder if you might be able to acquire me a decent handgun, fully loaded and a couple of blanks.'

'What the hell for?'

'It's just a ruse I have in mind. It'll probably come to nothing, but if an opportunity arises, I'd like to be ready.'

'I dread to think what this ruse is, Sep, but it'll cost you a monkey.'

'Five hundred? I thought you could get stuff cheaply.'

'Not that sort of stuff.'

'OK, five hundred it is. When?'

'Tomorrow with a bit of luck.'

'I don't suppose you have any inside info on the Strathmore case? Any knowledge or suspicion or anything that might interest the police?'

'Bloody hell, Sep! Everybody knows it's Formosa who's behind it and we know that Cope's in Formosa's pocket.'

'I'm just looking for solid information, I'm not saying how I'm going to use it. If I can turn it into misinformation to put Cope up the creek, that's what I'll do.'

'Does it bother you that Cope's with your wife?'

'Winnie, it enrages me, but mainly that he's living in my house – the house where my daughter lives.'

'Would you ever go back to your wife?'

'No, we're getting divorced.'

'On what grounds?'

'She cited cruelty, but I've denied it and asked for proof, which she'll never be able to produce. So I've cited her infidelity with Cope.'

'And that'll do the trick?'

'Yep. She's going for the house, which is fair enough considering it's where my daughter lives.'

'Can she sell it without your permission?'

'Not sure, must look into that.'

'Would you like it if she kicked Cope out?'

'I would. In fact it might make things easier all round if he didn't live there. Why do you ask?'

'Because I think I might be able to arrange that,' Winnie said.

'How?'

She tapped the side of her nose with a forefinger. 'Not entirely sure yet but I get the impression that he lives with your wife more for convenience and easy sex rather than love.'

'Probably.'

'So, in relationship terms he's a man-of-straw.'

'Is he?'

'Yes, and straw men are very vulnerable to women such as me.'

Sep smiled. 'I imagine most men are, choose what they're made of.'

She smiled back at him. 'What about you? Are you vulnerable to me?'

'To you? I can imagine circumstances where that might be the case.'

She leaned across the table and placed her hand on his. 'And is right now one of those circumstances?'

He looked down at their hands and felt the unusual warmth emanating from hers. He looked up at her and knew that this warmth was just part of the general warmth he always felt in her presence. Or could it be more than just warmth? He'd certainly never experienced this from his wife, whom he missed less and less as the days went by.

'Tell me what you want, Winnie.'

'I'm telling you that apart from being raped I haven't had sex in almost two years.'

'Hasn't your experience with Dragos put you off sex?'

'I'm hoping it's like falling off a horse. The quicker you get back on, the quicker you get back to enjoying riding.'

'And you want to get back on the horse now, do you?'

'I do.'

'You're an unusual woman.'

'So I'm told. How long has it been for you?'

He shook his head. 'I sometimes wonder if I've ever had it – with my wife that is. I suppose I must have at some time, with us having a daughter. I'm guessing Cope's having more luck than I ever did.'

'Nothing memorable then?'

'No.'

'What about outside marriage?'

'Not sure. I once woke up naked in a woman's bed after a really drunken night out but I wasn't sure if we'd had sex. She didn't know either.'

'Do you think there's something wrong with you?'

'Well, I hope not. I always used to joke about eating too much of that cake that restricts a man's sex life.'

'You mean wedding cake?'

'You're always a step ahead of me.'

'Tell you what. Why don't I, purely as an act of kindness, give you a try out?'

He gave it a moment's thought then said, 'Purely as an act of kindness?'

'Yes, I do have some professional experience in that field. I would hasten to add that I have long since lost my professional status, but I still have the talent.'

'You have talent?'

'Some. I wasn't cheap.'

'Then it'd be rude of me to turn such an offer down,' said Sep. 'I hope I won't need to shave or anything.'

'A shower will be sufficient. Perhaps we could shower together to kick things off?'

'I think that'd be an excellent idea.'

TWENTY-SEVEN

I t was nine o'clock in the evening and Rachel Black was ironing her daughter's school uniform when the telephone rang. Her daughter, Phoebe, took the call. It was a woman wanting to speak to Mrs Black. Phoebe handed her mother the phone.

'Hello, Mrs Black . . . No, I'm not trying to sell you anything. I'm ringing to do you a great favour.'

'Oh yes, what favour's that?'

'Well, I'm in the Tommy Wass public house in Beeston, do you know it?'

'I think so, yes.'

'Well I wonder if you might know who's also in here, talking to a local prostitute, called Molly Grogan. He often comes in and he often uses her services. He'll be off to her house in Harlech Road in a few minutes. It's a regular date they have. I think she gives him it for nothing, with him being a copper.

'If it's my husband, I'm not interested.'

'Your husband's not a copper any more, Mrs Black, but this bloke is. Not that he's on duty right now of course. You know him well, Mrs Black, his name's Lenny Cope. Oh, they're leaving now. Tell you what, I'll give you the number of the house and if you drive straight there you'll find his car parked outside.'

The caller gave her both the house number and postcode of the house so that she'd have no trouble finding it with her satnav.

'This isn't a hoax, Mrs Black, just someone who doesn't like to see women being made fools of. I'm telling you because the cockney bastard did it to me once.'

Rachel clicked off the phone, frozen with shock. No, it must be a wind-up. She rang Lenny's mobile but got a recorded message. She left one of her own.

'Lenny, could you ring me back the second you get this, it's very urgent.'

She sat down, staring at her phone. Phoebe was worried.

'What's wrong, Mum?'

'I don't know . . . nothing I hope. Look darling, I've got to go out for half an hour.'
'That's OK. I can do the ironing.'

Winnie was standing at the bar. She stuck her mobile back in her pocket and kept her back to Cope and Molly. Her head was tilted towards her drink but her eyes were on the mirror behind the bar as she followed the reflection of them leaving the room. She was tempted to ring Sep to tell him what she'd done, but maybe not yet. She just hoped he'd been telling the truth when he said he wouldn't take his wife back. Otherwise she might have just shot herself in the foot.

She'd known about Cope frequenting the pub and using Molly's sexual services but she hadn't thought it advantageous for Sep to know such a man was living in the same house as his daughter. He was depressed enough with his situation without making it worse. This seemed an ideal solution.

Fifteen minutes later Rachel Black parked her car fifty yards down the road from Cope's which, in turn, was parked fifty yards down from the address she had been given. But she figured no man in his right mind would park his car bang outside a known prostitute's house. After forty minutes Cope emerged, got into his car and drove off. Rachel sat there in tears, her worst fears now realized. Sep hadn't been her idea of an ideal husband but as far as she knew he'd never been unfaithful to her. She drove home.

Cope was already home when Rachel got there. He was surprised that she'd left eleven-year-old Phoebe on her own. She was normally over-protective of her daughter.

'Where've you been?' he asked.
'More to the point,' she said, 'where've you been?'
'Working.'
'Working in a pub?'
'Yes, as a matter of fact.'
'The Tommy Wass in Beeston?'
'How do you know?'
'I had a phone call from a friend who saw you there. You were talking to a woman, apparently.'
'Yes I was. I often talk to women in the course of my work.'

'Why were you talking to her?'

Phoebe could see this might end badly and she'd had enough of that when her dad was at home, so she excused herself and went to her room. The two adults watched her go then Cope said, 'What is this? Am I getting the third degree because someone you know saw me doing my job?'

'Just tell me about this woman. How come she's of help to you?'

'As it happens she wasn't of any help. I was just asking people about the whereabouts of a thief I'm trying to track down.'

'I thought that was the job of the lower ranks, the constables and sergeants.'

'I like to do my own legwork from time to time.'

'What job does this woman do?'

'I don't know. I hardly know her, just that she's in that pub a lot.'

'So, you talked to her in the pub, she was of no use to you so you came straight back here.'

'Not straight back, no. I called in another pub for the same reason, but there was no one there of use to me so then I came here.'

'I want you to leave, Lenny, right now. Pack whatever stuff you have and leave. You didn't come straight back here, you went off with that woman who's a prostitute.'

'I did no such thing.'

'Just go, Lenny. I saw you come out of her house. You'd obviously been screwing her. What's the arrangement? Does she give you freebies because you're a copper?'

His face turned savage. He raised a hand. 'Who the hell have you been talking to?'

'If you raise your hand to me, Lenny, I'll tell the truth about how I got those bruises that Sep took the blame for. He'll be back on the force and you'll be off.'

Cope put his coat back on and snatched his car keys off the table. 'Too late for that, girl. It's you who perjured yourself to get rid of him – that's a custodial offence.'

'Just go, Lenny.'

TWENTY-EIGHT

'Fiona, it's Sep. Do not say my name out loud.'

'Hi, Dad.'

'That's good,' said Sep. 'You now need to be somewhere where you can talk without being overheard.'

'I suppose that can be arranged.'

DS Fiona Burnside pressed her mobile closer to her ear lest any of the conversation leak out. She got up from her desk and walked out into a corridor, then into the ladies' toilet. She checked that all three cubicles were empty. Sep could hear this and knew what she was doing.

'Are you in the Ladies?'

'I am. What is it you want, sir?'

'I'm not a *sir* any more.'

'I know, force of habit.'

'I need to speak to you privately. There's stuff going on within the job that someone needs to know about and you're the only one who'll believe me.'

'What makes you think that?'

'Because I don't think you believed a word of all that nonsense about me beating Rachel up. I've never hit a woman in my life.'

'So?'

'I intend getting my job back and I need the truth to come out.'

'What's this stuff I need to know?'

'It's something we can't discuss over the phone. I'd like us to meet up.'

'Where?'

'My place would be good. I've just moved to Middleton.'

'I won't do anything that might compromise my job. I've been made up to detective sergeant since you left.'

'I know that. Congratulations, it's well-deserved. All I want to do is give you solid information. What you do with it is your own affair.'

'When?'

'ASAP.'

'I'm off duty in an hour.'

'I guessed that. Can you come straight round?'

'Yes, if you give me the address and postcode.'

After Sep had done that, Fiona asked him, 'Did you know your wife's kicked her boyfriend out?'

'I didn't know that, no.'

'Well, he came in today saying he was looking round for new accommodation because he'd had enough of her. Not ten minutes later she rang me with the full story. Apparently she caught him with a prostitute. She rang me because she knew he'd turn up with a different tale.'

'Who do you believe?'

'Oh, I believe Rachel. She even gave me the name of the prostitute – Molly Grogan.'

Fiona was a very feisty copper who didn't suck up to anyone. If she had she might have made inspector by now. When Sep was having his problems she'd been on a month's leave visiting her brother in Australia. Had she been working, she'd have been his only ally.

'I haven't done vice for years,' said Sep, 'so I don't know the woman.'

'I've already checked her out. She was with him all right. I got her to tell me.'

'Yeah, I'll bet you did . . . and she'll tell him you know about him.'

'What harm can that do me? Hang on – this stuff you're going to tell me, does that involve this person?'

'Well, it could do,' said Sep.

'See you shortly, then.'

Sep clicked his phone off and stared at the screen for a couple of seconds. He'd told Fiona he was aiming to get his job back, which was a commitment of sorts. DI Septimus Black was on the road back.

But was he going in the right direction?

TWENTY-NINE

Fiona double-checked the number on the door she'd just knocked on, before saying,

'Sorry, I think I might have got the wrong . . . er . . . does Mr Septimus Black live here by any chance?'

'Aye, if ye can call it livin'.' Sep was using his Glaswegian accent.

'Could I speak to him, please?'

'Y'already are, darlin'.'

'What?'

Sep dropped his accent and grinned at her, saying, 'Hell of a disguise this, isn't it?'

Fiona stared at him as he pushed his hair away from his face.

'What? Is it you, sir? Bloody hell!'

'Aye it's me, lassie, and yer not the first te be fooled.'

'Whoa! This is so weird . . . I'd prefer it if you dropped the accent, sir.'

'And I'd prefer it if you didn't call me "sir". Come in Fiona, and allow me to explain why I look like this and why I've asked you here.'

A large house had been converted into four flats. Sep lived on the first floor. Fiona followed him through a small hallway into quite a spacious lounge. She looked around it, approvingly.

'Not bad – bigger than my place.'

'It came furnished,' said Sep, 'so don't be too critical of my taste.'

There was a two-seater settee, an easy chair that looked to have its own adjustable foot rest, a dining table, three dining chairs, a chest of drawers, a thirty-seven inch flat screen TV and a computer table complete with computer and printer.

'The only things I own are the telly and the computer,' he said. 'There's a kitchen, bedroom and bathroom back there.' He nodded vaguely in the direction of the hallway. 'Sit down.'

She chose the settee, he sat opposite in the chair. 'Can't remember if you smoke,' he said. If you do, it's banned, part of the rental agreement.'

'I don't smoke – neither do you if I remember rightly.'

'No, I don't,' he said, 'but Jimmy Lennon does. I need him to be as little like Sep Black as possible.'

'Jimmy Lenn— Oh, I get it. He's your other self?'

'He is.'

'Scottish.'

'As they come.'

'And very scruffy, unlike Septimus Black.'

'Very unlike Septimus Black. Jimmy Lennon's a vagrant, fresh out of Barlinnie, just signed up with DI Cope as an informer.'

'You're joking!'

'I don't have too much to joke about nowadays, Fiona. I suppose you heard about the brothel Cope had raided?'

'I did.'

'Well that was all down to info given by Jimmy Lennon. Well, him and a certain female acquaintance of his.'

'You have a female acquaintance, do you?'

Sep remembered the bedroom activities in which he and Winnie had been involved. They'd spent an active night together in his bed. The best sex he'd had in his life, to the extent that he'd decided to invite her back for other nights of the same. All part of his rehabilitation, he told himself.

'Yes,' he said, 'I have a female acquaintance.'

'Good for you, sir.'

'Less of the sir. You do appreciate that I've taken you into my confidence and that if you tell anyone what I'm up to, the game's finished for me.'

'I had worked that out and you can trust me . . . what do I call you?'

'Sep or Blacky will do.'

'Sep, then. How does DI Cope come into this?'

'Ah, this is the dangerous stuff. This is where you really have to convince me that you trust what I'm doing and won't blab on me.'

'I've said you can trust me, what more do you want?'

'I don't know. I don't even know what I want from you, except that someone in the job needs to know what I know and can take that knowledge into account as the Strathmore case unfolds.'

'The Strathmore case! Don't tell me Cope's involved with that.'

'I'll tell you what I know, Fiona, and you can make your own judgement.'

'OK.'

'I know that a man called Lee Dench was the key witness against Vince Formosa.'

'I didn't know that until after he was killed and Formosa released,' said Fiona. 'It was Cope's case and Dench was Cope's informer.'

'True, and I assume you know that Formosa had him killed?'

'That's the general feeling, but there's no proof.'

'I assume CID were a bit perplexed as to how Formosa found out that Dench was Cope's informer.'

'The word is that Dench's girlfriend opened her big mouth and it got back to Formosa.'

'Well, I have another word. My information is that Cope was in Formosa's pocket all along – still is for that matter. That's how Formosa got to know about Dench.'

'Bloody hell!'

'Exactly.'

'Where'd you get this from?'

'My source is impeccable, and it's nothing to do with Cope having an affair with my wife. I believe Cope played a major role in getting me kicked off the force. I believe he was a crooked cop in London and that he's a crooked cop up here. I have no real proof of this, other than I'm sure Cope is in Formosa's pocket.'

'I know Cope spread a lot of poison around about you,' said Fiona, 'He was telling everybody that if they weren't careful they could all be tarred with the same brush as you regarding the MP's death. He was very good at it by all accounts. I was on holiday at the time but people were even warning *me* not to get too friendly with you.'

'Good God! The man hardly knew me. I checked him out and he's apparently an expert in propaganda. The Met taught him that and he comes up here and uses it against me.'

'That's because you were trying to turn people against him.'

'With good reason. I certainly lost that battle.'

'So Cope might know where the Strathmore children are,' said Fiona.

'I think there's a fair chance – that's if they're still alive.'

'Shouldn't we take all this upstairs, Sep?'

'I have no proof. My impeccable source is only impeccable to me. I trust her implicitly, but such is her reputation that she'd get laughed out of court, that's if it even got to court.'

'I assume this is your female acquaintance?'

'It is. Before Cope's raid on the brothel she went in first and put her life at risk for those girls. She's an unusual woman.'

'Were you there?'

'I was, as it happens.'

'I'm told one of the gang had his bits shot off and no one's been charged.'

'His name was Dragos.'

'Was?'

'Yeah, he's dead.'

'What exactly happened to him?'

Sep hesitated before answering this. Fiona was something of a feminist. The true story might bring her well and truly onside.

'Dragos had raped her and degraded her. Urinated on her naked body after he'd finished with her. I was involved in a fight with him. He dropped his gun, and she picked it up. What would you have done?'

'*She* did it?'

Sep nodded.

'Bloody hell! She wasn't gonna miss an opportunity like that. God, I bet it felt good!'

'She needed to show him who was really the boss.'

'Oh my god! Wish we could do that to all rapists.'

'She doesn't want it broadcasting.'

Fiona looked disappointed.

'I mean it, Fiona. The last thing she wants is to end up in court on a murder charge and having to answer a load of questions about her being raped.'

'Does Cope know she did it?'

'He does, but when I told him she was part of my team and if she was arrested my information would dry up, he let us both walk.'

'He didn't recognize you?'

'No, but neither did you, and you know me a lot better than he does.'

'So Cope saved your neck when he raided the place?'

'He did, but he also got the collar of a lifetime due to us

pointing him in the right direction. The best thing for him was that this gang has no connection with Formosa. It makes Cope look more of a Mr Clean than ever.'

'You better believe it, Sep. It was bigtime. Dozens of girls in three houses, plus a fair amount of heroin and coke. He's aiming for DCI is Cope.'

'Not if I can help it.'

'If it helps at all, I don't like him. He's an oily bugger.' She stood up and walked around the room in deep thought. 'Is there anything specific you want me to do?'

'I just want you to keep an eye on him, Fiona. It'd help if you could get yourself on the Strathmore case.'

'I'm already on it, Sep. He asked me today.'

'Anything specific he wanted you to do?'

'Nothing yet. Just to keep my eyes and ears open for information about the kids. He's of the opinion that Formosa will try to extort money off Peter Strathmore.'

'Well, that's a fairly obvious opinion. Is he of the opinion that they're still alive?'

'He thinks it's possible that Formosa's kept them alive so they can talk to their dad over the phone, but he doesn't think Formosa will honour any deal. He'll just take the money and kill the kids. What do you think?'

'I don't know enough about Formosa to have an opinion on that.'

'Would your female acquaintance know anything?'

'She's already told me all she knows, but she's got her ear to the ground.'

Fiona sat down again. 'A thought has struck me,' she said.

'What's that?'

'Strathmore's a rich man. He'd pay big money to a private investigator who got his kids back.'

'Fiona, all I'm trying to do is get my job back.'

'I know. But this might be a situation where us coppers, having to abide by the rules, find ourselves hamstrung. A private detective with your unusual talents might be able to circumvent a few rules.'

'Yeah. I might circumvent myself into prison or worse still, into a bullet.'

'It was just a thought. Those kids need all the help they can get.'

THIRTY

It was the twelfth week of their captivity. James and Milly were being kept in a cellar because cellars were habitats that criminals understood. As a boy, Formosa had often been locked in a cellar and it was where he'd felt the most helpless. He felt it was an ideal place to keep his enemies and an ideal place to subjugate those who needed putting in their place, and, of course, a cellar made an ideal prison and a man in his line of work needed a decent prison. He knew that, of all habitats, cellars were the most secure and soundproof. This cellar was beneath the centre of a building, surrounded by other empty cellars, all owned by Formosa. It had no access to daylight but it did have plumbing in the form of its own toilet and washbasin with cold, running water. Formosa didn't want the kids stinking his cellar out. They were fed meals through a four inch gap beneath the door. Cold food once a day; ten slices of bread and either two apples or two bananas each and they had one plastic cup from which to drink tap water. These were basic survival rations. No point wasting money on anything more as these kids weren't going to live too long. This cellar and these rations would be all they would ever know. His men had orders never to speak to them, never to give them any information about why they were there, what was going to happen to them, when they might be going home. All Milly had to live for was James's optimistic guesswork.

'We've been kidnapped 'cause Dad's rich. When Dad pays the money, they have to let us go. It always happens to rich kids.'

'Why hasn't Dad paid the money yet? We've been here flipping weeks.'

'I know. I think it's because they're maybe asking for too much. Dad'll have to do a deal with them. Dad's great at doing deals with people.'

'I wish he'd hurry up. If we get two bananas tomorrow can I have them both? I don't like the apples they give us. They give me tummy ache. I've still got today's apple.'

'OK.'

James wasn't a great fan of the apples they were being given but he knew it would do Milly good to have something to look forward to. Today he'd have an extra apple and tomorrow he'd live on his ten slices of bread and hope they'd bought it fresh that day, for a change.

His greatest worry was that his sister might cry herself into permanent hysterics. He tried to distract her from their situation by teaching her stuff she should be learning at school right now. Mainly he taught her mental arithmetic. Whatever he taught her had to be mental, with them having no means of writing anything down. He also taught her the art of storytelling for when she would have to do compositions at school. She enjoyed this more than the arithmetic as he often made up stories just for her benefit.

'What's seven nines?'

'Sixty-three.'

'Blimey! I couldn't have done that when I was eight. You're coming on our kid. Seven eights?'

'Fifty-six.'

'Twenty seven divided by three?'

Slight hesitation then, 'Nine.'

'That's it. You know as much as I know. OK, we need a new subject.'

'What about songs?' suggested Milly.

'That's a great idea. From now on it's stories and songs. Do you know *There was an old man called Michael Finnegan*?'

'No.'

He sang it to her, knowing she'd want to learn it. Michael Finnegan was a simple song which required repetition, and repetition was handy in their enclosed world. It was how they survived, by entertaining themselves. James considered that silence was their enemy. Silence led to her tears, and Milly's tears would lead to his tears before much longer. James knew he couldn't afford to cry. He was in charge and his mum and dad would expect him to look after his sister.

The cellar had no heating so the children had to be grateful that they'd been picked up in their school clothes, which included an outdoor coat. They each slept on a foam-rubber mattress, which had a thin woollen blanket but no pillow. There was a single bulb in the room which switched itself off on a timer at eight p.m. each day and came back on at eight a.m. When the light went out the darkness was so intense that the children couldn't see their own hands in front of their eyes. Should they need the toilet during this darkness, they had learned to feel their way there along a wall. Both had become quite adept at this. They had no real sense of time and assumed the light came on to indicate it was daytime, although their days often seemed interminably long. They were counting these electric light days and had got up to eighty-four.

'That's twelve weeks,' said Milly. 'Why is it taking Dad twelve weeks to come and get us?'

James didn't know the answer to this. Was he right about them being kidnapped for money – kidnapped by people who wouldn't even speak to him? Grown-ups often did stuff he didn't understand. When food was next pushed under the door, he shouted out.

'Excuse me. Can you tell us why we're here, please?'

It wasn't the first time he'd asked this question and it wasn't the first time he'd got no reply, just the sound of heavy feet going up the stone steps and the sound of a door opening and closing. He looked at Milly who had tears in her eyes. She knew her brother was losing confidence, and he was all she had.

'Sorry,' she said. 'I can't stop crying. I know it's not helping.'

James attempted a smile. 'It's OK,' he said. 'Cry more, pee less, that's what Dad used to say when I cried. It always made me laugh and I stopped crying – that's why he said it.'

Milly tried to smile back but failed. She hung her head and asked in a quiet and hesitant voice, 'I don't feel well. Are we . . . are we going to die in here, James?'

'No, no, don't be silly. They're keeping us here for money and Dad'll pay up even if it leaves him skint.'

'So why hasn't he paid them?'

'Dunno. There's stuff that grown-ups do that we don't understand. Sometimes we think stuff's easy to do when it isn't. Like going to a bank and drawing out a million quid.'

'A million quid? Do you think Dad's got a million quid?'

'I expect so. All rich people have a million quid at least.'

'He's not going to be too pleased with us if we've cost him a million quid,' said Milly. 'I only get three pounds fifty pocket money. How much do you get?'

'I get five pounds but that's because I'm older than you, and I have to keep my room tidy or I don't get anything. He's very careful with his money is Dad. Oliver Crenshawe gets ten quid and his dad works for our dad.'

'Do you think that's why Dad hasn't paid the money yet?'

'Dunno.'

'I bet if Dad has to pay a million quid, bang goes our pocket money.'

'Maybe,' said James, who knew his sister was trying her best to talk as if they lived in a normal world with normal problems such as pocket money. He'd had an abnormal thought preying on his mind for the whole twelve weeks of their incarceration. He hadn't mentioned it to Milly but now this ten-year-old boy needed to share his fear.

'I'm really glad these men aren't doing anything nasty to us,' he said.

'What? I think locking us in this cellar's very nasty.'

'I know, but . . .'

James had been made aware of child molesters by his mother and, much more graphically, by some of the kids at school, especially Oliver Crenshawe.

'But what?'

'I'm just glad they're not coming in here to, erm . . . to hurt us.'

'Oh? Does that happen sometimes?'

'Sometimes, but it's not happening to us, is it?'

'I hope they don't come to hurt us.'

'They won't,' said James, who felt he'd said too much. Milly nodded because she trusted him. James hoped she had good reason to trust him.

'Shall we sing *Zip A Dee Doo Dah*?' she asked.

'Uh?'

James's thoughts were now preoccupied as he stared into a dark corner. The dim lightbulb provided barely enough light to

illuminate the whole cellar. He got to his feet and walked over,
staring into the gloom at a small pile of bricks at the bottom of
a wall.

'What is it?' Milly asked.

'Just some bricks.'

'Oh.'

James looked up towards the top of the wall. Milly's question
about them dying in here still on his mind. Up until now he'd
thought it was just a question of waiting for their freedom, but
time was beginning to kill that hope and if there was anything
he could do to keep them alive he should give it a go.

There was a gap from where the bricks must have fallen. He
gave the matter some thought and began to build the fallen bricks
into a neat pile.

'Watcha doin'?'

'Buildin' these bricks.'

'Why? Why are you building bricks now?'

'There's a hole at the top of this wall. I wanna take a look
through it.'

'I don't 'spect it leads to anything.'

'That's what I thought, but it'll do no harm to look. It's something to do. I'm fed up of having nothing to do.'

She went over to watch him. Like he said, it was something
to do. She helped him pile up the bricks and even looked around
the cellar to find any other stray bricks. Eventually they had built
a solid pile about three feet high. James got on top of it and
reached up with his hands. He got a grip on the bottom course
of bricks in the hole.

'I bet I could get up there,' he said.

'Well, I couldn't and you're not leaving me down here.'

'I just wanna see what's on the other side of this wall.'

'Another cellar, I 'spect.'

'It might not be locked like this one is.'

'Have you just thought of that after all this time?'

'Well, I've always thought it might not even be a cellar. It's
mos' prob'ly small and horrible, but you never know.'

'You might end up trapped and can't get back.'

'If I do, you just tell them where I am and they'll let me out.'

James pulled himself up so his eyes were level with the hole.

'Can you see anything?' asked Milly.

'No, it's too dark.'

An idea struck him. He climbed off the pile of bricks and picked a half brick they hadn't used.

'What are you going to do with that?'

'This,' said James. He threw the brick though the hole and heard it land and skid across a hard floor. He guessed it had travelled some distance before it landed which meant that beyond the hole was a spacious room.

'It's deffo another cellar,' he said. 'I bet I could get through.'

'I don't want to be left in here on my own.'

'Milly, if I can get through I can always get back. I might even be able to let you out.'

'So long as you promise not to leave me here on my own.'

'I promise.'

He pulled himself up until his head was through the hole and his legs dangling on Milly's side. Normally James would have been over the wall in a flash but their meagre diet had reduced both his strength and energy, turning this into a Herculean effort. He lay in this position completely out of breath, planning his next move.

'Are you OK, James?'

'Yeah, just a bit out of puff that's all.'

He realized he needed to get his legs though first or he'd be landing on his head. He loosened a brick to his left and pushed it back to the floor, calling out to his sister.

'Watch out, Milly, I'm making the hole bigger.'

Milly took a couple of steps back as several more bricks fell to the floor. James now swung his legs right over until he was at the other side, just hanging by his hands and hoping the drop to the floor was no greater than in the first room. He let go. The drop was no more than four feet. He was OK.

Breathing heavily, he looked up at the hole he'd come through. It provided a dismal light into this new room, enough for him to see a door which was already open. He went through it into a narrow corridor and immediately found the door to his erstwhile prison. There was a key in the lock. He turned it and opened the door. Milly came out and hugged him, fearfully.

'What do we do now, James?'

'Try and get out of this place.'

In the gloom they saw stone steps at the end of the passage. 'Follow me,' said James.

She followed him up the steps. At the top was a door. James turned the handle.

'It's locked,' he told her. 'Listen, can you hear anything? Any voices or anyone walking about?'

They both listened for a full minute but they could hear nothing. 'I think they left us on our own,' said James. He ran his hand around the wall until he felt a light switch. A light came on. They both blinked in the unaccustomed brightness.

'What do we do now?' Milly asked.

'We think of an idea to get out.'

'I'm no good at ideas. What do we do?'

'We have a good look round. See what we can see.'

There was another light switch down in the passage. James switched it on and opened the door to the room he'd just crawled into, allowing in light. It was empty and dusty, just like the room that had been their prison. James was looking for some sort of tools that might help them break out. The ceiling looked very old and in desperate need of repair. The floorboards of whatever room was above could be seen between the holes in the crumbling plaster. They found a third room, much smaller than the other two. More of a store room but not much was stored in it. In the light from the open door, James kicked around in the piles of detritus on the floor and kicked against something hard and metallic. He picked it up and examined it. Recognizing it immediately. It was about five feet long with a flattened end.

'What is it?' asked Milly.

'It's a piece of scaffolding tube. This end is flattened so it can fit in a joint in the wall. It's called a putlog.'

'How do you know?'

'Because Dad told me. I go on his building sites with him now and again.' He took it out into the lit passage and looked up at the crumbling ceiling. 'I'll tell you something else, as well.'

'What?'

He pointed upwards. 'Them boards up there are floorboards and they're held down by two inch nails.'

'I bet they're rusty by now,' said Milly.

'I bet they are,' said James. 'I bet this place is a hundred years old and they had rubbish nails a hundred years ago. I bet I could knock a hole in them boards big enough for us to get through.'

'If you do, how do we get up there?'

'I can only solve one problem at a time, Milly.'

Holding the steel tube in both hands he thrust it up against the boards. There was a bang and a cloud of descending dust but nothing moved. 'I think I loosened it a bit,' James said optimistically. He thrust the tube up again, three times.

'I can see a gap,' said Milly.

'Can you have a go, I'm out of puff?'

Milly tried but couldn't reach. James took the putlog from her and began to bang along the length of the board until several feet of it was now bending upwards. He paused to catch his breath then turned his attention to the floorboard next to it and soon had a few feet of that bending up as well.

Completely exhausted he put down the tube and took stock of the situation. 'Well,' he said. 'The good thing is that there's no one in the place or they'd have been down here by now.'

'I was a bit worried about that,' said Milly. 'What will they do if they come back now and find out what we've been doing. They'll go mad.'

'Yeah, but they won't touch us. We're valuable merchandise we are.'

'What does that mean?'

'It just means we're valuable to them, so they won't do us any damage. You don't damage something that's valuable. Stands to reason.'

'Right,' said Milly.

James looked up again. 'If I could get up there high enough to push at them boards I bet I could push them right out.'

'There's a steel box thing in that little room you've just been in.'

'That's right. I wonder if it's fixed in to anything? Could be a water tank y'see,' he said, knowledgably.

'Dunno.'

They went back into the small room where they found the metal tank which once had contained water. It was three feet long by two feet wide and still contained the ball cock mechanism but it was attached to nothing. James checked all around it to ascertain this.

'I think we should be able to drag it out into the passage,' he said. 'Look, I'll move it away from the wall then I'll pull, you push.'

Despite his exhaustion, James was a strong lad for his age and between them they had no problem dragging the tank out into the passage. He sat on it for a while to regain his strength.

'Right,' he said, at length. 'I need us to stand it on its end so I can get up higher. I bet if I stand on it I can reach the ceiling easy.'

They stood it on end, James climbed on it and pushed up at the two loose floor boards. Gradually they came away from the rusty nails that had held them down for well over a hundred years. Above James was a gap about ten inches wide.

'I need to push another one out at least. Pass me that putlog up.'

'OK.'

James hammered away with the tube until he'd freed another board which he also pushed up until it came free of its nails. He threw it into the room above, along with the other two. He now had a gap big enough for him to climb through. He looked down at his sister, knowing that getting her out as well might be a problem. She knew what he was thinking.

'I don't want you to leave me down here, James.'

'I'm not going to. Once I'm out you climb on the tank and I'll pull you up.'

'OK,' she said, uncertainly.

It took the exhausted James some considerable time to pull himself up through the hole in the floor. He looked around at his new surroundings, lit only by the light coming from the street. It was a big room with many windows and chairs. A room a lot easier to escape from than the cellar.

'I'm still here,' Milly called up.

James laid flat on the floor and reached down to grab his sister's upstretched hands. She was a slightly-built girl, but it still wasn't going to be easy to pull her up.

'Grab hold of me as tight as you can. I'm going to pull you up until you've got your arms through the hole.'

'OK, James. Don't let me go.'

'I won't, honest.'

It took most of James's remaining strength to pull her up the two feet they needed for Milly to be through the gap and supporting herself with her arms and elbows on the floor. James then grabbed her by her armpits and, with a final massive effort, pulled her through. She stood in front of him, shivering with fear and holding on to him. Both of them were breathing heavily.

It was some time before Milly managed to say, 'Are we going to be all right, James?'

'Course we are. We've got this far, haven't we? Look at all these windows. All we've got to do is open one and we're outside.'

Milly shivered. 'I wish I'd brought my coat.'

'And me,' said James. 'Still, we can't think of everything.'

He went over to a window which, like all the others, was quite high off the floor. It was dark outside but some light came in from street lights. He found a window catch and opened it. Then he placed a chair beneath it and took a look outside. There was a five foot drop to the ground which he could manage all right but maybe not his sister. He picked up another chair and dropped it through the window.

'I'll go first then I'll help you out,' he said.

Once out he stood the chair against the window and helped his sister climb out. They took a few steps away from this building that had held them prisoner, wondering what it was. It was on a residential street of terraced houses.

'We should knock on one of those doors,' said James. 'If we tell them we're the Strathmore children who were kidnapped, I bet they'll ring the police for us.'

'Will they?'

'Course they will.'

Both of them unsteady on their feet from their efforts, they crossed the street and knocked on the first door they came to – number 17. To them it was as good a door as any. In fact it was the worst door they could have knocked on. There was no answer so they knocked again. The door opened and an elderly man stood there, glaring at these two exhausted and scruffy children, both very dirty from their ordeal in the cellar.

'What the fuck do you toe-rags want?'

The children were taken aback by such profanity coming from an adult. 'I er, we're the Strathmore children . . .' said James.

'So what?'

'We er . . . we were kidnapped and we've escaped.'

'What's that got ter do wi' me? Piss off!'

He slammed the door. James and Milly walked on, disconsolately, holding hands, both wondering if they should try another door, but not too keen on repeating the experience.

'I think we'll just look for a telephone box,' said Milly, 'and ring 999.'

A car turned a corner ahead of them. 'No,' said James. 'We'll stop this car. I bet the driver'll help us.'

It was a large, new car. Not the sort of car that would be driven by a foul-mouthed man who might swear at them rather than help them. James stepped into the road and waved at it to stop. It did. The driver's window buzzed down electronically. James went round to his side and said, 'I wonder if you can help us. My sister and I have been kidnapped. We're the Strathmore children, maybe you know about us.'

'Strathmore children? I certainly do know about you. And you've escaped have you?'

'We have, yes.'

'Well, I'd better get you to a police station. Get in the back, both of you.'

'Thank you.'

The children climbed into the back of the car as the driver said, 'I've just got to make a phone call.'

James and Milly listened to him in increasing dismay. 'The kids are in the back of my car. Where the hell are you? . . . Jesus Christ! . . . You're supposed to be guarding them not shagging some tart. Get yerself down here you idiot. What d'yer think the boss would've done if we'd lost 'em? He'd have had us wasted, that's what he'd have done!'

He then turned round in his seat and pointed a gun at them, just as Lee Dench had done at the beginning of their ordeal.

'Right, kids, we're going back. You've put me in a very bad mood. Any trouble and I'll shoot both of you.'

Milly began to cry. James put an arm around her.

THIRTY-ONE

'There must be a way of finding out where Formosa lives,' said Sep.

He and Fiona were in the Black Bull in Otley, a small, market town ten miles west of Leeds. Sep liked to keep his meeting places distant and varied.

Fiona shrugged. 'When he was arrested he gave the address of an office block in the middle of Leeds city centre. We checked it out and it has living accommodation that ties in with his personal tax returns.'

'He pays tax, does he?'

'Oh yes, religiously. He's got two scrap metal yards in London and one in Bradford.'

'Ideal for money-laundering?'

'We think so, but we can't find anything drastically wrong with his accounting. His books aren't bad enough to be called false accounting, just bad enough to be classed as incompetence. When he's given a fine he always protests before paying up. Anything less would arouse suspicion.'

'So, this address is his official domicile is it?' said Sep.

'It is, but I doubt if he spends much time there.'

'Have we ever had him followed?'

Sep used the word "we" through force of habit. Fiona noticed but didn't mention it.

'He has a real talent for disappearing off the radar,' she said. 'God knows where to.'

'Does he use disguises?'

'Dunno. He uses hotels a lot, especially hotels with more than one entrance and exit. There are times when he goes in one door and goes straight out of another. Without knowing exactly which hotel he's heading for makes it almost impossible to keep tabs on him.'

'If I were in charge of the investigation,' Sep said, 'I'd put another ten coppers on him. Try and anticipate his movements.

Find out everything there is to know about him. I know he drives
a Bentley, has anyone put a tracker on it?'

'There's one on it right now,' said Fiona, 'but he never goes
anywhere interesting. I'm guessing he's knows about the tracker
and is using it to his own advantage.'

Sep drummed his fingers on the pub table. 'If we can't keep
tabs on him we need to keep tabs on someone further down the
Formosa pecking order. There must be a couple of dozen men
in his employment . . . if you can call it employment. Do you
know any of them?'

'Only his driver. His name's Jez. He was a pro boxer but that's
all I know about him.'

Sep nodded. 'Yeah, I know about him. Formosa can't spend
every waking hour in that car. There'll be plenty of times when
his driver's out on his own. I doubt if he'll just stick a two
hundred grand, top-of the range Bentley on a parking meter
overnight. That car might be his Achilles Heel. We need to follow
it when Formosa's not in it. At some stage it should lead us to
his driver.'

'Then what? We can't just arrest a man for being Formosa's
driver.'

'I don't need to arrest him,' said Sep. 'I'm not a copper any
more.'

'Sep, I know you're a big feller but he's a man-mountain.'

Sep took a sip of his drink and said, innocently, 'Fiona, I'm
not going to fight him. All I want to do is talk to him.'

'Ah, you want to give him the old DI Black treatment. Do you
have any lies conjured up yet?'

'It's the truth that I find out about them that baffles them,
Fiona. It baffles them so much that they believe my lies, which,
I have to say, are sometimes works of art. He used to be a pro
boxer you say?'

'Yeah, he killed a man in the ring.'

'Well, there's a truth I can work with. I might have a story
that I can try on him. Could you get me details of the man who
died and when it happened and who was Jez's trainer? In fact
as much as you can on Jez in general. Was there any heavy
betting on the fight? Stuff like that.'

'I'll do what I can.'

'And let me know when he goes off in the Bentley on his own.'

'All I can do is alert our tracking people and see what can be done.'

Peter Strathmore was staring at the blank screen of his television when the phone rang. His wife was upstairs in bed. Peter was alternating between consciousness and sleep. He hadn't slept more than two continuous hours since his children had been taken. There were times when he'd been tempted by his wife's sleeping tablets, of which he was in sole charge after she overdosed, but he had a responsibility not to succumb to that temptation. The noise of the phone didn't immediately penetrate his consciousness. It seemed a distant noise that was nothing to do with him. It had rung six times before he became fully aware of it and picked it up.'

'Hello?' he said, dully.

'Strathmore?' It sounded like a woman with a husky voice.

'Yeah.'

'We still have your children.'

Strathmore squeezed his eyes shut, trying to make himself think straight.

'What?'

'You heard.'

'My children. They're alive?'

'Yeah, but we're getting bored with them. If we don't get two million within one week they will be dead and you will hear no more from us. That's a very generous amount of time for you to raise it. I'll ring you on this number in exactly six days.' The caller rang off. Peter stared at the phone trying to understand what he'd just heard. His mobile rang in his pocket. He took it out and turned it on.

'Peter?'

'Yeah.'

It was a two-man police telephone monitoring team working shifts in a van two hundred yards away from the house. It was the first interesting call they'd had in over a week.

'We're sending someone in to talk to you about this.'

'She said my children are alive.'

'Yes, we heard. It was probably a man using a voice changer.'
'You mean Formosa?'
'Possibly. My colleague is on his way to you now.'

THIRTY-TWO

'**A**m I speaking to Mr Septimus Black?'
        'You are.'
        It was that same evening. Sep was back in his flat.
The caller's voice was vague and defeated.

'My name is Peter Strathmore. I'm, er . . . ringing about my
children, who have been—'

Sep interrupted him. 'I know who you are, Mr Strathmore.
How can I help?'

'I don't know if you can, Mr Black, but I was told you're very
good at this sort of thing.'

'Were you told that I was kicked out of the police force?'

'Er, yes I was, and I was told why. But I'm also told that it
doesn't detract from your abilities.'

'Oh, the detective sergeant, she said that, did she?'

Strathmore didn't correct him on his assumption of the rank
and gender of his informant, which made Sep smile – Fiona.

'I'm quite desperate, Mr Black. The kidnapper rang today to
tell me my children are still alive.'

'Did you ask him to supply you with proof?'

'No, he didn't give me the chance.'

'Do the police know about this?'

'Yes, they heard the call. Detective Inspector Cope is in charge
of the investigation, but I'm not sure I have too much faith in
him.'

Your lack of faith is well-founded, thought Sep, whose sympathy
for the man was compounded by the knowledge that the lives of
his two children were also in the hands of a bent copper.

'I assume this call isn't being heard by the police?'

'No, it's not. This is my wife's mobile. The police have no
knowledge of it. I'm told you may have some unorthodox methods

of tracking people down and I would like to engage your services, Mr Black.'

'I understand the hot favourite for the kidnapping is Vincent Formosa?'

'That's right.'

'How much is he asking for?'

'Two million.'

'Can you afford it?'

'Probably. It's the time that's the problem. He wants it in one week.'

'If he thinks you're on with it he'll give you more time.'

'How can I convince him I'm on with it?'

Sep knew that if Cope got to hear that Strathmore was doing his best to raise the money he'd inform Formosa. But he daren't tell Strathmore this. 'I might be able to get a message on those lines to Formosa,' he said.

'The man's a slimeball. I'm not sure it'll get my children back,' said Strathmore. 'I'd much rather give you two million, Mr Black.'

'I won't take two million – that'll make me as bad as Formosa.'

'In that case, I will pay you one hundred thousand and I will insist on it.'

'Well, I'm not in a position to turn down good money, Mr Strathmore. If you insist, I'll take the job, but I'll do it on a no success, no fee basis.'

'Thank you. I want to leave no stone unturned in trying to get my children back. I will, of course, also pay any expenses you may incur.'

'Well, I don't have the resources that the police have and they certainly won't want me being part of their investigation. What I would like to do is to meet you and have a chat with you. Maybe I can turn something up that the police have missed.'

'Can we meet now? I can come to you.'

'Do you know if the police follow you?'

'No, they don't. They did at first but I objected most strongly. My life's bad enough without having to put up with such an intrusion.'

'OK, I'll give you my address and I'll see you in half an hour.

Oh, my unkempt appearance might take you aback. It's done for a reason.'

'I don't care a toss about your appearance, Mr Black.'

'That's just as well, Mr Strathmore.'

'Mr Black?'

'Yes.'

'You weren't exaggerating when you said your appearance was unkempt,' said Strathmore as Sep opened his door.

'I often need to work under the police radar.'

'I imagine the radar rarely picks you up.'

'I can't afford for it *ever* to pick me up, Mr Strathmore. Come in would you, please?'

Strathmore followed Sep into his living room where they both sat down and Sep immediately began to question the man.

'Tell me how this all started.'

Strathmore had told Sep the whole story of how the children had been taken in a car identical to the nanny's.

'It seems to me,' said Sep, 'that the nanny being late due to the car accident played a major part in the children's abduction. You say the nanny is completely trustworthy?'

'Yes, she is. She's greatly shocked but I'm sure she played no part in it.'

'Did Detective Inspector Cope or any other police officer ask for details of the car accident?'

'Er, not really.'

'Not really? I take that as a no.'

'Well it was something or nothing. A car hit her from behind and caused very minor damage to her car. The delay was caused by the exchange of insurance details.'

'Mr Strathmore, the delay was caused by the driver of the other car. I need to know if this was deliberate.'

'Why didn't Detective Inspector Cope check on this?' asked Strathmore.

'I don't know,' lied Sep, 'and it would suit my purpose if you don't question him about it. It's something I'll be better following up myself without being hampered by having to follow police procedure, which is why you've engaged my services, is it not?'

'Erm, I suppose so, yes.'

'The nanny, where is she now?'

'Well, she's still with us. She's been a big help to my wife since the children were taken.'

'So, is she at your home?'

'Yes, she is.'

'I'd like to speak to her. I assume she has a mobile.'

'She has.'

'Will the police know her number?'

'No. They only have our landline, my mobile number and my business numbers.'

'Would you ring her, please? I'd like to speak to her.'

Within a minute Strathmore was talking to Laura Graham. 'Hello, Laura, it's me. I'm with a man whose helping to find the children and he wants to speak to you. This is to be kept strictly confidential, especially from the police, do you understand, Laura?'

'I do, Mr Strathmore. I'm not sure I have too much faith in the police myself, especially that detective inspector.'

'I'm putting my man on now, Laura.'

Sep took the phone. 'Hi, Laura. You don't need to know my name but what I want to know about is the car accident just before you picked the children up.'

'What? You think that was part of it?'

'I think it might have been, yes.'

'The police didn't think it was important.'

'I understand you exchanged insurance details with the man in the other car. Did you give his details to your insurers?'

'Er, no, not yet. I've been too preoccupied with what happened.'

'I understand that. Would you do that first thing tomorrow and would you impress with the insurers that you think the man might have given you false details and could they check on this and get straight back to you?'

'I'll do that, yes.'

'Do you think you'd recognize the man if you ever saw him again?'

'I think so.'

'Can you remember anything about him or his car that might give us a clue to his identity?'

'You sound fairly sure that his insurance details won't do that,' said Laura. 'He was a smallish man and he spoke with a Birmingham accent.'

'Fat, thin, how old?'

'Average build. Fortyish . . . middle-aged, going a bit bald. His car was a dark blue Renault Clio. He was actually a bit of an old woman. I wouldn't have taken him to be a member of a kidnapping gang.'

'No, you weren't supposed to.'

'Oh, I see, sorry.'

'Don't apologize. He may well be completely innocent.'

'I don't think he was now.'

'Oh, why not?'

'Well, there was no reason for him to hit my car. I hadn't slammed on the brakes or anything. I'd been stopped at a junction for at least half a minute, signalling a right turn, and he came up behind and ran into me at about three miles an hour.'

'Did you take his registration number?'

'I did yes . . . do you want it?'

'Please.'

'You think it was a false plate, don't you?'

'Possibly.'

'Probably, more like.'

THIRTY-THREE

The Bentley Mulsanne, was parked beneath trees in a quiet lane beside the river Wharfe, ten miles north of Leeds. Its driver, Jez Copitch, was fishing in the river. It was a fine June morning and he had two days to himself, with his boss being away in London. DS Fiona Burnside had just arrived and was ascertaining her present postcode on her laptop. She needed to know the exact location of the driver before she contacted Danny. She got out of her unmarked car and strode, casually, along the path beside the road. Maybe Jez had picked up a girlfriend and impressed her enough with his car for her to go with him to a quiet spot where he could have his way with her. Fiona couldn't think of anything less innocent to explain why Jez had left his boss's car unattended. When she spotted him fishing it made her smile at how she'd misjudged him. Fishermen; who understands them? He was a good way away from the car, but the Bentley was almost thief proof, so why should he worry? Fiona knew this and smiled again. It was the word "almost" that should have made him worry. She took out her mobile.

'Danny?'

'Yeah.'

'It's me, Sep's friend.'

'Right. What have you got for me?'

'I've got a post code – LS23 8BQ.'

'Where's that?'

'It's parked on a country road by the river near Wetherby. You need to be here ASAP.'

'I'm in a truck, remember.'

'I know. The driver's fishing.'

'Fishing? Them fishing blokes have no sense of time.'

'No, but I have. ASAP, Danny. I'm in a silver Mondeo parked about fifty yards away from the Bentley.'

It was a good half hour before the breakdown truck arrived. Danny pulled up in front of her as if she was needing his services. Fiona got out of her car and pointed out the Bentley to him, then she wandered up to where Jez was fishing, with his back to her and half hidden from by trees. He was now unwrapping some sandwiches and unscrewing the top off a flask. He didn't look to be moving from there any time soon. She turned and waved to Danny, giving him the thumbs up.

Ten minutes later, Danny had winched the Bentley on to the back of his truck and was driving away. Fiona took one last look at the contented Jez before following the truck. After driving just out of sight she stopped and turned her car around, parking it so she had a distant view of the road where Jez would emerge at some stage. It was almost two hours before she saw him appear, carrying his fishing tackle. He looked left and right, at first assuming he'd come out at the wrong part of the road. He walked away from her, then turned and walked back. His arms went up in the air, hands on his head in bewilderment. Even from her distance she could see his deep anxiety, and he had every right to be anxious. He'd just lost a two hundred thousand pound car that belonged to the most dangerous gang boss in Yorkshire. How the hell was he going to explain that? Fiona started her car and drove slowly towards him.

When he spotted her, he stepped into the middle of the road as she hoped he might. He waved for her to stop, which she did, remaining in her car with the doors locked, as any sensible woman would, having been waved down by this giant man. He came round to her side. She buzzed the electric window down an inch.

'Did you pass a black Bentley up the road?'

He had an intimidating voice that came out as a low growl. His face was only inches from Fiona's, separated only by window glass. He had a scar running from the corner of his left eye down to his chin. It was the sort of scar that hadn't been caused by any accident. It dragged his left eye down a little and the left side of his mouth up, marking him with a permanently fearsome expression.

'Erm, yes, I think I did. About ten minutes ago.'

'Ten minutes, oh shit! He could be anywhere by now.'

'Why? Was it yours?'

'Mine? No, it was me boss's. I was doin' a bit of fishin' and someone took it.'

'Oh dear. I expect you're in trouble then.'

'Yer could say that. Look, girl, I want yer ter give me a lift.'

'Erm, I don't know.'

'I'm not asking yer. I'm fuckin' tellin' yer!'

She knew that all she had to do was put her foot down and drive away from him. Instead she pretended to be scared of him. It wasn't difficult.

'I . . . I'm going in to Leeds, if that's any help.'

'That's where I need to be.'

'Whereabouts?' she asked.

'Chapeltown.'

'Oh, right. I can take you right there if you like. Do you want to call into Allerton police station to report the theft? We'll be practically passing it. I can drop you off there.'

'Yer drop me off where I tell yer.'

Forty five minutes later she was on the phone to Sep. 'Right. We've got the Bentley and Jez's address.'

'What about the tracker? We don't want the tracking people knowing where it is.'

'It's in my pocket. In a couple of minutes it'll be in the back of a truck parked in the transport café car park where I'm ringing you from. It belongs to a Scottish haulier who's heading north – probably north of the border.'

'You'll do for me, Detective Sergeant.'

'It's as far as I go, Sep. I offered to take him to the police station to report the theft, but he declined. He's a scary man, Sep. I hung around until I saw him go into his house.'

'He should have reported it in Wetherby.'

'Silly me. I never thought to tell him that.'

'Did he know you were a copper?'

'Oddly enough, I didn't tell him that either.'

Sep smiled at her sarcasm. 'OK, you did really well. I owe you a big favour.'

'You also owe Danny a monkey. What will he have done with the car, by the way?'

'It'll be under tarpaulin in a corner of his garage.'

'I'm amazed he's taking that risk for five hundred quid.'

'He owed me a big favour did the lad.'

'Not as big as the one you owe me.'

'Is Jez worried?'

'Well, he's big and he's fearsome but I'd say he's a broken man. Apparently his boss had to wait over a year for that car to be delivered. Two hundred grand and there's people queueing up to buy 'em. Formosa's pride and joy by the sound of it. Good idea of yours to get it nicked. Shame *we* can't do stuff like that.'

'Broken, eh? That's how I want him.' He paused, thoughtfully and added. 'Last night Strathmore rang me. I wonder where he got my number?'

'You know he got it from me, Sep.'

'Yes, I do know that. He wants me to do the job directly for him . . . as if I need to tell you that.'

'Formosa has a serious edge on us,' said Fiona, 'especially with you not being on the job anymore.'

'He's got the edge on everybody with Cope being in charge of the investigation.'

'I know,' said Fiona, 'and I'm thinking about those poor kids.

When I heard Strathmore had been contacted and told they were alive, I gave him your number and told him you might be able to help but he mustn't mention it to Cope or to anyone at the station.'

'That puts your job on the line, Fiona, never mind you helping me with Danny.'

'Like I said, I was just thinking about those poor kids. So, what did Strathmore have to say to you?'

'He offered me a hundred grand to find them.'

'Did you accept?'

'I said I'd do what I can.'

'You know Formosa's asking two million for them.'

'I do, but there aren't too many people who can raise two million in readies in a month, never mind a week. Strathmore certainly can't.'

'I know.'

'Which is why you gave him my number.'

'Correct. You've got more chance of finding them than we have – especially now.'

'I'm not too sure about that. This Jez character's an unknown quantity.'

'I know, but I also know that you're not – not to me, anyway. He's got no chance once you get to work with your outrageous lies.'

'I only lie to the criminal classes, Fiona. Oh, I have a car number for you to check. It's supposed to fit a blue Renault Clio.'

THIRTY-FOUR

The children had been hooded and manhandled for thirty minutes. When the hoods were taken off, both of them had eyes red with tears; the cast in Milly's left eye was more pronounced and both of them had wet themselves with fear – the fear that they might be being taken to their deaths. Their situation was exacerbated by them still wearing the same school clothes in which they'd been abducted all those weeks ago. James spotted Milly's problem and felt it might ease her embarrassment if he admitted to his own problem first.

'I've was so scared I peed myself,' he said, after their captors had left them alone in yet another cellar.

'So did I. Is there a lavvy or anything down here?'

'Dunno. I'll take a look through that door.'

The only source of light was a tiny window which was set at outside ground level. It cast a bleak light across the room, adding to its gloomy ambience. There was a rickety door in the corner. It opened on to a tiny room lit only by the dim light from the cellar. James peered into it until his eyes became accustomed to the darkness. There was a toilet and a tap, underneath which was a large square sink. It was squalid room, laced with cobwebs and dirt and smelling of damp, rotting wood and distant drains. He looked into the toilet bowl and saw dark water, probably brown. He pulled the chain. The toilet flushed, dismally, but probably enough for a couple of kids on a starvation diet. He then tried the tap water which was initially brown, but after a while it cleaned up, perhaps even drinkable. He collected some in the palm of his hand and drank it. As far as he could tell it was OK.

He checked a single pipe leading from one wall and out through another, then he reported back to his sister.

'There's a lavvy and a tap but it's really dark in there so if you need to use the lavvy you'll have to leave the door open to see. If you need to wash anything you could do it under the tap and hang it over the pipes.'

'I think my pants and tights are a bit pongy.'

'We do pong a bit, don't we?' said James. 'I think my under-pants could do with a bit of a rinse. There's a hot water pipe in there that'll help with the drying.'

'What? We've got hot water, have we?'

James shook his head. 'Just a hot pipe coming in and going out – better than nothing. There is some toilet paper in there though, so they are looking after us. You don't give people toilet paper if you don't want to look after them. Stands to reason.'

'Looking after us? I thought they were taking us somewhere to kill us, James.'

'Yeah, but they didn't. That means we'll be OK.'

'Does it really?'

'Yeah,' he assured her. 'We're very valuable we are. Most prob'ly worth thousands, mebbe millions.'

'I wish Daddy would hurry up and come for us. I hate these horrible men, James.'

'We won't be here much longer, Milly.'

She was only slightly buoyed by her brother's optimism and her bottom lip began to quiver. James put his arm around her as she wept profusely and noisily. In a way it saved him doing the same. His sister was weeping for both of them. The light went on, but it didn't brighten their lives much. It would take more than a forty watt bulb to do that.

It wouldn't have saddened them one bit to know that their two captors would soon be dead.

THIRTY-FIVE

J ez was seriously thinking of leaving town. The trouble was that Formosa had fingers in many pies and in many towns and countries. He had methods of tracking people down that Jez couldn't understand. It involved Formosa having access to records that civilians weren't even supposed to know existed, never mind have access to. He'd have to change his name, he knew that. The trouble was, he couldn't change his appearance. He was a giant of a man who was further identifiable by the nasty scar on his face. He was sure Formosa could track him down eventually, no matter where he went. The knock on his door scared him rigid. No one ever came to his door at night. He went to a window and looked out at a large, scruffy man with long hair and a beard. He was holding a bicycle that he'd apparently arrived on.

'Who the fuck are you?' he muttered to himself.

The man saw him in the window and waved a hand. Jez hesitated and went to the door, mainly out of curiosity. Vince wouldn't know about the car yet, so he had nothing to fear from that quarter. As he opened the door the man on the step held out a hand of greeting that Jez didn't take. Instead he repeated the question he'd just asked of himself.

'Who the fuck are you?'

'Ma name's Jimmy Lennon and I know ye name's Jez Copitch and ye work fer Mister Vincent Formosa who's a very dangerous man.'

'How d'yer know that?'

'Because I'm in the business of knowing things. It's how I make ma livin'. I might be able te help ye . . . for a small consideration.'

'Help? What sort of help do I need?'

'I know many things, Jez. For example I know ye're in desperate need of help, which is why ye'll let me in ye house purely out of curiosity. I know about kidnapped children and murdered men and women. In fact, it has been said I know too much fer ma own guid.'

'All right yer can come in.'

'Can I bring ma bike in? I've heard it's a bit dodgy around here wi' all the bike thieves. I think maybe they do it te take the piss out of the polis by committin' bike crime under their noses.'

There was some truth in this, so Jez said, 'What? Oh, I suppose so.'

Sep wheeled his bicycle in and left it in the hall. Jez's house was as Sep might have expected. It was a rented establishment with rented furniture. He would have done well to hire a housekeeper for a day or two a week, such was the state of the place. Much worse than Sep's, who considered his own house to be fairly untidy. Without being invited he sat down at a table, Jez sat opposite.

'Right, Jimmy Lemon.'

'Lennon, like the Beatle, only I'm trying to ensure you don't end up like him, with a bullet in your back.'

'Why would anyone want to shoot me?'

'I think you know.'

Jez frowned. He certainly did know, but how did this scruffy bastard know?

'Tell me how yer can help me an' how much is it gonna cost?'

'From a financial aspect, nothing,' said Sep.

'What the fuck have you got that might be worth anythin' ter me?'

'I'll tell ye what I know. I know the names of five people who know where the Strathmore kids are bein' held. You're one of 'em and another's that wee baldy twat from Birmingham or some such place.'

'Kev Clarkson?'

'Aye, that's the feller.'

'Kev knows fuck-all about where the kids are.'

'Well I'm sayin' he does. He's the one who rammed the back of the car going ter pick 'em up from school.'

'I don't know about that.'

'That's because you don't know as much as I do, Jez. Kev rammed the back of the woman's car who was going to pick the kids up. It delayed her long enough fer Lee Dench to pick 'em up in an identical car.'

Jez frowned. Maybe this Lennon character was right about Kev. Shit! How did he even know about Kev?

'How d'yer know all that?'

'I also know that Detective Inspector Cope is as bent as a nine bob note and your boss is arrangin' with him for ye to take a fall for them kids. I know so many things, Jez.'

It was the fact that this man even knew about Cope which held Jez's attention. Only Jez was supposed to know about him and he was sworn to secrecy under pain of execution. This Lennon guy was a man to be taken seriously.

'What else d'yer know?'

'Oh many things. They say ye killed a guy in the ring but what ye didn't know was that the dead guy had been taking steroids which affected his heart and that was the cause of his death.'

Sep had made that one up. He knew about the death in the ring but not about the steroids. He'd heard of such a thing happening and Fiona had told him all about Jez's past. 'Ye didnae ken that, did ye?'

'Maybe I did. So, what's all this bollocks about Formosa setting me up for a fall?'

'It's nae bollocks, man. Formosa's gonna collect two mill for the wee kids and fit ye up wi' killin' them. Ye'll go down for it, leaving him no longer under suspicion by the polis. Formosa's a man who tidies up after himself, right enough. Life fer you wi' zero fuckin' parole – that's ma guess. Doin' time as a child killer's the worst kind o' time, as ye probably know yerself.'

Jez gave this much thought. It definitely sounded like something Vince might do. He knew all about Dench and his whore girlfriend.'

'And you're here ter help me are yer?'

'Well, ye definitely need help from someone.'

'And do I need ter pay for this help?'

'Well, I like to be paid by exchange of information. For example, the information I require is the whereabouts of the Strathmore children. If I get that, it'll get Formosa off the streets for good thereby making your life much healthier.'

Jez clenched his fists and glared at Sep, who held his gaze. 'How do I know this isn't all fuckin' lies just ter get information outa me?'

'Ye know I'm telling the truth about Cope and about the guy ye killed in the ring and about Kev Clarkson. How would I know about that? How would I know ye know where the kids are? How do I know these things, Jez?'

'This is shit! What's ter stop me knockin' fuck outa you right now?'

'Me,' said Sep, calmly. 'I were trained in the army – Special Forces. I know twenty-seven ways te kill a man and you were just a boxer.'

Jez looked Sep up and down. 'Army trained? What army was that – the Salvation Army?'

'Don't let the whiskers fool ye. I'm a bit past ma best but I'm not in bad shape. Yer way past your best. I reckon I could take ye, as big as y'are. Trouble is, I take ye, I might kill ye, or we end up enemies, both wi' pain and broken bones. I don't want that. I'm here on business.'

Jez's face relaxed into something slightly more amenable. He shook his head in confusion and got to his feet. Sep sat there and watched him walk around the room; a man troubled by what he'd been told, unaware they were mainly lies, albeit reinforced by an injection of the truth that Sep knew about Cole's association with Formosa.

What Jez needed was one more piece of impressive information to bring him over to Sep's side. Sep could see the man was deeply troubled and desperate for help, but he also needed to be sure the help was genuine. Jez, confused and deeply worried by his desperate situation, turned his back on Sep and began walking up and down the room. He was walking away from Sep when he spun on his heels and pointed at him.

'OK, what else?' he said. 'What else d'yer know what can help me?'

'Well, I know ye've lost Formosa's car.'

Jez was astounded. 'Jesus fucking Christ! How the fuck d'yer know that?'

'I might even know where it is,' Sep said it casually as if it were information of no great moment, then added, 'given enough incentive te go out and find it.'

'What?'

'Ye asked me if I knew of anything else that might help ye. I imagine getting Formosa's car back might ease things for ye in the short term – until he comes to fit y'up as a child killer. I cannae help ye wi' that. Ye can only help yeself wi' that.'

'How the fuck d'yer know about the car?'

'Man, I keep tellin' ye! It's ma business to know things.'

Sep's muscles were tensed in case Jez lost it and launched an attack on him. His story would only wash with a man grasping at straws, a man desperate to believe anything that might get him out of the deep hole he was in. Sep looked up and saw a red-faced mountain of rage and despair, so he now spoke in the friendliest of tones.

'Come on, man. Neither of us want te see the wee children killed so that Formosa can keep lining his pockets. Ye not a child killer, surely?'

'No, I'm fuckin' not!'

'Tell me where the kids are, Jez, and I can straighten ye life out, man.'

'Why d'yer wanna know?'

'If ye must know I'm working for their father, and if you tell me what I want te know I'll also be workin' fer you insofar as I'll be making sure they lock that bastard Formosa away fer the rest of his unnatural life.'

'Why? What's he done to you?'

'When I was down in the Smoke he fitted me up with an

armed robbery that was nothing te do with me. I did six years fer the bastard. No man whoever worked for him came out on top.'

Sep was fairly certain this last bit was true and he hoped Jez would think it to be true as well. He added: 'Do you know of any man who made a success of working for Formosa? Any man who lived to enjoy his money?'

Jez couldn't think of anyone, but it didn't occur to him that this question might be asked of any criminal gang boss without producing a positive answer. Gang bosses didn't work for the welfare of their employees.

'Where are the kids, Jez?'

'Yer know where the Bentley is do yer?'

'I know who to ask.'

'You bring me the car and we'll talk about where the kids are.'

'This is something of an impasse, Jez. How do I know that ye won't just drive off in the car and tell me nothing? My alternative is to go to one of the other guys who knows where they are and bollocks to the car. Mebbe I'll try Kev Clarkson. I reckon he'll be easier te crack than you.'

Jez looked unhappy at this suggestion. He was at his tipping point and just needed a nudge. Sep looked around the room and spotted a boxing trophy on top of a shelf. He pointed to it.

'I take it that's something from your boxing days.'

'Yorkshire ABA heavyweight champion,' said Jez. 'I won that when I was eighteen years old. Youngest ever senior champion.'

'Never really made it as a pro, though, eh?'

'Wi' better management and a decent trainer I could have done well.'

'Tell ye what. Let me take that cup. I'll be back tomorrow wi' a photo of it on ma wee camera, standing on the bonnet of the Bentley just te prove I've found it. I'll also let ye in on Formosa's plan te fit ye up as the kiddies' murderer.'

'This guy who took the car,' said Jez. 'He'll let you walk in and take it from under his nose, will he?'

'He will if it's who I think it is. I'll tell him that Formosa will definitely find out who nicked his Bentley and the best thing he

can do is hand it over to me and I'll get it back without Formosa
ever knowing it was taken.'

This sounded immensely plausible, especially to a man in as
much trouble as Jez. Sep pressed on by imparting more baffling
knowledge.

'Your alternative is to tell yer boss that ye lost his pet car
while ye were out fishing and take what comes – and the best
of luck wi' that.'

'How the fuck d'yer know I were fishin'?'

'I'm a man of unusual knowledge and talent, Jez. To the extent
that I can tell y'of a much better place on that river to fish. A
place where ye can catch a nine pound barbel without much
problem. Have y'ever caught a nine pound barbel, Jez?'

Jez shook his head and sat back down. His senses completely
defeated by this tramp-on-a-bike who had come to his door and
baffled him with so much dangerous knowledge. He certainly
wouldn't put it past Vince to fit him up with the kids' murder.
He didn't hold with killing kids and this way he could stop their
murder and save himself a life stretch. *If this tramp were to be
believed.* Shit! There was something believable about the man;
something assured; something that belied his appearance. Jez felt
he could trust him. Jesus! He'd lost Vince's car which was a
death sentence in itself. What the hell else did he have to lose?

'How much do you get from the father?'

'Enough to give ye ten grand.'

It was another lie but it was Sep's final card.

'How do I know I'll get it?'

'We're playing a trust game here, Jez. It's probably not a game
y'ever played before but I make all my connections by being a
man of ma word. People trust me, as will you after this is over.'

Jez hung his head and thought long and hard about what to
say. 'OK,' he said, at length, 'you bring me that photo and I'll
take you to where they are, then you take me to the car. But you
didn't get any of this from me.'

'No problem,' said Sep. 'Are the children guarded?'

'No, they're locked up tight. A man takes them food once a day.'

'That will probably be about noon or thereabouts?'

'I would think so.'

                              *   *   *

Sep left it until the next afternoon before turning up with a video rather than a photograph. It might have aroused suspicion had he turned up with it too quickly. Jez peered at it and saw the car number plate, then the camera pulled back to reveal Jimmy Lennon in all his scruffiness standing by the car, holding Jez's boxing cup.

'Right,' Jez said, 'about Vince fitting me up. How's he gonna do that?'

'Well, he'll nae be doing that when I get the kids. No dead bairns te frame ye with.'

'Oh . . . right.'

'If ye must know, the cops have a sneaky way of transferrin' fingerprints using an adhesive lifter and transferrin' 'em on to a surface sprayed wi' a chemical called ninhydrin. Cope's an expert at it and he's already taken ye prints off the Bentley and he's ready te transfer them on to the gun that was supposed to have killed the children.'

In fact the expert at this was Sep who had only used it once to persuade a killer to confess to a murder that Sep was certain he'd committed, in the hope of getting a reduced sentence. The man confessed to many murders, justifying Sep's illegal subterfuge, insofar as he'd taken a serial killer off the streets.

'The bastards!' said Jez, looking at his fingers.

'Vince wants rids of you,' said Sep.

'Why?'

'You've been with him too long and you know too much. Like I said, how many of his men live long enough to enjoy their money? Formosa killed Dench because Dench was informing on Formosa to Cope who's in Formosa's pay. You won't be in any danger if you turn Queen's Evidence, with you being in a safe house.'

'You mean go to court and give evidence against Vince?'

'It's the only way you'll get him off your back, unless ye want to kill him yourself. By the way, did ye realize the Bentley's registered in your name and at your address?'

'What? No I didn't. Why would he do that?'

'Agh, them wise guys like te keep their names away from officialdom as much as possible. When Formosa's banged up the Proceeds of Crime guys'll strip him of every penny they can

track down to him, but that won't include the car. Ye'll be able
to keep it, sell it if ye like. It's legally yours.'

'Bloody hell! It's only done six thousand miles.'

'Anyways, all that's up te you. All I want is te know where
the bairns are.'

'I'll take ye there, only I ain't gorra car and I don't fancy
having you saddle me there on yer bike.'

'I'll be in a van. Where are they?'

'Pudsey.'

Sep smiled. It seemed he was practically home and dry now,
on his way to pick up the children.

'Pudsey, eh? That's where the pigeons fly backwards te keep
the muck outa their eyes.'

It was one of two aphorisms he knew about Pudsey but Jez
saw no humour in it, so Sep didn't bother with the other one.

'What sort of place is this?'

They were in Winnie's van. Sep had pulled up at a gate in a
high, wire fence. The surrounding area was industrial. It was
a gate to a compound, empty except for the two snarling
Dobermans that had raced over to greet them. There was a stone
building that might once have been offices, and various sheds,
some of them open-fronted. The whole place looked to have
fallen into disrepair some years ago.

'It used to be a builder's merchants,' said Jez. 'It was owned
by a man who ended up owing Vince money.'

'I don't see any vehicles. Does that mean there's no one
guarding the kids?'

Jez shrugged. 'Not unless someone was dropped off to be
picked up later.'

'How do we get past them dogs?'

'I've got some meat in me pocket that'll keep 'em busy.'

'I wondered what that smell was.'

Jez got out of the van and went to the gate, pulling up the
hood on his coat. It was raining. Using a pair of bolt croppers
he'd brought with him he cut through the padlock. Then, from
his coat pocket, he took out two pieces of meat wrapped in a
newspaper and threw them, with all his might, over the fence
and twenty yards into the compound. The two dogs spun on their

skinny legs and hurtled towards the food. Jez then opened the gate and signalled for Sep to drive in, Jez closed the gate behind him. Sep drove up to the door to the building and got out. The dogs were busy eating. Very poor guard dogs, Sep thought, but probably their very presence kept intruders away. Jez came over to him.

'I suppose the kids are inside the building,' said Sep.

'In a cellar.'

Sep went to the door and was surprised to find it unlocked. He opened it and had taken one step inside when he heard a noise that didn't appear to be coming from the cellar. He stepped back. Unlocked doors and unknown noises weren't to be trusted. He held up a hand to stay Jez, who was right behind him. A shot rang out and a bullet splintered the door frame an inch away from Sep's head. Another shot came from Jez's gun. It drew a shout of pain from someone. Sep dived to the floor as bullets shot to and fro above him. He saw a desk and scuttled behind it as the firefight progressed. He heard Jez call out. He seemed to be in pain.

'What the fuck's all this about? I'm Vince's driver! He sent me ter see the kids.'

'Lyin' bastard! The kids aren't here. They've been moved. Yer've just killed Bazza. Vince'll kill yer for that.'

Jez screamed back. 'Fuck Vince! He wants rid of me anyway. He'll get rid of you eventually.'

Sep could now see Jez, who had blood streaming down through his coat sleeve from a wound to his left arm. In his good hand he was holding what looked like a 9mm automatic. Now he was firing again. The other man returned fire. The exchange lasted ten seconds which seemed like an age to Sep who was trying to work out how he could get out of the building without crossing the line of fire. Would he get out *dead or alive?* Jesus! Those three bloody words again!

Jez went down. Sep saw bullets striking his body. The shooting stopped. Jez was now silent. Moaning was coming from the surviving adversary.

Sep crouched there quietly, not sure what to do. He heard the man stumbling about and crying out in pain. Jez's gun had dropped to the floor and was only six feet away from Sep, but all six of those feet were in the line of the man's fire. More moaning. Sep darted out and snatched the gun. The man let off a single shot, too late to do damage. Sep crawled around the desk to try and catch a glimpse of the wounded man who was scoping his gun left and right, waiting for him to appear. Sep kept his head down and checked his weapon was ready to fire and still had ammunition in it. It was a Smith and Wesson with a fourteen round magazine and still had seven rounds left in. Sweat ran down his face as the tension of that moment hit him. He knew there was only one way out of this – alive or dead. His adversary was injured, he knew that, but he didn't know how badly. But what he did know was that injured men with nothing to lose, fight fiercely, like injured animals. Sep crept to the end of the desk and peeped around the corner to where he figured the man wouldn't be expecting him to appear. He saw the lower half of a man on the floor, just a pair of legs. It could be the dead man or the live one, he couldn't be sure.

He then stood up quickly, to find the legs belonged to the live man who had anticipated this move and had him in his sights already. The man's finger tight on the trigger. In that same instant Sep had figured he could get a reasonably accurate shot off in less than a second. The man got a shot off first but his pain caused him to waver and his shot missed Sep's head by a millimetre, by which time Sep had brought his arm round and fired almost simultaneously, causing the man to jerk backwards as a bullet hit his body from close range. It was the last thing he did.

Sep put two more bullets into the man's body, as per his police fire arms training. If you must shoot leave no room for doubt. Sep went over to him. There was no room for doubt that the man was dead. Sep's feelings were mixed. Deep relief that he'd survived this unexpected firefight and a sickness at having taken a man's life. He checked the pulse in the man's neck to confirm what he already knew. The man was stone dead. He then confirmed that there were three dead men in the building. One killed by a clean shot between the eyes. Jez was a good man with a gun under pressure.

Jesus! He hadn't expected anything like this, just two kids happy to be freed. Then he remembered what one of the men had said. The children weren't there. Had he been telling the truth? Shit! Surely he hadn't been through all this for nothing? He listened for external sounds, wondering if the shots would have been reported to the police. He heard the sound of heavy machinery coming from a nearby building, plus banging from a sheet-metal works next door. The shots might well have been mistaken for industrial banging. There was a lot of that in the district. He took a look around the building, searching for a cellar, which he found. He went down the stone steps to find a two room basement, both empty. One of them showed signs of recent occupancy. Two flimsy mattresses, bits of bread scattered about, apple cores, banana skins. There was a WC with a wash basin, but no children. No children at all in the building. Time to go.

He made a dash through the rain for the van. Slamming the door on the snarling teeth of the dogs which had finished off the meat. Then he realized he still had Jez's gun in his hand, along with his fingerprints. He thought about the consequences of this: to take the gun away would prove to the police, or to Formosa, that there was a missing shooter who wasn't Jez. To wipe off Jez's prints and leave it there would also arouse suspicion. He had to go back to tidy up those loose ends. Make it look as if this was an action between the three dead men and no one else. The dogs could cause him no end of problems, unless . . . he really didn't want to have to do this.

He wound down the window and stuck an arm out, the arm holding the gun. Both dogs jumped up at him, trying to bite him. It took him four shots to kill them both, which sickened him somewhat. The dogs had done no wrong, just doing their jobs. But their job might have put him out of action or worse, in very serious trouble with the police and completely knackering his plan to get the kids back. Dead dogs versus live kids – no contest really. There was a rag in the door pocket with which he wiped the gun clean of his prints. Then he got out of the van and went back into the building. Holding it by the rag, he pressed the gun into Jez's hand, wrapping his dead fingers around the butt. Then he placed the gun on the floor and looked around to see if anything might be amiss. There were footprints on the dusty floor, some of his and many others. He'd throw his shoes away the minute he got back. No, he'd get rid of every stitch of clothing he was wearing. Wrap it in a plastic bag and throw it in a skip or a dustbin that had no connection with him.

He hadn't stepped in any blood – maybe his police training was kicking in automatically, so no problem there. The FME lot would be uncertain as to how many people had been involved. Time to leave. He drove away, leaving the gates wide open. The rain was heavy now, which suited him as it would wipe out any tyre marks. The yard was in an area free of street cameras; an industrial area free of curious eyes; an ideal area for keeping kidnapped children. Formosa had done him a favour with his choice of location, and Winnie had done him a favour by lending him a pair of false number plates.

But where were the kids now? All this for nothing.

THIRTY-SIX

Cope adjusted his tie nervously before he knocked politely on Formosa's office door and opened it. Formosa was sitting at his desk, reading a newspaper. He looked up and gave a stiff smile.

'Come in, Lenny. Sit down.'

Cope sat down. Formosa hadn't taken his eyes off him. They were small and mean and deep set, glittering like black diamonds.

'Have you any idea why I've asked you to come here, Lenny?'

'None at all.'

'The reason I asked you to come is because I've suffered a major loss.'

'Oh, what?'

'In order of importance; I've lost my car, two dogs and three men. All gone, Lenny.'

'What do you mean by all gone?'

'I mean my car is missing and possibly irretrievable. I can't even claim insurance on it; two of my guard dogs are shot dead, as are three of my men.'

'You need to tell me the how and where and when.'

'Oh, I know the how and the where and when. What I don't

know is why. The when is yesterday when I was in London, and the where is the compound where I was keeping the Strathmore kids. The how is with guns.'

'I never knew where the kids were being kept. Not since you moved them from the last place.'

'I have a compound in Pudsey with offices and a cellar. Two of my men were there. Jez turned up and all I know is all three are now shot dead, including Jez. It looks as though they shot each other.'

'What about the kids?'

'I had the kids moved the day before. They'd been too long in one place. My caution proved correct. What I'd like to know is what went on and why?'

'Do you want the police to investigate it?'

'No, I want *you* to investigate it. I don't want the police and their forensic people anywhere near it. The five bodies have already been disposed of.'

'Five?'

'Including two Dobermanns . . . five dogs altogether.'

'Vince, it doesn't sound as though there's much left there to investigate.'

'Weapons and bullet holes is all you have to work with. The rain wiped out any vehicle track marks in the compound. I'd also like you to track down my Bentley and figure out a way of returning it to me.'

'I'll need police help for that.'

'There is a minor problem. The car was registered in Jez Copitch's name and he's now dead but no one knows that. When it's found, how do I get possession of it?'

'What? Why did you do that?'

'We live in a ridiculous computer age, Lenny. An age where everyone knows everyone's business. In this business it's wise for a man to put his name to as little as possible. The more a man's name is in the public domain the more dangerous it is for him. What I require from you is the means to recover ownership of my Bentley.'

'I'm not sure how I can do that. It'll remain Jez's vehicle until such time as he's properly declared dead and then it'll become part of his estate.'

Formosa's eyes narrowed. 'You will get me my fucking car back or I will not be pleased with you.'

'I'll do whatever is required to secure its return.' Cope spoke without any confidence then, by way of changing the subject, he added, 'I could give you one piece of advice, though.'

'What's that?'

'Get rid of the kids. It seems to me to be too much of a co-incidence that all this occurred exactly where the kids were supposed to be. Do you think Jez was working for their father and attempting a one-man rescue? Would he have known you had two men there?'

'No, he wouldn't have known that. But if that's the case Jez had an accomplice who is still alive.'

'Why's that?'

'Because there was no vehicle there. My men had been dropped off to be picked up. Jez'll have brought his own transport to get there and to get the kids away – probably my Bentley. Someone other than Jez drove it away.'

'So, neither Jez nor his accomplice will have known the kids had gone?' said Cope.

'No,' said Formosa. 'Nobody knew except the other two who are dead. They're the ones who moved them. They went back to the compound to tidy up all evidence of the kids ever being there, but as far as I can see they hadn't even made a start. Judging from the empty beer cans left lying around I think they were both pissed which is a serious offence in my book. Jez did my job for me.'

'Jez might have had more than one accomplice,' said Cope. 'He and whoever it was took out two of your men. Vince, we need to know who was with him. If you take my advice you'll just kill the kids and dispose of their bodies. This is getting out of hand.'

'If I take your advice I lose two million pounds. I need these kids alive long enough to talk to their father. I'm already missing a two hundred grand car. I'm in no mood for more losses.'

'In that case you could forestall any future attempts to free them by assuming Strathmore was behind this attempt, and you should mention it when you talk to him. Tell him Jez is dead, as will the kids be if he doesn't go along with you. It'll make him realize the futility of not complying with you.'

'Futility of not complying with me. I like that, Lenny. I will say that to him.'

'How will you pick up the money?'

'I will give him the number of a bank account in Lichtenstein into which he will transfer the money. Within minutes of it being deposited it will set off on an exotic journey around the world's banks ending up in an impregnable bank account eight thousand miles away from here. I have a highly paid banking expert who is something of a wizard at this sort of thing. He is the most indispensable man on my team. However, he knows that if I do dispense with him I will find a suitable replacement for him, as should you.'

His eyes fixed Cope with a humorous stare. Cope didn't respond. Formosa went on to say, 'I will also tell Strathmore that I have the means to know if the money is being tracked, and if it is he will never see his children again.'

'And do you have the means to see if it's being tracked?'

'No, but I'm told that my man's method of moving money means it can't be tracked. But I'll make the call anyway, to stop them trying. Even if they did track it, all they'd end up with is a numbered bank account that they can't touch without starting a war.'

'I'm impressed,' said Cope. 'You could keep your word and let the kids go. If they disappear completely the police will never let it go. It'll only take one loose tongue in ten years' time and they'll be knocking on your door.'

'And whose tongue will that be . . . yours?'

'Hardly. They knock on your door, they knock on my door.'

Formosa shook his head. 'No, once they've outlived their usefulness the kids are toast. I've got no way of knowing how those drunken idiots at the compound handled the move. Maybe they shot their mouths off, mentioned my name or some such stupidity. It's safer for us all if the brats are never seen again.'

'I agree,' said Cope.

'I do not like this child kidnapping business,' said Formosa. 'It's too difficult to read the unbalanced parents. They don't always obey the rules.'

'Maybe you should try kidnapping rich businessmen.'

'Now that's a good idea, Lenny. I must check me out some

Arab oil sheiks. The pickup might be more complicated, but the high value guys are worth the extra trouble.'

'They tend to go round with bodyguards.'

'Bodyguards aren't bulletproof. We can handle bodyguards much better than unbalanced parents. Yeah, it's about time I got me a share of the oil business.'

THIRTY-SEVEN

The following day, Winnie drove her van into the hand car wash on Roundhay Road. It had picked up a lot of mud during its one day on loan to Sep. The car wash was run by Eastern Europeans, as were all such car washes it would seem, but they were cheap and did a good job. She stepped out of the van and walked over to the office, as was her usual routine in this place. She'd become quite friendly with the manager, a young Romanian she was on first name terms with.

'Morning, Marku.'

He smiled, broadly. 'Good morning, Winnie. Hey, I have a question for you.'

'Oh?'

He lowered his voice, despite them being the only people in the office. 'Yes, my question is about a police raid on a brothel in Spencer Place.'

Winnie was immediately on her guard. 'Really? I read about that in the papers.'

'I think you know all about it, Winnie.'

'What are you talking about, Marku?'

'Well, one of the girls who was rescued from that place was my girlfriend. Five months ago she was supposed to come here from Romania to join me but she did not arrive. I thought she had left me. I just try to get over it. But she'd been a foolish girl and she fell for some trick those people were playing over there to get girls from Romania to Leeds very cheaply. She was there four months when the police bring her out.'

'So, what's that got to do with me?'

'Your name and that van,' said Marku. 'When she was being driven away from the place in a police van, the police were talking to each other and they talk of a woman called Winnie who shot Dragos in his private parts – only they didn't say private parts. They say she drive a blue Transit van and it has me wondering how many Leeds women called Winnie drive blue Transit vans.'

'Marku, have you told anyone else about this?'

'I haven't, no. I thought I should mention it to you first.'

'What about your girlfriend?'

'Corina is still in shock about the whole thing. Since she tell me about the conversation in the police van she has not been able to talk about it at all and I do not press her. In fact I do not think I want to hear what she might have to tell me as there is nothing I can do about it, so I am trying to help her forget about the whole thing. I think she might have forgotten about the police conversation but not about her time in the house.'

Winnie considered denying she was the woman in question, then she thought about this logically. Marku was right when he asked how many women called Winnie drive around Leeds in blue Transit vans. She didn't even know anyone else called Winnie, never mind a Winnie with a blue Transit van. There was a silence between them as she considered her two options – admit or deny. Marku interrupted her thoughts.

'They said Winnie must have been very brave and that she must have been working for the police undercover . . . Is this true?'

Winnie looked at him. He'd all but denied her one of the options.

'No,' she said.

'Are you working for police?'

'Marku, I came in here to get my van washed and you're giving me this third degree.'

'What is a third degree?'

'It's . . . Oh never mind.'

'I was only saying this because I believe my girlfriend owes her life to you, and you give her back to me, which means I owe you my life as well. It was you, wasn't it?'

Winnie looked at him and knew it was hopeless to deny it.

'OK, it was me. I was helping a friend and, due to my stupidity, it got out of hand – and I would rather you didn't talk about my involvement in it to anyone. The police captured most of the gang but probably not all of them, and they're the ones I need to be afraid of.'

'I understand. I will never do anything to cause you harm.'

'Not a word to anyone?'

'Not a word.'

'Thank you, Marku.'

He smiled at her and a question arose in her mind. 'Tell me, Marku, how has this affected your relationship with Corina?'

'You mean the knowledge that she was forced into prostitution?'

'Exactly that, yes. That can't be easy for you.'

'No it isn't easy for me, but she is still the girl I fell in love with and my love is still as strong, in spite of all the things that filthy men have done to her. None of this was her fault.'

'I'm proud of you, Marku, but how has it affected your relationship?'

'It is not good at the moment. I am a man, and she doesn't want me anywhere near her. She is talking about going home to Romania, but I remind her that she has a father and three brothers who all treated her like a servant.'

'How do you treat her?'

'I treat her like the woman I love who is an honoured guest in my home. What else can I do?'

'I think that ought to do it eventually.'

'Do you know that Dragos is dead?' he asked her.

'I do, yes.'

'Should I tell Corina he's dead?' Marku asked her.

'Oh yes, I think you should. He will have humiliated her and what I did to him was the ultimate retribution for the humiliation he heaped upon all the girls, as well as myself. I know I have beaten him and she should know something similar. It will help her, I can assure you. But please do not mention my name or that you know me.'

'I will tell her he die in the agony of having his manhood removed by an angry woman.'

Winnie smiled. 'Oh, yes, you tell her that. I think it should do the trick.'

'Winnie, if there is anything I can ever do for you I will be most honoured to help. I will never charge you for washing your van.'

'You'd better not let your boss hear you say that.'

'Do you often help police?'

'Sometimes.'

'I ask this because in my world I hear many things that may be of interest to the police, but I say nothing to them as they think we Romanians are all people who commit crimes, which is not true.'

'No, I don't believe it is either, Marku. What sort of things have you heard recently?'

'What is it you wish to know about?'

'Well, have you ever heard of a man called Vince Formosa?'

Marku's face lost its animation. He stared at her with frightened eyes. 'Yes, I have heard of him. I know he is a most dangerous man.'

'I know that, but have you heard anything specific about him?'

'What is specific? I no understand.'

'It means . . . do you know of some actual crime he has been involved in?'

'What sort of crime?'

'Such as the abduction of children.'

The frightened eyes returned. His eagerness to help was fading. Winnie pressed home the only advantage she had. 'Would your girlfriend like you to help me?'

'I think she would, but she would not like me to put my life in danger.'

Winnie got to her feet and went over to the window. Her van was covered in foam which was being cleaned off by three very industrious young men. Marku came to stand beside her.

'You talking about Formosa reminded me that Lucian, one of my people, went back to Romania last week,' he told her.

'And what did Formosa have to do with that?'

'Well, I promised Lucian I would never to tell anyone. He is terrified of Formosa.'

'I think you can tell me without jeopardising his life. Is it to do with the children?'

'No, it is to do with the murder of two people. A man called Lee Dench and his girlfriend.'

'I knew his girlfriend but not Dench,' said Winnie.

'No, I did not know him either. Not a very nice person I am told.'

'So, what about their murder?'

'I know who did it.'

'How?'

'Because Lucian was in the house at the time. Two men came to kill Dench because he grassed up Formosa. They kill both him and his girlfriend but left the rest of them alive, this included Lucian. He tell me all about it the day before he goes back to Romania. I have never seen a man so terrified.'

'I'm guessing he didn't give a forwarding address.'

'You guess correctly. I give him all the money he was due and wish him good luck.'

'Did he give you the names of the killers?'

'No, but he give me a description. A black man and a white man who Lucian thinks was Irish which makes me think it was Spud and Sharky.'

'I'm guessing the Irishman's Spud,' said Winnie.

'That is right,' said Marku. 'How did you know?'

'Just a wild guess.'

'Well if the white man is Spud then the black man will be Sharky. I also know they haven't been seen around in Hull since the murders, which is unusual because they're always out and about in some pub or other.'

'Why Hull?' asked Winnie.

'It's where they both live. They're regular hitmen. Live in Hull and work over this way, where no one knows who they are.'

'Except you.'

'Well I worked in Hull before I was asked to run this place. We have a branch in Hull and I asked the manager about them. He's like me, gets to hear all sorts of stuff.'

'Why do you think no one's seen them? Will they have gone to ground?'

'Gone to ground? What's that mean?'

'It means are they in hiding somewhere.'

'Doubt it. I think they've either left the country or Formosa have them killed and I don't think they will have left the country.'

'Why not?'

'It means they have to go through security checks. Men like that do not like being checked by anybody.'

'Well, I don't blame Lucian for doing a runner,' said Winnie.

With her van cleaned, Winnie drove away. She wasn't thinking about Marku and his information, she was thinking about the man she had killed and would she be in trouble for it? The fact that she had killed Dragos didn't trouble her as much as it would have had she killed an actual human being. Retribution for her rape and humiliation was now complete, but she was worried about the consequences. Best get hold of Sep and see how the land lies.

THIRTY-EIGHT

Sep was at home, fitting a more comfortable saddle on to his bike. Something he'd promised himself to do should it ever be returned to him. It was leaning against the dining table in his living room, when his mobile rang. The caller's name came up on the screen.

'Fiona.'

'Hi Sep, how are you?'

Her unaccustomed familiarity took him aback. 'If you must know,' he said, 'I've got a sore arse from riding this damned bike.'

'You've got it back?'

'Yeah, I've been riding round on it this morning. The tracker did its job. It was a local kid. It was found three streets away. I promised myself a new saddle if ever I got it back.'

'Ah, I did wonder about that saddle. Bit on the sharp side is it?'

'Like riding round on a razor blade.'

'I was wondering how you went on with Jez. Did he know where the kids are?'

'He thought he did but they weren't there.'

'Is that it?'

'It'll have to be, Fiona. Better that you don't know the whole story.'

'I see.'

'It got a bit ugly. What have you got for me?'

'Er, the car number you gave me fits a Peugeot 405 registered in Nuneaton. What do you mean by "ugly"?'

'Honestly Fiona, I'm sorry to keep you in the dark, but it's best you don't know.'

'OK, all the insurance details were false as well. So, the bloke who bumped into the nanny was obviously part of it. What about the name Kev Clarkson?'

Sep had asked her to run the name through the PNC soon after he'd got the name from Jez.

'I couldn't find a Kevin Clarkson who fits that description. In fact I only found two in Yorkshire; one's an eighteen-year-old burglar from Rotherham and the other's a Jamaican drug dealer from Bradford, and both of 'em are currently banged up.'

'I imagine our Kev Clarkson's got half a dozen other names.'

'Nothing came up that's of any use. I suppose I could let Laura look through the mugshot files,' said Fiona.

Sep smiled to himself. 'It'd be interesting to see Cope's reaction when you tell him you're getting the nanny to check out the mugshots.'

'I don't need to tell him.'

'You'd bloody well need to if I was in charge.'

'He's not you, Sep, and if I ask Cope won't Clarkson just get to know and just leave town?'

'Good thinking. OK, don't ask him. In fact if she identifies anyone you'll need to keep his identity to yourself until you pick him up.'

'I'll bring her in on Friday evening. He likes his weekends off does Cope.'

'What? Whole weekends? How does he manage that?'

'He sets it off against the overtime he puts in at night, which is mainly pub-crawling, as far as I can tell.'

'Pubs are where all the prostitutes are,' said Sep. 'His night work should suit him down to the ground.'

'And maybe he spends his weekends working full time for Formosa.'

'If I was still in the job I'd put a tail on Cope this weekend.'

'I'd have to do the tailing myself. A mere sergeant can hardly authorize for an inspector to be tailed. In any case I'll be tracking down Kev Clarkson . . . if Laura can identify him.'

'You just tell Jimmy Lennon where Kev Clarkson is. Jimmy'll deal with him.'

'Bloody hell, Sep, I could get drummed out of the force for this!'

'Not if we find the kids and expose Cope for what he is. I get my job back and you'd be in line for a promotion – at least you would if you got your finger out and took your inspector's exam.'

'I've only just made sergeant, Sep. I'm at least ten years off trying for inspector.'

'Sometimes opportunities arise out of the blue, Fiona, and you need to be ready to take them – as in already having your paper qualifications. It's how I got bumped up fairly quickly. Two years as a DS then a DI got the push for improper conduct and I was both available and qualified to take his place.'

'That's not what I heard. I heard you had some magical powers when it came to getting the truth out of villains.'

Sep grinned. 'It's not magic, it's a talent for lying convincingly. It's a practised art I've acquired. Villains don't expect cops to be as dishonest as them, and as far as lies are concerned I can see through their lies but they can't see through mine. A lot of it's educated guesswork but you don't need much education to know the truth when a villain's lying to you. All you need is a bit of detail that takes him by surprise and he thinks you know everything. I ask around, check him out and sometimes I dig out damaging information that's got nothing to do with the case. There's always a skeleton in his cupboard and a villain's skeletons tend to rattle louder than most. That's what I do. I rattle their skeletons at 'em, and that's when they spill the beans, hoping you might go easy on them. This knowledge works a charm coming from a nobody like Jimmy Lennon.'

'How did that work?'

'Well, when Jimmy Lennon told Jez he knew about him losing Formosa's Bentley while he was out fishing, it shocked the hell out of him. I mean, how the hell could a no-account tramp know that? He probably thought Jimmy had mystic powers. It's a case of using what little you know to its best advantage . . . and being a talented liar.'

'You must teach me that. Was Jez of any help?'

Sep sighed to himself. 'I'd better tell you, Fiona, Jez is dead. His information led to a shoot-out with two of Formosa's men, also dead. If the police haven't found out about it I'm guessing Formosa's got rid of all evidence.'

'Were you involved?'

'I was, unfortunately, but Jez did most of the shooting.'

'Did you . . .?'

Sep chopped her off. 'Honestly, Fiona, you don't want to know any more. Just keep in mind that at the end of this Cope'll get the push and there'll be a vacancy.'

'Which will be given back to you,' Fiona said.

'Maybe they'll take me back as a DCI to make up for all the injustice they've heaped upon me.'

'Do you really think that might happen?'

'You have to admit, there's a kind of logic to it . . . copper's logic admittedly, but logic nevertheless.'

'So you see all these problems as a means of fast-tracking up the promotion ladder?'

'I see it as the light at the end of the tunnel.'

'You're a very positive person, Sep.'

'It's better than going crackers.'

Fiona switched the computer to the police-booking-photographs archive, better known as the mugshot file. She was sitting next to Laura Graham.

'You saw him in Harrogate, so I suppose we'd better bring up all the Harrogate and district villains – that shouldn't take long. Then we'll try Leeds.'

'OK,' said Laura. She scrolled through the mugshot pages, bringing up twelve at a time. It took two minutes to rule out the known Harrogate villains. Fiona went to another file showing Leeds criminals. After ten minutes, Laura came to a photo that looked vaguely like the man she was looking for.

'He's that type but it's not him,' she told Fiona. 'I could be here for hours. How many are there?'

'It depends how far back we go. Thousands altogether.'

'Is there some way of separating them into age groups?'

'Yes, I can do that. Middle-aged you say? Shall we try forty to fifty-five?'

'OK. What about type of crime?'

'Yep. Let's try fraudsters. He gave you a lot of false information?'

'He certainly did.'

It took fifteen minutes and several false alarms for Laura to point to a photograph. 'That could be him, but he looks a lot younger there.'

Fiona brought up the man's details. 'Well it was taken fourteen years ago. He'll be fifty three now. Kevin Kennedy, arrested for fraudulent accounting. They often hang on to their first name to avoid confusion. He fiddled the books of his employer by the looks of it, to the tune of eighteen thousand three hundred pounds. Got two years for it.'

'Are there any more recent photos of him?'

'We've got all his identity details. I'll try the Passport Office, see what they've got.'

Five minutes later Fiona brought up a passport photo of Kevin Kennedy taken two years ago. Laura stared at it intently. 'That's definitely him,' she said.

'Well, if he's still living at his passport address, which he should be, we've got him,' said Fiona. 'Some things are so simple. I bet he didn't tell Vince Formosa he had a criminal record.'

'Does this help in finding the children?'

'If it does, the Strathmores owe you a big debt.'

'Maybe it will make up for me being late picking them up. I haven't forgiven myself for that.'

'I'm sure the Strathmores don't hold it against you.'

'I think they might. Someone steals your children, you blame whoever's handy. I'm amazed Mr Strathmore hasn't tracked down this Formosa character and beaten it out of him.'

'If it turned out *not* to be Formosa, that'd put Mr Strathmore in a lot of trouble – with the law as well as Formosa, and I don't know which is worse.'

*   *   *

'His name's Kevin Kennedy, he's fifty three and he lives at 13 Bayswater Drive in Harehills. I'll be passing this on to Cope when I speak to him.'

'Which will be Monday.'

It was Friday evening. Laura had just left the police station. Fiona had rung Sep. 'Sorry, Sep. He'll be down on me like a ton of bricks if I leave it three days before telling him. I'll ring him in the morning at his home.'

'Where's that? He doesn't live in my house anymore.'

'No idea, but someone must know.'

'Fiona. Don't ring him before Jimmy Lennon's talked to Kennedy. Tell me everything you've got on him, and anything you haven't got on him but might be true. Can you email his picture to me?'

'Bloody hell, Sep! If I get found out doing thi—'

'It's for a good cause Fiona, and no one'll know but me.'

'OK. I'll trust you with that, but this is as far as I'm going with it, Sep.'

'You're a diamond, Fiona.'

Sep put the phone down and rang Winnie. 'Winnie, is Bayswater Drive near you?'

'Not far away.'

'There's a bloke I need to check out in connection with the kidnapping. His name's Kevin Kennedy. He lives at number 13. Is there any way you can help?'

'Possibly. I know someone who lives in the Bayswaters. Could be the Drive, I'm not sure. Is there anything special about him?'

'Not really. He's a bit of a nonentity apparently. Lives on his own, but about fourteen years ago he did two years for fraud. I think he does work for Formosa.'

'Ah, I've heard there's a bloke around there who does dodgy driving licences and passports and stuff. I imagine Formosa could use a man like that. Don't know his name but I can find out soon enough. I'll ring you back, Sep.'

It was an hour before she rang him back. He was thinking it was too late to call in on Kennedy with it being Friday night. He'd most likely be in some pub or other by this time.

'Kevin Kennedy did you say?'

'Yes.'

'There's a bloke calling himself Kevin Kitson who lives on Bayswater Drive.'

'Is he the forger?'

'Yes.'

'I'm thinking he's my man. Did you find out anything of interest?'

'Possibly. I've got a contact who tells me there's a bloke doing life in Wakefield nick who tried to do a runner using one of Kitson's passports.'

'What's he in for?'

'Double murder. Real nasty type. He wasn't pleased with Kevin's work one bit, and this was before they introduced these new hologram jobs. Word has it that he didn't blow the whistle on Kevin because Formosa put the frighteners in.'

'What's this bloke's name?'

'Pete Devlin.'

'Devlin? Bloody hell!'

'You know about him do you?'

'Yes, he's bad news,' said Sep. 'Do you know what Kitson looks like?'

'No, but I imagine my contact does. Do you have a photo of him?'

'I do, but I've promised to keep it to myself. Look, I'll email it to you.'

'Sep, how can you do that if you're keeping it to yourself?'

'Because I expect you to keep it to *your*self. Can you print it and take it round to your contact?'

'You want me to show it to my contact?'

'Yes.'

'How can I do that if I'm keeping it to myself?'

'Winnie, can you do it?'

'Sure. I'm only five minutes away from her.'

'It's a she, is it?'

'Yes. Women are much more reliable – much better at keeping things to themselves than men. Send it and I'll ring you back in fifteen.'

'If there's anything else she knows as well, and don't mention Formosa's involved in this.'

'We're not stupid, Sep, us women.'

*   *   *

'Kitson and Kennedy are one and the same, Sep. My contact is certain.'

'Well done, Winnie. What's the betting that Kennedy has half a dozen passports for half a dozen Kevins? Do we know anything else about him?'

'You'll find him at home right now because he rarely goes out at night. My contact's mother knows him quite well. He was married briefly but his wife left him when he went to prison and he has no idea where she is. According to him she left with all the money he embezzled. They have a son who he hasn't seen since he was a baby. That's about all.'

'Would you say this information is widely known?'

'I would doubt it. My contact's mother was told all this in confidence. I believe they had some sort of affair and people tend to open up under such circumstances.'

'Are they still having this affair?'

'No. It didn't last long. He's not exactly God's gift to women. It seems she befriended him when he came into some money, presumably from his nefarious activities. She dropped him when he lost a testicle to cancer and ran out of money.'

'So it wasn't a hearts-and-flowers love story, then?'

'I've met her. She's a real old cow. Is all this of any help?'

'Oh yes.'

'Oh, by the way, I think I know who killed Dench.'

'You do?'

'Yes.' She went on to tell him about her chat with Marku the car wash man and how Dench was killed by two hitmen, most probably called Spud and Sharky. All the details Marku had given her she passed on to Sep.

'Never heard of them,' said Sep.

'That's because they live in Hull.'

'How sure are you that it was them?'

'About ninety per cent. I'm also ninety per cent sure Formosa's had them killed.'

'Why's that?'

'Because they're not around any more. Can you use this?'

'I imagine so. Spud and Sharky. Do you know anything about them?'

'Spud was Irish, Sharky was black. Both regular hitmen, that's all I know.'

Ninety per cent certainty was plenty for what Sep would use the information for. In fact ninety per cent was a luxury.

THIRTY-NINE

The door to number 13 Bayswater Drive looked to have been there since the house was built over a hundred years ago and it hadn't weathered well. Paint flaked off as Sep knocked. He heard a muttering voice inside. An internal door opened. Then the front door opened a crack. Sep saw half a face.

'What do you want?'

'I want te know if I'm speaking te Kevin Kennedy or Kevin Kitson or Kevin Clarkson or one of the other Kevins who live here.'

Sep was in his guise as Jimmy Lennon and didn't look too much of a threat.

'Go away.'

'Right. Shall I tell Pete Devlin ye told me to go away? He knows Vince Formosa's not looking after you anymore.'

'Who says so?'

'I just did. Are ye deaf?'

Sep was playing it by ear as he often did. If he was wrong about anything he'd be able to make it sound right. The door opened fully. Kevin was a tidy man. Balding and clean shaven with sharp eyes, dressed in a clean white shirt and trousers held up high by red braces.

'Are ye inviting me in, Kevin? It would be in yer interest te invite me in.'

'Why?'

'Because Devlin's got unfinished business with ye and I might be able to help y'out in a way that keeps ye breathin'.'

Kevin stood there, undecided for a few moments then he stood back to allow Sep through into his living room.

It wasn't a luxurious room but it was as tidy as the man. Two
easy chairs, a dining table, two dining chairs and a television set
on top of an old fashioned dresser. The carpet was cheap but
clean, as were the curtains. There was a smell of coffee in the
air but no evidence of a coffee cup.

'Have ye got some coffee brewin', Kevin? Wouldn't mind a
cup.'

Kevin looked at this disgusting tramp of a man who had invited
himself into his neat and tidy home. Had it not been for his size
he might have told him to bugger off, but Sep could be an intimidating man, with or without his Jimmy Lennon disguise.

'Who the hell are you?' Kevin said. 'If you're after money, I
haven't got any.'

Sep sat down in one of the easy chairs. Kevin remained
standing.

'What?' said Sep. 'Have ye spent the money Formosa gave
ye for that fake crash?'

'What fake car crash?'

'Did y'ever know what that was about, Kevin?'

'No idea what you're talking about?'

'It was about two bairns bein' abducted. Ye were a party to
the abduction. In all probability the bairns will soon be murdered
and ye'll be a party to that as well. That's if Formosa or Devlin
don't get ye first.'

This shocked Kevin. He sat down opposite Sep. 'Just who are
you?' he asked.

'I'm either ye best friend or ye worst enemy. Ye must take ye
pick. If I'm an enemy I'll leave right now and let the bad guys
and maybe the polis do they're worst. The guy who took that
Picasso yer crashed into had his head blown off by Formosa.
Did ye know that, Kevin? Blown clean off wi' a fuckin' shot
gun. His woman took a bullet in the mouth. His name was Lee
Dench. He was killed because he was involved in the abduction,
as were you Kevin. Devlin's a pussycat compared te Formosa,
and Formosa's not locked up. He's a free man te kill whoever
he pleases, and I think it might please him te have you killed.
I'm amazed ye still livin' in the same town. In fact, I'm amazed
ye still livin' at all. Did it never occur ter ye te move towns,
Kevin?'

'How did you find out where I live?'

Sep smiled. It was the first sign that Kevin was cracking. He was telling Sep that his information was correct, which Sep already knew. It was always wise to get off on the right foot in these interviews. Tell the truth to start with, lie later.

'Well, I know because it's ma job tae know stuff, Kevin. It's how I make ma living. I know ye have a son ye haven't seen since he was a wee bairn.'

Kevin leaned forward in his chair. 'Do you know where he is?'

'No, but I could find out, right enough. I might even be able te track that ex-wife of yours down and find out what she did with yer money. The money ye served time for. I can do many things, Kevin.'

'What is it you want? I have no money, but I can make you a passport.'

'Aye, I know all about ye dodgy passports, Kevin. Wouldnae be interested, man. What I want is information.'

'About what?'

'Information about the whereabouts of the missing children.'

'I'm guessing you've been privately hired to find them.'

'Ye know they're missing?'

'I've read about it, yes.'

'And ye say ye had no idea ye were involved in it?'

'None at all and I've got no idea where they are.'

Sep shook his head. 'I believe ye, Kevin, but I cannae see a jury believing ye – not when yer bein' paid by a man like Formosa. The man's poison.'

'I didn't know *he* was paying me. I was just given five hundred pounds to bump into a car, keep the driver waiting for ten minutes and show her false documents. It was all pretty harmless. I hardly damaged her car.'

'In that case I'll just turn ye in ter the polis. The woman driving the Picasso'll identify ye as the man who started it all. When the polis check ye out ye won't stand a chance, man. It'll be a lot more than the two years ye got last time, man, and it won't be in a Cat D either. Cat B fer ten years minimum as a kiddie killer.' Kevin's face betrayed how scared he was.

'What if I tell you who hired me to do it?'

'That seems mighty brave of ye. Are ye no scared of repercussions?'

'He doesn't know I know who he is.'

'Ah.' Sep pretended to give this some thought. 'That might help. Who is he?'

'He's an estate agent who has dealings with Formosa. I think he handles Formosa's property portfolio.'

'Formosa has a property portfolio, does he? How d'ye know that?'

'I'm a bit like you. I'm a nosey man and I know stuff I shouldn't. He has property all over the place, including London.'

'How come ye know this estate agent?'

'I hadn't seen him for over twelve years but remembered him from prison. He didn't remember me. Well, he wouldn't. I was an insignificant nobody; kept myself to myself. He was a loud mouth, thought he was bigtime. We were both in Ford Open Prison in Sussex. Cat D place for white collar crime as they call it. The word was that he'd got away with a light sentence for a half million pound property fraud.'

'How did he get the light sentence?'

'Because he had money and he had a top brief. I was skint and I had a Legal Aid plonker. Anyway, I think the owner of this house is one of his clients, and he must have found out I was five hundred in arrears, and he came round pretending to be a debt collector. I recognized him but I didn't let on I knew who he was – well, for all I knew he *was* a genuine debt collector. Then he mentioned how he could get me off the arrears if I did the crash job. He said he knew I did dodgy documents, but he didn't know I knew him and I wasn't going to make him any wiser. The less people know about me the better I like it.'

'I know the feeling. So you did the crash job?'

'Course I did. Money for jam. He even supplied the motor. I just did the documents and drove the car. All I was asked to do was hold her up for ten minutes, which I did. I'd no idea what was happening after that.'

'So, who's this estate agent?'

'His name's Derek Manson. I checked him out and he's got a place on Street Lane, Manson Estates, it's near the Deer Park pub.'

Sep got to his feet to go. 'So, what do I get out of this?' Kevin asked. 'Are you going to find my son for me?'

'What I'm going te do, Kevin, is not tell Devlin. I'm amazed Formosa hasn't sent someone round already with him being linked te the guy who owns the place. I would advise ye to move right out of this town and use a name that Formosa doesnae know about. I don't need te find your son because if I do find him, I won't know where you are.'

'I'd rather take that risk and see my son.'

'Kevin, one way or another this abduction case is going to be resolved. If it turns out badly, the police will come looking for anyone who was involved in it, which includes you. Even if it turns out well for the children and yer still around, it might not turn out too well for ye.'

FORTY

'I've brought you a cup of tea, love.'

Juliet Strathmore didn't open her eyes which were red raw from continuous crying. It was early evening, she was in bed and spoke without looking at her husband. 'Have they got my babies back yet?' Her voice was hoarse and barely audible. Peter's voice wasn't much better.

'Not yet, love. But we'll get them back, even if I have to *give* the damned land to Formosa.'

'Why can't the police just arrest him?'

'Not enough evidence, so they say. If I ever get my hands on him I won't need evidence.'

'If you hadn't made so much damned money he wouldn't have picked on us in the first place,' said his wife. 'We were happy enough when you were just a bricklayer but you had to go bigtime didn't you? I want my babies back, Peter.'

'I know, love, I'm doing my best.'

'I know I'm blaming you but it's their fault really – them bloody partners of yours. They shouldn't have gone to the police without telling us.'

'I know, love.'

'I rang one of them up. He was out but I told his wife what I thought of him. I called him all the lousy bastards under the sun. She didn't know what to say to me.'

'Dave Tomlinson, I heard. I'm breaking the partnership up after this is over.'

'What do you mean by over, Peter?'

'I mean when we get the kids back, choose what I have to do to get them back. I'm the majority shareholder. I'll just take my share out and leave them to it.'

'Why can't you just let Formosa have the land?'

'Because I haven't got a controlling interest in the company. I've got forty-six per cent, they've got the rest between them – twenty seven per cent each. I wish I'd never sold it to them.'

She closed her eyes and said no more. This had been their longest conversation since the children had been taken. Peter stood and looked down on her; his lovely Juliet, whose beauty had been draining away, day by day, until she was almost unrecognizable. He'd met her when they were both twenty-three. He was a bricklayer and she was a backing singer getting plenty of work through a Leeds agency. They'd met at a club in Leeds and had hit it off straight away. They'd bought a house together then sold it after house prices rocketed. He used the profit to buy a piece of land on which he'd built a house which he'd sold for further profit and ploughed every penny back into his company. Juliet's singing career came to an end with the birth of their first baby, James, but they didn't miss her money, not with Peter's business growing year by year.

For the past twelve years he had worked sixty hours a week and had built up a company with a multi-million pound turnover; they lived in a five bedroom house he'd built in Harrogate and their children went to a select private school. As he looked down at Juliet, he knew that all this money and success could not buy what he valued the most, his wife's happiness and his children's safe return.

'What's it all about, Strathmore?' he murmured to himself as he went back downstairs. He answered his own question. 'It's about me letting Formosa get away with it. What's the worst that can happen to me if I nail the bastard myself?'

FORTY-ONE

His heart was racing. He wasn't by nature a violent man but he'd had his moments when pushed. A man doesn't get to the top in his business without throwing his weight around a little, and Strathmore had plenty of weight to throw around. His hand tightened on the steel bar in his hand. It was an eighteen inch long piece of reinforcement bar which he'd sawn off to length for this particular purpose. Behind his heart rate was a deep hatred of the man he was about to confront; the man who had taken his children; the man who might even have already killed his children. This was why Strathmore didn't care what happened to him. Such a man is the most dangerous of all. He was a man ready to explode with grief and rage.

Formosa arrived first, but Strathmore made no move. Despite his heightened tension he was still thinking straight – just. He knew Formosa wouldn't be alone. He knew there would be a man close behind him. He even knew the man's name and his capability. His name was Fowler – Foxy Fowler, and he was a big and brutal man, highly paid to watch Formosa's back. Formosa walked past quickly, totally unaware of Strathmore's presence in the dark, side alley. Jazz music could still be heard from the club the two men had just left. Every man has a weakness and Formosa's was modern jazz. He loved its harmonic complexity which, he thought, suited his own complex personality.

Fowler was close behind him. Almost walking in step with his boss. He looked into the alley where Strathmore was lurking but the bar was already descending on his head. He had no time to call out a warning. The bar struck him a heavy blow and knocked him completely unconscious. The thud of the blow was lost in the music. Strathmore caught the big man, lowered him quickly to the ground, and stepped out behind Formosa, picking up on Formosa's step without the gang boss noticing. Formosa, without looking round, walked quickly to the club's car park where a black Lexus was parked. Strathmore knew the car, but he also knew the van parked alongside it. As Formosa half-turned for his man to work the remote door-opener the bar came down again, this time on Formosa's head. Within seconds Strathmore had loaded him into the back of the van, climbed in beside him and closed the door to await him regaining consciousness. He would have been wiser to have driven him away, but wisdom and rage rarely go together.

Formosa shook his head and glared into the torch light Strathmore was shining in his eyes. His head was slow in clearing. Strathmore said nothing. He just looked down at this piece of shit who was now at his mercy and he was sorely tempted to just bludgeon him to death there and then. Formosa spoke.

'Who the fuck are you?'

'Where are my children?' Strathmore's voice was low, and saturated with rage.

'What?'

'You've got ten seconds to live. I want to know where my children are.'

Formosa regained some of his senses. 'If you kill me you won't see them again.'

'Well, I think you've already killed them you scumbag. I'll give you ten seconds then I'll do what I've been aching to do since you took them. Once you're out of the picture we'll find them without your help. Nine . . . eight . . . seven . . . six . . . five . . .'

Formosa knew this man wasn't bluffing.

'OK . . . OK . . . I'll tell you.'

'Four . . . three . . . two . . .'

'Do you want to know or not?'

'I'm not sure I'll believe you. Better that I kill you and question the scumbags who work for you. There's one lying in an alley back there. I bet he'll tell me.' He raised the bar. Formosa could just see him on the edge of the torchlight.

'OK. You can talk to them right now if you like!'

'Get them,' said Strathmore.

The chance of talking to his children was a chance he couldn't miss. Formosa fumbled in his pocket for his phone. It lit up as he turned it on and went to the contacts page. The van door opened and a man reached inside, grabbed hold of Strathmore and dragged him out. Formosa was shouting. 'Kill the bastard! I want him dead!'

The man was doing his best to obey his boss's orders as he rained blows down on Strathmore who was waving his steel bar around trying to hit his adversary who took one damaging blow then snatched it out of Strathmore's hand and began to beat him with it. A loud whining noise came from behind, accompanied by a flashing blue light. Formosa cursed as two uniforms jumped out of a police car and ran to where Strathmore was lying on the ground. His attacker was running away. One of the officers gave chase but fell to the ground as the flailing arm of the fleeing man, still holding the bar, hit him in the face. The other officer was leaning over Strathmore. Formosa made to get out of the van. The officer looked up and called out.

'You, stay where you are!'

He got to his feet and handcuffed Formosa to the door handle. Formosa was protesting loudly. 'He's the one you should be arresting. He attacked me in the back of this fucking van!'

'I've no doubt we'll sort it out down at the station, sir. First I need to get an ambulance for this man who you say's been attacking you. He looks in a bad way to me.' He shone his torch on Formosa's face. 'Has he injured you, sir? I can't see anything. Who's the man who ran away? Was he helping you to fight this man off, sir?'

'I've got no idea.'

'Well, I think he was bleeding so I've no doubt he'll have left some DNA around. If he's known to us we'll soon track him down. Could I have your name, sir?'

'No, you can't have my fucking name.'

'His name's Formosa,' said Strathmore from the ground. 'Vincent Formosa. He abducted my children. I was just asking him where they are.'

'He says you attacked him, sir.'

'Does he look as if he's been attacked? It's me who's been attacked.'

'I'll get you an ambulance, sir.'

'Thank you. He needs locking up.'

Foxy Fowler, who had recovered sufficiently to make his way to the car park, was listening to all this from a safe distance. He walked away, quickly, having a good idea where he could meet up with the colleague who had just helped their boss. The woman who had called the police, after seeing Foxy Fowler knocked out, was climbing into a taxi, relieved to get away from this place of violence.

'Where have you brought me?' Strathmore asked Cope, who was standing by his bedside.

'You're in Leeds Infirmary.'

'Am I in trouble?'

'That's to be decided. If Mr Formosa decides to press charges.'

'Press charges for what? He wasn't injured.'

'He had a head injury.'

'Did he? Well, I might have tapped him on the head to get his attention.'

'It required four stitches.'

'Four? I've had twenty-four. I was attacked by one of his knuckle-draggers. I was just asking him what he'd done with my children. Am I not entitled to ask him that?'

It was a question Cope had no answer for. He simply said, 'Do you want us to contact your wife, Mr Strathmore?'

'My wife is in St James's. She took an overdose of sleeping tablets last night, not for the first time, either. I was lying awake beside her, thankful that she was getting some sleep at last, then I noticed something odd about her. She was stopping breathing for long periods, then starting again. I tried to wake her up but I couldn't. She was completely out of it. I switched the light on and saw the zopiclone tablets on her bedside table.'

'What are they?' asked Cope.

'Sleeping tablets, she'd only just been prescribed them. She was supposed to take one at the most. I looked in the packet and it was empty. She'd taken the lot – twenty-eight. I rang for an ambulance.'

'How is she, Mr Strathmore?'

'She's going to be all right. They gave her an antidote that worked, thank God. She didn't want to kill herself. It's just that being awake was too much for her. If I hadn't been awake, she'd have died. I know Formosa's got my children. We all know he's got my children, but you lot are so useless I thought I'd

ask him myself. If that thug hadn't turned up I'd have them back
by now.'

'How's that?'

'Because I'd persuaded him to tell me where they were.'

'You mean you threatened him.'

'I did, yes. As a matter of fact, if he didn't tell me I fully
intended killing him because with him gone I thought his death
might make it more likely for the rest of his mob to hand over
my children.'

'You would have gone to prison for that.'

'Maybe, maybe not. Who cares, so long as I get my children
back?'

FORTY-TWO

Sep suspected he wasn't the type of man who would be
welcome in an estate agent's office. His reception bore out
his suspicion.

'Can I help you?'

The questioner was a frosty-faced young woman standing
behind a counter. She was dressed in a dark business suit and
she had a false tan. Sep saw no reason to alienate her.

'Ay, I hope so, lassie. I hope so. I wish te speak wi' Mr Derek
Manson.'

'Do you have an appointment?'

'No, but I'm an old acquaintance of his. We served time
together in prison and I'm here te be of great assistance te him.
Tell him that, will ye please? Ma name is James Lennon.'

The frostiness left her face and was replaced by astonishment,
and relief that there were no other potential clients on the premises.

'Er, wait there one moment, please.'

The receptionist returned within a minute followed by a
bemused man in his forties, dressed in a dark grey suit, a loud,
silk tie and a matching handkerchief in his breast pocket. His
tan was real and accentuated his unusually white teeth. If Sep
had gone in to buy a property he would have been on his guard

instantly. This man had a lot of show but did he have any substance?

'Mr Lennon you say? Are you sure you haven't made a mistake, Mr Lennon? I don't believe I know you.'

'Well, I believe my appearance might have changed since we did bird down in Ford Open – as have my financial circumstances. I have a matter to discuss with you that you might want to discuss in private. It concerns a mutual friend; Mr Formosa.'

Manson's fixed smile turned to a rictus grimace, 'I see, perhaps you'd like to come through to my office.'

Sep touched a subservient forelock to the receptionist and followed Manson through a door into a businesslike office, designed to impress. It had certificates on the wall and photographs of impressive-looking houses. The desk was large and made of polished oak and leather. On it were three computer monitors, two telephones and various other pieces of electronic equipment. The room was expensively carpeted and the windows had complicated-looking Venetian blinds. Manson's chair was leather and comfortable-looking, as were the three other chairs in the room. Sep sat down in one of them, without being asked, and folded his arms. Manson sat in his own chair and leaned forward with his elbows on the desk.

'I'd like to start wi' an apology,' said Sep. 'I've never seen ye in ma life before and I've never been to prison, but I am curious about one thing.'

'What's that?'

'How ye got mixed up wi' Formosa and how far ye'll go to extricate yourself from the trouble he's about to get you in.'

'I don't know what you're talking about.'

'Och! And how many times have I heard that line in the past few days? Of course ye know what I'm talking about. I'm talking about the kidnapping of the Strathmore children. Your part in it was to delay the arrival of the nanny at their school. Ye paid a man five hundred pounds to crash into her car. Are you aware that Mr Formosa wishes he hadn't started that particular caper wi' all the trouble it's causin' him. In fact he's locked up as we speak, did ye know that?'

'I didn't, no.'

'Well, he had an altercation with Mr Strathmore which ended

up with Mr Strathmore in hospital and Formosa locked up in a police cell. I've no doubt his lawyer will have him out on bail soon enough, but ye can see why all this is just too much trouble for him.

'He's killin'' off all the guys involved. He started with Lee Dench, of course, then his driver, Jez, then the two men he sent Jez tae kill, then Spud and Sharky who killed Dench. All wasted. If ye add Dench's girlfriend, it adds up tae seven so far. Man, he's certain tae come for ye at some time and it wouldnae surprise me if he took out his tame copper, Detective Inspector Lenny Cope.'

Manson had gone white with fear. Sep was only guessing that Spud and Sharky had been killed, but it was a fairly safe guess. Even if they were alive, it was unlikely Manson would know who they were. As it happened, Manson knew about Lee Dench and his girlfriend but that was all. He knew Formosa had recently lost both a Bentley and his driver, so he had no reason to suppose this man wasn't telling the complete truth.

'Why are you here?'

Sep dropped his pretend Scottish accent and said, 'I'm here because I'm a policeman and I believe you can help me find the children, and if you help me I can ensure the police won't touch you.'

'You don't look like a copper.'

'I'm not supposed to.'

'Is James Lennon your real name?'

'No, and my real name is no concern of yours.'

'How do I even know you're a policeman?'

'If I wasn't, why would I be doing all this?'

'Doing all what?'

'That's a good question, Mr Manson. You see, it's up to you to tell me what you can do. I need information about Formosa, information as to his whereabouts, and with you running his property portfolio I imagine you'll know where he's likely to be at any given time. If I get useful information from you, the police will grant you immunity from prosecution. Now that's a life-changing offer I'm making.'

'Would I be required to give evidence against him in court?'

Sep smiled, this was his breakthrough. The man was about to admit to his involvement.

'I don't know. It depends on the strength of evidence we get against him. Right now it's certainly strong enough for a conviction but, for obvious reasons, we don't want to move against him until we find the children.' He paused for a few seconds then asked, 'Mr Manson, are the children still alive?'

Manson's brow furrowed. 'I think so, but I don't know for sure.'

'Do you know where they are?'

'All I can say is that they're not in any properties I know about.'

'How do you know that?'

'Because I've checked. Look, when I got involved in this car crash thing I had no idea what it was for. Had I known, I wouldn't have done it.'

'Really? You'd have said "No" to Vince Formosa?'

'I like to think so, yes.'

'Well, I think not. Formosa *will* go down for it, no question of that, but the question is, when he does, will you be going with him? It's a ten year stretch for you at least. A ten stretch as a child killer. You won't want to do that in the general population. Cons don't like child killers.'

'I'd rather not go to prison at all.'

'Tell me, Mr Manson. What do you do for Formosa?'

'I run his property portfolio and advise him when to buy and sell.'

'I want this portfolio,' said Sep.

Manson stared at him long and hard. 'I might be able to let you see it.'

Sep's demeanour turned aggressive. His voice was a low, menacing, mentally unbalanced growl that he'd perfected over many years.

'Might? How do you mean, might? You're in no position to negotiate. Please hand me the portfolio right now, or I will bring police to arrest you and ransack this office and take away your computers and any evidence you may have here. Other officers will do the same with your home. I am not here to be pissed about, Mr Manson!'

Manson got up from his chair, went to a filing cabinet and opened the bottom drawer, from which he took a box file, simply marked, VF. He handed it to Sep who took it and said, in the same aggressive voice;

'I assume you have this on your computer.'

'Yes, I also have it on this memory stick.' He took a memory stick from the box and gave it to Sep.

'Bring it up on the computer and put another memory stick in.'

Sep went around to Manson's side of the desk as Manson brought up a file entitled VF Portfolio.

'Scroll down it all.'

Manson did as instructed. There were sixteen properties on the file, on which had been scanned all the title deeds and associated contracts and paperwork.

'Is this up-to-date?'

'Yes it is.'

'Because if it isn't, any deal you and I have is terminated.'

'It's up-to-date. This is all he has.'

'Save it on the other stick while I watch.'

Two minutes later, Manson unplugged the memory stick and gave it to Sep, who now had a box file and two memory sticks containing details of all Formosa's Manson Estates property.

'Right. If the children are found on any of these properties, our deal is terminated, as is your future. So, I'll ask you for one last time. Are the children on any of these properties?'

'No.'

Sep stared at him, trying to glean the truth from his eyes. He decided this man wasn't lying.

'Does he have any property other than these?'

'Possibly. These are all the properties he has given me to handle. I believe he has property in London which is handled by a London estate agent.'

'Whose name is?'

'Peter Hamilton.'

'Do you have his details?'

'Yes.'

Manson opened a drawer in his desk, took out a file from which he produced a complimentary slip from the London agent, which he gave to Sep, who glanced at it, then back at Manson, his aggressive manner still in place.

'I assume it was you who advised Formosa to buy the land off Strathmore for a knock-down price?'

'It was me who told him about it and what potential it had, but I didn't advise him to kidnap Strathmore's children so he could get the land almost for nothing.'

'So Formosa always pays the market price for his properties, does he?'

Manson hesitated before answering. Sep jumped in. 'He doesn't, does he? I want a list of all the dealings you think might have been done using strong-arm methods.'

Manson stared at him with frightened eyes. 'You've just asked me to sign my own death warrant.'

'It's information that won't be used until *after* he's arrested and safely locked away. Once he's arrested we'll freeze off all his assets and once he's convicted we will strip him of every penny he has. He'll be the poorest man on the wing. Money is power to an imprisoned man and he'll have none of either.'

Sep got to his feet and handed Manson a small mobile phone and its charger.

'You will keep this on you at all times. It is only for you to receive calls from me. Always keep it charged. My caller name will be J Lennon, just like the late Beatle. I will contact you, as and when I need you. Answer the phone the instant my name comes up on the screen. I do not want to hear any automated voices telling me I can't speak to you. And remember, the more you cooperate with us, the brighter your future.'

He turned to go, then he hesitated and turned back, saying, 'You might be tempted to tell Formosa all about my visit in the foolish hope that he'll somehow be the one to keep you out of prison. Of course that's up to you, but you've just confessed to me that you were involved in the abduction. That alone will send you down, no matter what Formosa does to protect you.'

'I could simply deny I said any such thing to you,' Manson blurted.

'No you couldn't.'

Sep reached up to his lapel and, among all his lapel badges, he pulled out what looked like a tiny camera lens which he showed to Manson. Then he opened his coat to display a wire running down his shirt and into his trouser pocket. 'You can deny it all you like, I've got your confession on video – sound and vision. You're on my side now, you piece of shit, whether you like it or not.'

'I didn't say I *would* deny it, I just said I could,' said Manson.

'And now you know you can't.'

'Yes – now I know I can't.'

'And don't forget the list of his strong-arm dealings I asked you for. I want financial details, names and dates. I'll call back later to pick it up. I should get it done now if I were you, with me being an impatient man.'

Sep left the office and walked to his bicycle, pulling the wire from his trouser pocket. It was a good idea he'd had to video his interview with Manson but, in view of the fact that he didn't have the right equipment at such short notice, it was a better idea just to fool Manson with a lens from a broken camera and a length of wire leading from behind his lapel to an empty pocket. He made up his mind to buy himself some decent equipment ready for the time when he really needed it. All that was needed right now was for Manson to believe that this undercover policeman had him bang to rights.

Sep put the boxfile into his capacious saddlebag and cycled off. As he rode home he pondered on the balance he'd achieved between the lies and truth he'd told Manson. He had a tried and tested theory; that an alarming truth will always trump a casual lie, especially in a terrified man, but it was very important to get the balance right. Yes, he was happy that he'd got Derek Manson completely fooled.

FORTY-THREE

To say that Cope was apprehensive was an understatement. Being summoned into Formosa's office meant one of two things: a severe bollocking or a particularly dangerous job that no sane man would take on. Or perhaps three things. In certain circumstances it could mean the ultimate punishment and Cope was racking his brains to figure out what he might have done so wrong to merit a bullet. It was at times like this that he wondered if the money he was getting from Formosa was worth it. He tried to keep any timidity out of his brief knock, but he was not so bold as to knock and enter. He knocked three times and waited for Formosa to call out, 'Come.'

The Maltese gangster was sitting behind a desk which dwarfed him. On his face was a look of annoyance, but not with Cope who sat down opposite him.

'What's the problem, Vince?'

'Problem? I'll tell you what problem. Twenty-four hours locked in a police cell was something of a problem.'

'There wasn't much I could do about that, Vince, not without revealing my connection with you. I had to pretend that you being banged up was of no concern to me. You could have pressed charges against Strathmore, you know. He admitted to me that he would have killed you if you didn't tell him where the children are.'

Formosa glared at him. 'Charging the bastard would be a complication I do not need. In fact, I am totally unhappy with this kidnapping business. It is something I will never do again. Violent parents; too many loose ends; too many people knowing my business. These people need to be eliminated.'

'Such as?'

'I sent someone to bring Manson in this morning, but he hadn't gone into work. His wife said he left at the normal time but he did not arrive. My man asked his receptionist if anything unusual had happened and she said no, apart from an odd-looking character who called in to see Manson yesterday. In her opinion he made Manson nervous.'

'What was odd about him?'

'He was some sort of a tramp. A man Manson should have kicked off his premises but he didn't. He took him back into his office. The receptionist mentioned something else as well. She said the man told her that he knew Manson from prison. He said they'd both done time together some years ago.' Formosa looked up at Cope. 'If this is true, I knew nothing about it and I rely on you to vet everyone who works for me.'

'I vet every new man who comes, but Manson was already with you when I arrived here. I assumed he'd been vetted already.'

'It is wrong to assume anything in this business!' snapped Formosa. 'You can vet him now. He gave the receptionist a name – James Lennon.'

'Jam—! Oh shit. I think I know who he is. I have an informer called Jimmy Lennon. He's a Scottish vagrant but he's very useful. Let me ring Manson's receptionist. I need to know if he spoke with a Scottish accent.'

Two minutes later, the receptionist had confirmed that James Lennon spoke with a Scottish accent and that his description fitted Cope's man to a tee. Cope put the phone down and said to Formosa, 'It's definitely him.'

'What the hell was he doing at Manson's place? How would he even know about Manson?'

'I've got no idea. He's a man who gets about a lot and gets to know stuff. He's been quite useful to me.'

'A man who knows too much is not useful to me. It appears he's getting to know things about me and I want him dead. If he's your informer you should be able to get hold of him.'

'I can.'

'Then I want you to bring him back here today. I want him in my furnace by close of business tonight.'

'I'll get him.'

Cope took out his mobile and tapped in the number Sep had given him for Jimmy Lennon. Sep answered in a Scottish accent.

'Aye?'

'Jimmy?'

'Aye.'

'We need to meet.'

Sep knew full well who he was. 'Who are ye?'

'The last time we met I saved your skin in a pimp's cellar.'

'Och aye, inspector. Where'll we meet eh?'

'Where we first met.'

'Jesus, this is all very cloak an' dagger by the way. Am I being paid fer what ye owe me?'

'You are.'

'Guid man, yersel'. Will I see ye there in an hour, eh?'

'Yes. One hour from now – ten o'clock.'

Cope clicked his phone off and looked at Formosa. 'He's

meeting me in an hour. He thinks I'm giving him five hundred. The trick is to get him back here.'

'When he gets here I want him to tell me what went on between him and Manson, who'll be the next to go, and then the Kennedy man. I want all three gone, Lenny. This tramp is just the first. I need to tighten up this organization.'

'What about the kids?'

'I'll let them stay alive for a day or two until I decide. Why not? Hell, they still might be worth a couple of million.'

FORTY-FOUR

Cope was already there when the man he knew as Jimmy Lennon walked in the Horse and Trumpet, ten minutes late. The policeman was sitting by a window with two glasses of beer in front of him, one half drunk. He was not looking forward to being joined by the most unsavoury-looking man in the place. With a small movement of his head he indicated that Sep join him.

'You're late.'

'It's why I never got on in life.'

Cope scowled. 'I got you a pint of bitter.'

'Aye, guid man. Did ye bring me ma five hundred notes?'

'Not with me. You'll have to come with me to get it.'

Sep sat down and picked up the full pint, asking, 'And where will I have te come?'

'To the ex-gratia payments office.'

'Ex-gratia, hey? They have such a place, do they?'

'For larger sums, yes.'

'And what do they call the guy who pays it out, by the way?'

'What do you mean?'

Sep leaned forward so that his words would only be heard by Cope. 'I mean, would his name be Formosa and would he be payin' me out in bullets? Tell me, how did he enjoy his night in a polis cell? It's something he'll need te get used te, by the way.

'Yer see, Mr Cope, I know too much about ye te trust ye. I

know yer in Formosa's pay. I know that Lee Dench grassed Formosa up te ye and I know that's why Dench was killed by two of Formosa's heavies – a black guy called Sharky and an Irishman called Spud. Sharky killed Dench with a shotgun and Spud killed the girl with a handgun – shot her through the mouth then they fucked off back te Hull where they used te live when they was alive.'

Cope's eyes widened in alarm at the mention of these names. Not only the names but their descriptions and details of who killed whom. Apart from him and Vince, no one in the whole Formosa organization was supposed to know the identity of any hitman. It was one of Formosa's golden rules designed more to protect him than the hitmen.

Sep continued: 'I know Jez Copitch had a shoot out wi' Formosa's men and they were all kilt. This was all set up by Formosa himself just te rid himself of excess baggage. I also know that he's got Manson on his hitlist, along with Kevin, the guy who crashed his car into the nanny's car, and of course yer good self. He's clearing the decks is Formosa to prepare for an influx from the Smoke. Have ye no heard he's got men coming up frae London te join him?'

Cope listened to all this with mounting concern. 'Jesus Christ! Where the hell did you get such rubbish?'

'Rubbish is it? Can ye swear hand on heart that Formosa hasnae mentioned he wants rid of Manson? Can ye swear he wasn't the one who got rid of Dench when he grassed Formosa up te ye? And what d'ye think happened te Sharky and Spud, the two guys who did fer Dench and his woman? Why has no one seen them around lately? Tell me, Mr Cope, what makes ye think ye so fuckin' bulletproof. D'ye really think Formosa holds ye in such high regard? Has it ever struck ye how Superintendent Ibbotson can afford a new Lexus every year?'

'What?'

'Aye, yer boss was in Formosa's pay well before ye came on the scene and that makes one too many coppers for Formosa's liking. He's asked ye ter take me back wi' yer so he can take me out, has he not? After which, ye'll go as well. Killin' two turds with one stone, that's how he looks at it.'

Sep was taking wild stabs at what might be the truth but his stabs seemed to be hitting home. The Ibbotson comment was taking it almost too far but it was the one that might tip Cope his way – if he believed it.

He tried another one.

'He's just got back off yet another holiday has Ibbotson, has he not? So where's he been?'

'He went to the Algarve, golfing.'

'No, he went to Monte Carlo, gambling with ten grand of Formosa's money. We both know Ibbotson likes a gamble, do we not?'

'He bets on horses, nothing more.'

Cope had heard rumours of the superintendent's gambling, but Sep's knowledge ran to a lot more than rumours. This gave him an advantage.

'Five years ago he nearly lost his house and his job in a wee game of poker. It was Formosa who bailed him out. He's been in Formosa's pocket ever since. You, Mr Cope are nothing te Formosa. He gave ye a try and ye've been a waste of his money.'

The gambling story was true. The Formosa connection wasn't, but it was too much of a possibility for Cope just to discount. He took a nervous sip of his drink as he pondered what had been said.

'Why are you telling me all this?'

'I'm tellin' ye because it's true, and I'm tellin' ye because if ye come in wi' me, it could be te the advantage of both of us.'

'What advantage?'

'What's he do with all his bodies?' Sep asked this question very quickly, as a quick question often prompts an instinctive but careless answer, as it did this time.

'He puts them in a furnace . . . shit!'

Sep smiled at him through his whiskers. In those few words Cope had given himself away. The policeman closed his eyes in anger at himself, then he thought for a moment and said. 'OK, you got me there, but why should I believe anything you say?'

'Because the bits yer know about, ye know to be true. The only things yer doubtful about are the things ye don't know about. Me? I know about everything. As far as Formosa's concerned yer a dead man walking, Mr Cope. If I get up from here and leave ye to it, and ye go back te Formosa without me,

I'll guarantee ye'll be dead within a minute ye walk through the door, and burning away in the furnace five minutes after that.'

At that point Sep turned off his Scottish accent and spoke with his own voice. 'As for me I'll shave off my beard and try another way to set the kids free.'

Cope stared at him, trying to place the new voice. 'Have I met you before all this?'

'Yes, you met me in my house. My name is Septimus Black.'

Cope stared at him. 'Bollocks!' he said.

'True,' said Sep. 'You helped lose me my job and lived with my wife for a while until we set you up for her to see what a low-life you really were.'

'Really? Then I can assume you're not here to help me.'

'You can assume that I'm not interested in you. Your punishment awaits you. The only thing you have to decide is how severely you're punished. It will range from dismissal from the force without pension, to a long prison sentence.'

Cope went quiet, absorbing the shock of what he was hearing. There was just too much truth in it for him to dismiss it lightly.

'How come you've got so much influence?' he asked at length.

'Because on the day I was supposed to leave the force to save myself from being punished for killing Johnstone and attacking my wife, I was approached by a covert unit of the West Yorkshire Police Force who have been watching you from the minute you moved up here from the Smoke. They believed my story of being set up for everything and they agreed with my opinion that it was you who set me up. They were briefed by the Met about you being investigated for corruption and saw an opportunity to use you to bring Formosa down. As much as they hate bent cops, they hate the Formosas of this world a lot more.'

Sep had crafted this story very carefully in readiness for such a showdown with Cope. As far as he knew it was flawless. Cope would already know that the Met had been looking at him and he would now know that he was still within their grasp. Sep's story about working for them was also plausible as the Met knew Cope had certain skills in influencing people's opinions – it was the Met who had trained him in this. All Sep knew about him was what he'd learned from his friend down there, but Sep knew how to make a little knowledge go a long way.

'I just asked you how come you've got such influence,' said Cope. 'I'll ask you another question. If I've done all this to you, why would you do me any favours?'

'*I'm* not doing you any favours. This offer comes from the Met, via West Yorkshire Police. I've been instructed to make you take that offer. It was my phone conversation with them that made me late. Ibbotson won't be so fortunate. They're aware of your dealings with Formosa and those of Ibbotson. I answer to a much higher police authority than Ibbotson. So far we've had to tread very carefully, with the lives of the children being at stake but now it's crunch time. The only question that matters is, do you know where the children are?'

'No, I don't.'

'If you did, both our lives would be a lot easier, so I'll ask you one last time, 'Do you know where they are?'

'No, I don't. Never have.'

'Next question then, are you with us or with Formosa? Please bear in mind that Formosa is planning to kill you, and our plan keeps you alive. I've already saved Manson's life by telling him to clear off before Formosa gets to him. I think you know this to be true.'

Cope did indeed know it was true that Manson had cleared off. He also knew that Formosa wanted Manson "eliminated".

'Mr Cope, answer me this: How do you think I know about Sharky and Spud killing Dench, who was killed for grassing Formosa up to you? And how do you think I know that Sharky and Spud are both dead on Formosa's orders?'

Cope shook his head in despair, indicating that he had no idea how Sep had got hold of this impossible information. Sep pressed home his advantage with another credible lie. 'We have Manson in a safe house. We can do the same for you if you cooperate fully.'

A defeated Cope looked up at Sep and asked him. 'OK, what do you want me to do?'

FORTY-FIVE

The children lay on the cold floor in complete darkness in the room next to the one they'd been previously kept in. Milly had been crying ever since she found out they'd been captured again. James was inwardly cursing the man in the house who had sworn at them. If ever they got out, he'd report that man to the police. Their plight now seemed worse than ever. They had angered their captors who, up until their attempted escape, hadn't mistreated them. That had all changed. They had been roughly manhandled from the car, dragged down the cellar steps and thrown into this pitch-black cellar with nothing to lie on and nothing to keep them warm. Their coats were still in the cellar next door.

'My leg hurts, James. It's bleeding, I can feel it.'

'The bleeding will stop, Milly. I've got a few cuts and bruises myself.'

'I feel really poorly.'

'Yeah, so do I. It's this rubbish food they give us. When we get home Mum'll feed us up.'

'I don't like what that man was saying, James. He was talking about coming back and killing us.'

'I know. I heard him but it was just to make us behave, like when he threatened us in the car with his gun.'

James wasn't at all sure this was true. The man had said he was going back to contact his boss and find out what to do with them and that the odds were that his boss would tell him to kill them both to save a lot of trouble, and that they could still get the ransom money even if they were dead. It all seemed to make sense to James, but he didn't tell Milly.

'What if he comes back to kill us, James?'

'He won't, Milly.'

'Promise?'

'I promise.'

They now heard loud voices from above. 'I bet it's that man he was talking to on the phone,' said Milly.

'Could be,' said James, trying to listen. But, although the voices were loud, they were indistinct. It could be that they were arguing about the children escaping and whose fault was that. Then the main cellar door opened, heavy feet clattered down the stone steps and a loud, angry voice was shouting.

'James, it's him!' screamed Milly.

'I know. I can hear him.'

A shot rang out, then another.

'He's mad! He's coming to kill us!'

Milly was screaming with fear. James felt like screaming himself but, in the inky blackness of their prison, he just held on to his sister to offer what comfort he could in their final moments. He began to say the Lord's Prayer. Milly joined in. Both of them praying with eyes tightly shut and streaming tears as the door was kicked open.

James briefly opened his eyes and blinked away the mist of his tears to see a man silhouetted against the light from the passageway behind him. James recognised the silhouette as that of the man who had manhandled them earlier. He knew the man hadn't come to manhandle them this time. This time the man was holding a large gun; this time he'd come to kill them, no doubt about that. James now closed his eyes again as he didn't want to see any more of this horror that was about to befall them both. Milly's eyes remained firmly shut. They clung to each other, praying more quickly now as they wanted to finish their prayer before this man killed them.

FORTY-SIX

Formosa looked up as Cope came through the door with a man who had to be Jimmy Lennon. Opposite him were two chairs. He signalled his two visitors to sit in them. Cope sat down, but Sep just stood there.

'Do you have a problem, Mr Lennon?' asked Formosa.

'I do,' said Sep, but not in his Scottish accent. He took a handgun from his pocket and pointed it at Formosa. 'My problem is you.'

Formosa wasn't fazed by the gun. He had one of his own in an open drawer in front of him. Sep kept his gun trained on Formosa's face as he rounded the desk, kicked the drawer shut with the underside of his foot and spat out a harsh order.

'Get up, Formosa, you piece of shit!'

Suitably intimidated, Formosa got to his feet.

'Now walk around the desk and sit next to that crooked cop.'

Formosa complied. Sep sat in the chair Formosa just vacated, with his forearm resting on the desk and the gun pointing at Formosa's face.

'He was expecting my call, Vince,' said Cope.

'What I wasn't expecting,' said Sep to Formosa, 'was to hear from the crooked cop that he was going to pay me money in one hour. Took me by surprise that. So much so that I rang up Manson's, only to find him gone and his girl wondering why so many people were interested in him and the visitor he had yesterday.'

'Who are you?' asked Formosa, belligerently. 'You do know I have men in this building who will come running if they hear a shot they're not expecting.'

'I know there is no one in this building but the three of us,' said Sep. 'Now I want you to tell me where the children are or I will shoot you.'

'You won't shoot me,' sneered Formosa.

'I will, actually,' said Sep, 'but it might not be necessary if the crooked cop gives me the right answer.'

'I don't know where they are,' said Cope.

'Cope,' said Sep, 'I figure you to be number two in this organization which means you must know where they are. I'm going to count down from three and put a bullet in your heart if you don't tell me before then.'

He took careful aim at Cope's heart and counted. Formosa maintained his sneer. 'Three . . . two . . . one . . .'

Sep pulled the trigger. Bang! Blood spurted from Cope's chest as both he and his chair fell backwards to the floor. Formosa looked down at him and at the blood staining his shirt, then back at this lunatic who had shot him dead so casually.

'Well, he's dead,' said Sep, with an air of casual indifference that unnerved Formosa. 'Just you left. I assume I can stick him in your furnace.'

The gang boss was sweating now and wondering how the hell this madman knew about his furnace.

'Out of interest, how many bodies have you burned in your furnace?'

'A lot.'

'Thought so. OK, Mr Formosa, where are the children?'

'If I tell you, how do I know you won't shoot me?' said Formosa.

'Because Cope did me a lot of personal damage, but I have no such problem with you. You are just a means to an end.'

'I'm guessing you're working for Strathmore not the police,' said Formosa.

'Of course I am. Your man Cope did me too much damage with the police, no doubt with your help. I was always going to kill him.'

'Who exactly are you?'

'My name is Septimus Black.'

'Ah, the disgraced copper who beats up his wife.'

'I was kicked off the force for killing a paedophile who died from an epileptic fit, but your man blackened my name too much for me to keep my job, especially after he beat up my wife and got her to say it was me. Was that your idea as well?'

'No, that was all his own idea. So, how do you want to play this?'

'All I want is the reward money for the kids. If I get the kids you get your life, simple as that. If the kids are dead, so are you. So there's no point lying to me, you'll only prolong the agony. If they're dead tell me and I'll pull this trigger, stick you in your furnace too, job done. I'll be happy just having dealt with Cope.' He aimed the gun at Formosa's forehead, as if in readiness to shoot.

'I'm not waiting all day,' he said, harshly. Sep allowed his finger to tighten on the trigger just enough for Formosa to notice it.

'They're alive,' said Formosa, quickly.

'You don't sound too sure.'

Sep tried to detect a lie in this man's eyes and he saw nothing. He remembered Winnie's description of him. "Eyes like a shithouse rat".

'They were alive the last time I saw them. Who knows what stupid men will do behind my back?'

'How far away?'

'Ten minutes in a car.'

'That might be how long you have to live if you're telling me a lie.'

'How do I know you won't kill me anyway?'

Sep laughed. 'Put it this way. You've got more chance of living than those kids ever had. Even if the ransom had been paid, you'd have killed them.' He fired a shot that almost took off Formosa's left ear before burying itself deep in the door.

'OK, you piece of slime, it's crunch time. Where are they?'

'Do I get to go free?'

'What you get is a head start, but you'll definitely need your passport, and you'll need to be in a hurry.'

'Why would you do this for me?'

'Just think, man! I've just killed a cop. I'm not doing anything for you, I'm doing all this for me. Do you think I want to get involved with the cops any more than you do? The second I'm told the kids have been found, I'm out of here to collect my reward and you can make your own arrangements. Your future is of no interest to me.'

Formosa nodded. It kind of made sense. Sep knew it needed to make some kind of sense. 'OK,' said Formosa, who could foresee an opportunity for revenge on this man, maybe even forestall him in his planned escape. 'I'll tell you. The kids are in the cellar of a derelict church hall I own in East End Park. Number 18 Cross Park Terrace.'

'Any of your people with them?'

'One, maybe two.'

'If this isn't true I won't piss about, I'll instantly kill you. I want you to understand that.'

'I understand.'

'No second chances if this is a lie. If it's the truth, who knows?'

'How do you mean – Who knows? You said you wouldn't kill me if I told the truth.'

Sep snarled at him. 'I'm not sure you have told me the truth, and I'd certainly enjoy pulling this trigger on you. You're a useless slimeball who inflicts pain and cruelty and misery on this world for your own gain. It might be too much of a temptation to resist!'

'But—'

'Just shut the fuck up!' roared Sep, thrusting his gun forward and allowing it to appear as if his finger was tightening on the trigger – a trick he'd taught himself many years back. He adjusted his aim slightly and fired another shot that missed Formosa's head by a fraction of an inch, leaving the gang boss wide-eyed and shivering with shock and terror. Beads of sweat had appeared on his brow. He held his shaking hands up and was having trouble keeping them still and Sep knew from the fear in his eyes that the man was telling the truth. It was probably the first time in his life that Formosa had been subjected to such terror.

Sep took out his phone and called Fiona. '18 Cross Park Terrace, East End Park in the cellar of an old church hall. Probably two armed men there. Take an armed response unit and go in heavy-handed. I'm at the address I gave you. I assume you've got a unit ready to come in here as well . . . Good, I've got them covered.'

Formosa screamed at him. 'You're supposed to let me go free.'

'Free? Did I say that? No, I meant I'd let you live.'

'You bastard! You'll get life for killing a copper.'

'No I won't – get up Cope.'

Cope got to his feet to face Formosa's wrath. Sep fired again. This bullet just whistled past the gangster's nose. 'I only put one blank in the gun. Sit down, Vincent. If you try to run I'll put the next one through your knee. I'll definitely enjoy that.'

Formosa sat down, glaring at Cope who looked anywhere but at him. 'The blood came from an exploding capsule,' Sep explained, as if to pass the time. He knew a casual conversation wouldn't interest Formosa, it would just annoy him, and Sep liked annoying such people.

'I worked it by remote, but I did need Inspector Cope's full cooperation of course. After finding out what I have on him, he's turning Queen's Evidence in return for leniency, although I did record all our conversation just now, including how you burned a lot of bodies in your furnace. It's not all bad news, though.'

Formosa glared at him.

'I assume you want to hear my good news,' said Sep. 'I should get my job back. Might even get it back with a promotion to compensate me for all my troubles. They'll *need* me back of course, with Mr Cope having to leave suddenly. Come on, you've got to be happy for me, Mr Formosa.'

'Hang on. You're not a copper. You can't arrest me.'

'Of course I can, I can make a citizen's arrest and hold you until the proper coppers get here. And when they do get here and arrest you, that's when all your assets are frozen pending the courts taking everything off you and they'll hold it until the proceeds of crime guys get working on you. Hey, compared to you, Mr Formosa, Jimmy Lennon's a billionaire.'

FORTY-SEVEN

Ten minutes passed in relative silence, broken only by the occasional cursed threat from Formosa to Cope, who was feeling very sorry for himself. He was now totally unsure if he'd done the right thing, going along with this man, whose house he'd been living in, whose wife he'd been sleeping with, and whose life he'd all but destroyed. But it was all too late now, he must hope for the best and place his trust in this man. Sep read his thoughts.

'You're wondering if you've done the right thing?'

Cope shrugged. Sep turned his attention to Formosa. 'Tell me, Vincent, if I hadn't twigged your game, would Cope here have lived much longer than me?'

'Maybe five minutes longer.'

'Honesty at last,' said Sep, still pointing the gun at Formosa. He swapped hands.

'My right hand was getting tired,' he explained. 'When your hand gets tired you instinctively tighten your grip which often ends up with you firing off a shot. Did you know that, Vincent?'

Sep's mobile rang. With his free hand he switched it on.
'. . . Really? . . . Excellent. How are they? . . . Well that's
only to be expected . . . Yeah, come in now.'

He turned his phone off and smiled at Formosa. 'It would
seem you've been having severe attacks of honesty, Mr Formosa.
The children were where you said they were. Two men arrested
and on their way to the clink; two children freed and on their
way home.'

'It's a pity *you* haven't been having an attack of honesty,'
grunted Formosa.

'I know and I do apologize but I find that dealing with lowlife
and being honest never work together.' He looked at Cope and
added, 'and I look upon you as lowlife, Cope, which means I
haven't been exactly honest about what will happen to you. The
truth is I've got no influence whatsoever, not with anyone. They
don't need your Queen's Evidence, they've got you bang to rights
as it is, apparently. I'm guessing you'll be an old man when you
get out. Mind you, Formosa here will die in prison as an old and
useless lag, so it could be worse.' Sep smiled at Cope as he
added, 'You made a big mistake when you tried to destroy my
life, you should have left me well alone and I wouldn't have
come after you. Hey, remember when I said I'd catch up with
you? Well, consider yourself caught.'

Cope's eyes bulged, his face reddened and he looked to be
about to explode with rage. Sep pointed the gun at him to calm
him down but Cope ignored it, got up from his chair and
approached Sep as if to attack him, which would have been
awkward. Shooting him would complicate the situation no end.
Shit! Why did he have to rile the man?

Then, as if on cue, the door was kicked open and four armed
officers burst in, followed by Fiona who looked at Sep's gun,
raised a censorious eyebrow and shook her head. Sep was sticking
it in his pocket as she said to him, 'The children will be on their
way home by now. I've already notified Mr Strathmore in hospital
of your part in this. He's delighted, as is the superintendent,
although the super does have one or two things he needs to talk
to you about.'

FORTY-EIGHT

4 July

Juliet Strathmore was looking in the mirror and she didn't recognize what she saw. The face looking back at her from the glass was a stranger's face. She scarcely remembered the beautiful woman who used to look back at her. Her blond hair was mousy and dank, her skin sallow, her blue eyes empty of life and surrounded by dark rings. The emptiness inside her was giving her constant nausea. She wanted to throw up but had nothing to throw. She had sores at the sides of her mouth that she'd been told were caused by lack of vitamins, but the only thing she lacked were her babies. She didn't care about vitamins or skin or hair or eyes. She didn't even care about her husband who, she'd been told, was in hospital after attacking Formosa.

'Did he get my babies back?'

'No.'

'Oh.'

'Would you like to visit Peter?'

'No.'

It was a large mirror in the hallway of their house in Harrogate. She'd returned there that morning after spending some time in hospital recovering from the overdose. She wasn't really aware that she'd taken an overdose; she was only aware that her children had been taken from her life, and her children *were* her life. The mirror went from head-height down to the floor. It had been designed by at interior decorator who said it would reflect the light coming through the windows on either side of the front door and light up a dark corner of the spacious hallway. But Juliet wasn't interested in light. Her world of choice was cheerless and dark. She didn't deserve any better because it was probably the same world as her babies were living in – that's if they were still alive. And that was the deep cut; not knowing if her babies were dead or alive, not knowing if they had been murdered by these vile people, and if they had, what sort of terror had they been through in their final hours. She lived in a world of the deepest sorrow, emptiness and fear and dread – the dread that came when yet another police car arrived because this one might be bringing the news that her babies were dead and if that happened she might as well be dead.

'You really need to eat something,' her sister was telling her. 'You need to keep your strength up for when the children come back.'

But this desperate optimism was now falling on rocky ground. Juliet had heard it so often she knew it for what it was. Eliza was ten years younger than Juliet, and had once been given the same treatment by her big sister that Juliet gave to her children.

'All you've done is sip tea and nibble at biscuits. At least take some of these multi-vitamins. Two a day is all you need.'

Juliet could see her sister standing behind her. Through the mirror she could see the reflection of her whole desolate world. Just her and her sister. She loved her husband but he didn't need her love right now. He was big and tough and he was kind to her and he loved her, but she blamed him for allowing their children to be taken. And now he'd gone off to beat up the man who had taken them, and he had failed at that – failed her and their children. Jesus! He was a bloody useless man at times!

'Peter will be in hospital about a week,' Eliza had told her, but it didn't register. Eliza was there to replace Peter as Juliet's guardian. She was never to be left alone. Eliza even slept in a spare bed in the same room as her sister. The sisters' parents lived in Australia and were standing by the phone awaiting a call to come through from England. They had wanted to come over but Peter had put them off that idea. He had enough to cope with looking after Juliet without her parents adding to the problem. Eliza kept them up-to-date with events, such as they were. She was bright and practical and, if anything, could lift Juliet's spirits far better than Peter could. She was also beautiful, just like her big sister.

As Juliet stood there she wanted to scream away all her fears and her sorrow. She wanted to scream at the mirror until it cracked and disintegrated just as she wanted her fears and sorrows to disintegrate. But she had no screams left in her, no tears left, no voice, nothing with which to vent her complete desolation.

To cap it all, she had been seeing things. A face in a window of a grandfather now long dead. She'd been talking to him, asking him if he knew where her babies were when Peter had come into the room and asked who she was talking to. Her grandfather faded away and she blamed Peter for that.

'I was talking to my granddad to see if he knew where the children are. You spoiled it.'

'Sorry – maybe if I go out he'll come back.'

'No, he won't come back, he never liked you.'

What she didn't realize was that Peter was just as distraught over the abduction of their children as she was, only he had to hold things together for her sake. Not now, though; sometimes he needed to relax his hold.

'For God's sake, Juliet, you're not talking to anyone. You're seeing things!'

'Am I?'

'Yes . . . I'm sorry but you are, and for your information I got on very well with your granddad!'

This was why she didn't believe what she was seeing just after Eliza went off to make a cup of tea. She saw the reflection of two children standing in the doorway – holding hands. Juliet froze, trying to hold the image before it faded away. They looked familiar: albeit emaciated, unwashed, with dirty, untidy hair, scabs here and there – a couple of real tykes, but they looked very much like her babies. She spoke to them in the mirror, not daring to turn around lest they disappear.

'Are you . . . my children?'

They didn't fully understand her question.

'Hi, Mum!'

James's voice had her turning round. Yes, they were still there and they were smiling at her. No mistaking those smiles. Eliza appeared and screamed with shock and delight. Juliet looked at her sister and asked, 'Can . . . c . . . can you see them?'

'Of course I can see them!'

'Are they my babies?'

'Of course they are. It's James and Milly. They're back, Juliet!'

Juliet was now shaking with shock, but a kind of shock she

had never experienced before. This was unbelievable news shock. Long-gone tears now made a reappearance. Her mouth quivered as she made her way towards them, her steps unsteady, feeling faint. Eliza saw the problem, stepped forward to help her sister and sat her on a chair.

'We're scruffy because we've been kidnapped,' said James.

'We know that,' said Eliza.

'And we pong a bit,' said Milly.

'We pong a lot,' said James. 'Some policemen came and got us out. I thought I saw a man coming to kill us but it was a copper with a gun.'

'Oh you poor, poor darlings,' wept their mother.

'I bet Dad's a bit poorer now,' said James. 'Did he pay them a load of dosh?'

'Yeah, how much did we cost him?' asked Milly, eager to know their value. 'I bet it was a million.'

'I bet it was more,' said James.

Dumbstruck, her lips quivering, Juliet took her daughter in her arms and knew that she was real, not a mirage. Here was her daughter and there was her son. A bit worse for wear but she'd got her babies back – and James was right, they did pong.

Two policewomen appeared in the doorway. They had sent the children in first to give their mother a nice surprise. They were now concerned that it might have been a bad idea. It appeared that the mother was in shock.

'No money was paid,' called out one of them, in an effort to alleviate this delirious trauma they'd imposed on Juliet. 'The kidnapper and his gang have been arrested. The children have had a hard time, I'm afraid.'

'Oh thank you, thank you, thank you.' Juliet was now holding on to both of her children.

'Does their father know?' asked Eliza.

'He should be finding out round about now.'

Juliet's face was contorted with confusion. Her bleak world had spun around in the space of a minute. The sun had come out from behind a black cloud and she was ill-prepared for this sudden sunshine. She looked up at the two policewomen. 'Please, I . . . I've got my babies back. I don't know what to do . . . *Have* I got them back?'

'Yes, Mrs Strathmore, of course you have.'

'Mum, we're not babies,' said James.

'Of course you're not, darling.' To the officers she said, 'I er . . . I'd like my husband here. Can you bring him here, please? He's in hospital but I think he'll want to be here.'

'It might be as well to take you and the children to him. They need to be checked over in a hospital. In fact they're not in the best of health so they might have to stay there for a time.'

'Oh,' said Juliet, still unsure of how much authority she had in all this. 'Can I come with them, please?'

'We insist on it. If they're kept in you'll be able to stay with them.'

'Thank you. I think they'll both need a shower first, and some clean clothes.'

'We really need to take them as they are, Mrs Strathmore, so that our FME can make an assessment of their treatment at the hands of the kidnappers. They'll have to be photographed as well, but by all means bring spare clothes. They can shower and dress in the hospital.'

'Am I allowed to feed them?'

'Of course you are.'

'Fish and chips,' said James.

'And scraps,' added Milly.

'I'll nip out to the chippy and get us all some,' said Eliza. She looked around at everybody. 'Fish and chips six times?'

Six nods.

'Don't forget my scraps,' said Milly. 'I need building up.'

'I'll ring the hospital and make the arrangements,' said the police officer.

'Have I really got my babies back?' said Juliet.

'We're not babies, Mum,' said James. 'Not any more.'

EPILOGUE

Sep stood on the door step, making no move to go through the door his wife had just opened to his knock.

'I won't come in, Rachel.'

'Too right you won't come in. This is my house, or it will be when our divorce comes through.'

Sep had made a point of visiting the hair solutions man before he paid this visit to his wife. He was wearing a new blazer he'd just bought from Marks and Spencer along with appropriate trousers, shirt and tie. Sep was looking respectable, some might say handsome – at a stretch. Jimmy Lennon was history. Behind him he had parked his other recent acquisition, a gleaming one year old, Jaguar XK in bright red, the same colour as his beloved Audi. He had told himself that he wasn't presenting himself to her at his best to show her what she was missing – but he hadn't convinced himself.

'I think,' he said, 'that you'll find there's a bit of a snag with that. In fact, the house might end up all mine.'

'What are you talking about?'

'Well, your ex-boyfriend has been arrested for perverting the course of justice, among many other things. He was involved in the kidnapping of the Strathmore children and he was in the pocket of one of the biggest gangsters in Yorkshire.'

'You mean Lenny Cope?'

'Who else? He'll go down for ten years – if he's lucky.'

Phoebe came to the door and stood behind her mother with bitterness in her eyes, which Sep couldn't help but notice.

'Why the nasty look, Phoebe?'

'It's because I'll never forgive you for hurting Mummy.'

'But I *didn't* hurt Mummy, darling. I'm afraid that was something Mummy cooked up with Lenny. It was Lenny who hurt her just to blame it on me.' He returned his attention to his wife. 'He's admitted it, Rachel. In fact it's the least of his worries. I'm just curious as to why you went along with it.'

'Is this true, Mummy?'

Rachel didn't answer because she had no answer. 'Yes, it's true,' said Sep,' and I'm not too impressed with you, young lady, in believing I could do such a nasty thing. Perhaps your mother can explain to you why she did it.'

'Leave her out of this,' said Rachel.

'Why? *You* didn't leave her out of it. *You* made her believe I beat you up.'

Rachel glared at him. 'What's this nonsense about the snag with the divorce and you getting the house?'

Sep gave a shrug. 'Well, in the divorce papers you swore an affidavit saying I assaulted you, which wasn't true, and which means you committed perjury. So you could go to jail for perjury and I could end up with the house.'

'What?' screamed Phoebe. 'Daddy, you can't send Mummy to jail!'

'He's talking nonsense, darling, as usual.'

'I'm not, actually, as you well know. Phoebe, it was Lenny Cope who gave your mummy all those nasty bruises, darling. He's admitted to beating her and persuading her to blame it on me. And Mummy told a lie on what's called an oath, which is a very naughty lie in the eyes of the law.'

'I don't want Mummy to go to jail.'

'Well, Mummy shouldn't have told such horrible lies about me, Phoebe. She made you hate me, didn't she?'

'I bet *you* could stop Mummy going to jail.'

'Maybe I could, I don't know.'

From one step below her, Sep looked up at his wife. Her good looks were turning on her, turning her into something hard. Perhaps her face was punishing her for her behaviour towards him, or was that just wishful thinking? He had no means of punishing her without hurting Phoebe. In fact he knew he'd do his damnedest to get Rachel off a perjury charge.

He wondered if he had ever loved her, or had he simply been in love with her good looks and the easy sex she put his way before they were married? He wouldn't be the first young man to fall for that. Then the sex dried up and all he was left with was her. It was Phoebe who'd kept him at home. But none of this explained why she'd lied about him hitting her . . . unless. Oh, God you're so thick, Sep Black! Of course that's why.

'Rachel, I didn't think things were so bad between us for you to do that to me. Why did you do it? Was it because he was a posh cop from London who promised you a better life? You turn up at the station with a battered face and blame me so my colleagues would turn on me. That MP dying at my hands must have been a real bonus for you and Cope. Dead MP and a battered wife. Game set and match to you two, eh?'

The expression on her face told him he was near the truth. For Phoebe's sake he kept his voice low and restrained. Just a man having an everyday conversation with his wife.

'I'm right, aren't I? Rachel, he didn't want you. All he was doing was trying to destroy my good reputation because I knew how corrupt he was, and I was telling everybody down at the nick about him. They all fell for *his* story because he was trained in that sort of propaganda, and so did you, but I'm married to you so I was entitled to expect better from you. Now you're about to end up with an ex-husband who wants nothing to do with you and an ex-boyfriend whose about to do very serious time for abducting children – among many other pending charges.'

Phoebe smiled up at him. 'You said you'd catch up with him, Daddy, I remember you saying that.'

'Do you, darling? I'm glad you remember that.'

Rachel burst into tears, turned and ran into the house. Sep looked at his daughter and said, 'Your mummy's been very silly darling. Sometimes grown-ups do silly things that can never be explained, but if she ever explains it to you, perhaps you'll explain it to me.'

'Daddy, are you going to stop being my daddy?'

'What? Never in a million years. I'll always be your daddy and I'll be there whenever you need me and if I do end up with the house, you and Mummy will always be able to live here, although I'll decide who else gets to live here – and it won't be the likes of Lenny Cope.'

'I didn't much like him, Daddy. Please don't let them send Mummy to jail.'

'I'll do what I can, Phoebe.'

Phoebe summoned up a tearful smile. 'That means you *will* do it. I love you, Daddy.'

'Well, that's probably all I came to hear. I love you, Phoebe. Bye darling, take care of your mummy, she'll need you.'

The faces of James and Milly stared out at Charlie Bickerdike as he picked up his Yorkshire Evening Post. Where the hell had he seen them before? He'd been wondering what all the police commotion in his street had been about, with them taping off the old church hall across the road. He hadn't asked them; associating with the police had never done him any good. Then he read the names, James and Millicent Strathmore . . . Strathmore? Where had he heard that name before? Jesus! It was them two scruffy tykes who'd come knocking at his door the other night. They said they'd been kidnapped or some such bollocks, and here it says they *had* been kidnapped and there'd been a reward out for anyone helping find them. Twenty five thousand pound reward, and he could have had it. There was a knock at his door. He went to open it, this time deciding he'd be more civil. It was a young woman, smartly dressed and smiling.

'Mr Charles Bickerdike?'

'That's me, who are you?'

'My name is Suzanne Hogan, I'm with the *Daily Mail* and I wonder if I might ask you a few questions about the Strathmore children who were kidnapped and held in the church hall cellar over there.'

'Why should I know anything?'

'Well . . . this is number 17, isn't it?'

'It is.'

'Good, according to the children they actually escaped from the church hall and were recaptured by their kidnappers, but before this happened they knocked on your door and asked for help.'

'They didn't ask for anything.'

'Did they tell you who they were?'

'Mebbe . . . an' some nonsense about bein' kidnapped.'

'They said that, rather than help them, you swore at them and you shut the door on them. I'm just wondering why you did that, considering there was a twenty five thousand pound reward, which would have been yours.'

'Same reason as I'm shuttin' the fuckin' door on you, love.'

As the door slammed in her face Suzanne stood there and smiled at the number 17. 'I trust I can quote you on that, Mr Bickerdike.'

A police car pulled up alongside her and a uniformed sergeant got out. 'You the papers?' he asked.

'Yes. *Daily Mail.*'

'Have you just talked to him?'

'Well it wasn't much of a talk, but yes. His name's Bickerdike.'

'We know that. I think I'll see what Mr Bickerdike's got to say for himself.'

'Oh, good. I'll listen in, if I may.'

The sergeant shrugged, 'Suit yourself. I just want to give him a good bollocking. Two kiddies in obvious distress come knocking on his door needing help and he slams it on 'em.'

'Is he known to you?'

'Yes, he's what you might call a recidivist – if you can spell it.'

Suzanne had already written the word down in shorthand. This was an angle that would give her story even more human interest than it had already. Readers loved to hate the Mr Bickerdikes of this world. The man might end up having to move out of the street, but what the hell? It was no more than he deserved.

There was a rare knock on Sep's door. It could have been a meter reader or someone trying to sell him something, but it wasn't.

'I came to see Jimmy Lennon. Is he not at home?'

'Never heard of him.'

'How're the hell are you doin', Septimus? You're certainly looking smart, without all that hair. Clean shirt as well.'

'I'm doing OK, Winifred.'

'Gotcha job back?'

'Not yet. I'm due to see the super tomorrow.'

'Divorced yet?'

'Nope.'

'So you're still married to that liar and you still haven't got a job. How come you're doin' OK?'

'My daughter loves me, I'm still alive, I've got my reputation back, I've got my bike back, I'm allowed back in the Sword and Slingshot and I've been paid for my private-eye services.'

'Strathmore paid up?'

'He insisted on it. In fact I qualified for the twenty five thousand pound reward as well – me being a civilian. I put that towards my new car.'

'*Towards* it?' She jabbed a thumb over her shoulder at the Jaguar. 'Is that it?'

'Yes.'

'I thought it looked out of place in this street.'

'This street's OK, anyway, I won't be here much longer.'

'It's a smart-looking machine. You bought it brand new?'

'Not quite – it just looks new. And before you say anything, I got myself a seriously good deal, paid in full, cash money, much haggling.'

'Did you threaten them with anything?'

Sep pulled a sad face and shook his head. 'Nah, they're a respectable dealership. I had nothing to work with.'

'That's what you get when you deal with respectable people.' She turned to look at it. 'Wow! You really like your self-esteem.'

'Winnie, I really like that car.'

'So do I. Can I have a drive in it – with the hood down? I might get one myself.'

'Why, have you come into money?'

'Not yet, but I'm about to. I'm selling my story about Cyril Johnstone to the papers. I tracked down those two girls you told me about and they're happy to talk to the press. I think they're gonna make a big deal of it. Am I still not allowed to mention your name?'

'Best not. I haven't got my job back yet.'

'Sep, when you get your divorce, would you marry me?'

'If you're going to propose to me, you'd better come in.'

She followed him inside. 'Well, at least you didn't say no. I own my own house, no mortgage or anything. Did you know that?'

'No, I didn't.'

'And I'm currently free of all sexually transmitted diseases.'

'Winnie, your proposal is damn near irresistible – if only you owned a brewery.'

'Well, what do you say?'

'Winnie, tomorrow I'm applying to get my job back as detective inspector. I don't wish to be indelicate but I will have to divulge all my personal details which will include my pending divorce. Now, if I divulge that I intend marrying a former prostitute, how do think that will go down with the West Yorkshire Police? Do you think that will persuade them to have me back?'

'There's no need to tell them, surely.'

'Not tell them what? Not tell them I'm getting married or not tell them I'm marrying an offender with assault and prostitution on her charge sheet?'

'Do you have to keep saying that word, Sep? I haven't done any of that stuff for years and even then I was only part-time – as and when I was skint, and I never worked the streets. Upper end of the market, selected clients.'

'That's right, you worked in Henrietta's Whorehouse.'

'There you go again. That was a name the police gave the place. It was actually very well appointed inside and was just called Henrietta's to the clients. All I ever did was to avail myself of her business facilities from time to time.'

'I'm guessing it paid for this house you own.'

'Do me a favour. What I made doing that wouldn't have bought me the garden shed. The house came from a husband of mine who died.'

'I didn't know that. Sorry to hear it.'

'Don't be.' Winnie took out her pipe and proceeded to load it with tobacco. 'He got drunk one Christmas Eve and walked under a bus. The mortgage was paid off by his insurers and I ended up with the house. I was twenty-three, he was forty-three and he treated me badly.' She lit her pipe, blew out two smoke rings and added, 'Best Christmas present I've ever had.'

'I've never known anyone who could blow smoke rings with a pipe.'

'It takes years of practice. Oh, and I've got an apartment in Benidorm, courtesy of one of my clients.'

'What? A punter left you an apartment in his will?'

'Yeah, they've got to leave their stuff to someone – and he wasn't even a proper client, just an old man who needed a young woman to stroke his head and talk to him now and again. I was very good at that. So, what do you say?'

'Winnie, I'm not sure that being your husband's a smart career move. Look, it's not what you've been, it's that I don't want to jump out of the frying pan into the fire.'

'So I'm the fire am I?'

Sep grinned, 'You're certainly fiery.'

'Maybe I can just stay the night with you from time to time, and you can stay with me. You know, avail ourselves of each other, as and when the need arises.'

'Sounds like a good arrangement,' said Sep. 'We can start right now if you like.'

'Right now I'm going to see my bank about buying a brewery, and I'm going in a flash Jaguar just to impress him.'

'Formosa's denying everything,' said Superintendent Ibbotson.

Sep was in his office having officially applied for reinstatement as a DI, but Ibbotson seemed more interested in the Formosa case, which still might hold problems for Sep.

'He told me where the children were, sir. Isn't that enough?'

'You'd think so, Black, but the CPS are scared of this top barrister he's got. We've only got your word that Formosa told you.'

'What about Cope's word? He was there.'

'The defence will try to brand ex-Inspector Cope as an unreliable witness, with him admitting to being in Formosa's pay.'

'But that means everyone who turns Queen's Evidence is unreliable.'

'Some of them are, and Formosa's brief is just arguing on one particular point – the point where Formosa told you where the children were. It's Formosa's word against your word and Cope's, and neither of you have got great track records.'

'Unlike Formosa's great track record.'

'I know, I know. But we need to nail him properly, once and for all. He's also saying you threatened him with a gun and even fired off a couple of shots. Being in unlawful possession of a firearm might well render your evidence as unreliable. The forensic people have dug out two bullets and found a couple of casings on the floor.'

Sep was mentally kicking himself for not picking up the casings. 'I did what I had to do to get the children free, sir, and I used Cope as part of my subterfuge.'

'Subterfuge? You must tell me more about this subterfuge.'

'Well, as you may know, sir, when faced with a stubborn miscreant I often stretch the truth to scare the real truth out of them.'

'Yes, I'm aware it's one of your interview techniques.'

'How are the children, by the way, sir?'

'As well as can be expected. They were interviewed in some depth and it appears that the boy is some sort of a hero – certainly to his sister. He helped them both escape and it would have worked had it not been for some old scrote whose door they knocked on for help and had it slammed in their faces.'

'So the end justified the, er, the unconventional means I was forced to employ, sir – and in this case, the end was saving the lives of those children.'

'And a payment of one hundred thousand pounds to you. The CPS know all about that too.'

'It was actually a hundred and twenty five thousand, but the CPS probably know I risked my life doing it.'

'Well, they might wonder about your sanity in doing such a thing.'

'I wasn't working simply for the money, sir. I saw a way of frightening the truth out of him and I took it. It wasn't something I could have done had I still been a policeman.'

'No? Please explain.'

'Before I do, sir, I would need to request immunity from prosecution regarding my unlawful use of a firearm.'

'Really? And why would the CPS grant you that?'

'Because I have video evidence of Formosa's confession, sir.'

Ibbotson's eyebrows shot up in surprise. 'Video evidence? Why the bloody hell haven't you told me that before?'

'Because I'm behind the camera firing an illegal gun.'

'Ah.'

'I hoped we might have enough on him without it. I threatened him with a gun and I knew it might get me into trouble. Anyway, I videoed it all, and there's no editing. What you see is exactly what happened, including Cope's part in it.'

'And what *was* Cope's part in it?'

'He was Formosa's right-hand man. I told him I had enough evidence against him to send him down if he didn't cooperate with me against Formosa. He agreed and it worked like a charm, sir.'

'What worked like a charm?'

'I pretended to shoot Cope dead for not telling me where the children were. I put a blank in the gun and fitted Cope up with an exploding blood capsule. I got Formosa and Cope to sit side by side then I asked Cope to tell me where the children were, he said he didn't know, so I pretended to shoot him dead. I pulled the trigger quite casually, as though I was a psychopath who didn't care a toss about killing people. Cope fell backwards, chair and all, with blood all over his shirt. It was very realistic, sir. Then I turned the gun on Formosa and told him, quite casually, that I'd shoot him dead as well if he didn't tell me where the kids were – which of course he did.'

'Good God, man! And you want me to put this to the CPS do you? The first question they'll ask is where did you get the gun?'

'I acquired it from a contact.'

'Does the contact have a name?'

'Yes, but for me to betray their identity would lose me a lot of valuable information in the long run – that's if I were to get my job back.'

'Is that so?'

'Well, it might be to my advantage to point out to the CPS that DI Cope, the officer leading the investigation, was corrupt and that I was aware of this and had made my suspicions known to my colleagues, but none of them believed me.'

'And that includes me,' grunted Ibbotson.

'I don't know what to say about that, sir. The truth is that the Strathmores were having to rely on an officer in Formosa's pay to get their children back. Had I not intervened, the children would have been killed whether or not the money was paid. I think the CPS need to be told that, sir.'

Ibbotson sighed. 'That will no doubt damage me, but you're quite right. Better that it comes direct from me than from anyone else. They'll be told about your suspicions, and the fact that you were ignored.'

'Thank you, sir. Along with my video recording of Formosa telling me exactly where the children were, plus many other things, including him admitting that he's burnt a lot of bodies in his furnace. He also exonerates me from beating my wife. That was all Cope's doing.'

'And *did* you have enough evidence to send Cope down?'

'Not really, sir. I made a few educated guesses when I discussed things with him, but I seem to have hit enough nerves for him to go along with me.'

'You appear to have a wonderful knack with the educated guess, Mr Black.'

'I think by now you have enough against him to send him down.'

'Is that what you think? Did you tell Cope I was as bent as him? That I was in Formosa's pay as well?'

'I just said that to throw him, sir – to make him believe he wasn't indispensable to Formosa.'

'And he believed you?'

'He did, sir.'

'The bastard!'

'That's what I thought, sir.'

'According to him,' said Ibbotson, 'you told him that you could get him off with no more than dismissal from the force, loss of pension and no prison time if he cooperated with you. And you told him you were employed as an undercover man by the West Yorkshire Police, which was why you could make such an offer.'

'Is that what he said I said, sir? Well, I do tend to ramble on a bit when I'm being creative. But a man would have to be really gullible to believe such a rubbish.'

'Or really desperate.'

'True, but I needed him to be really desperate – and there's no one more desperate than a copper facing long prison time. Lying to him was the only way I could get to those children. Let's face it, sir, Cope had this nick believing all sorts of terrible lies about me.'

'Well, it strikes me, Black, that you've beaten Cope at his own game. The CPS think that if they get a conviction he'll get life with a ten year tariff at least.'

'*If* they get a conviction, sir? I thought there'd be no *if* about it.'

'The *if* is down to your unconventional methods of extracting evidence.'

'I was concentrating on getting the kids free, sir, using any method I could.'

'I know that, but a top brief might well spot a loophole.'

'Can the CPS spot a loophole?'

'They're a bit non-committal at the moment.'

'What about Formosa?' asked Sep.

'Do you have one of these iPhone things on which you can show me this video?'

'I do, sir.'

Sep took out his iPhone and played the superintendent a video of his interview with Formosa, complete with the fake shooting of Cope, and Formosa telling him exactly where the children were.

'Is there any reason why this might not be allowed in court, sir?'

'I don't know. The judge would have to be swayed by the overall weight of evidence against Formosa.'

'Good God, sir! How much evidence do they need? Oh, I've got a memory stick with details of Formosa's property portfolio.'

'How did you obtain this?'

'I was given it by Derek Manson who handles all Formosa's property. It would be interesting to have Formosa tell us where he got the money from to buy it all, and were they bought without the sellers being put under duress, such as what happened to Peter Strathmore.'

'And Manson just gave you this, did he? Not under any duress or subterfuge?'

'Subterfuge, sir?'

'Yes. Did he think you were a police officer?'

'Er, yes, sir.'

'The defence counsel will crucify you when you tell him that. What we need is evidence that doesn't involve Formosa being threatened with an illegal firearm by a man kicked off the force for killing a member of parliament and then impersonating a policeman to obtain a property portfolio. Their defence will have a field day with that.'

'I didn't kill Johnstone, sir. His death was not my fault.'

'So, when you're in the witness box and you're asked why

you left the force so suddenly, you'll tell them you were kicked off the force for something that wasn't your fault.'

'Of course I will – it's the truth.'

'Cope will have given them his version of the truth, which they'll twist beyond recognition. When their barrister's finished with you the jury will be wondering why *you're* not up for murder.'

'But it'll be out in the open why Johnstone was arrested that night.'

'Will it really? How come?'

'There was a certain amount of publicity in the papers about me being responsible for his death. I expect Cope gave them that.'

'I expect he might have.'

'Well, I was approached by a reporter called Suzanne Hogan of *The Mail*, for my side of the kidnapping story.'

'Yes, I've read all about your heroics. The story did the police no favours, I might add.'

'That was all her doing, sir. I just gave her the facts, she put her own interpretation on it.'

'I know, it's what reporters do. So, what has this to do with Johnstone?'

'Well she knew about me being involved in his death and she asked me for a statement giving my side of that story.'

'I do hope you didn't give her one.'

'I didn't sir. All I told her was that he died in custody.'

'Did you tell her *why* he was in custody?'

'Of course not, but she does have the names and addresses of many of Johnstone's victims.'

'Oh hell! And where would she have got those from?'

'Difficult to say, sir. Where these reporters get their information from is a mystery to me.'

'Is it really? Would she tell us if we asked her?'

'I hope not, sir.'

'Yes, so do I. Still, if the stories don't come from us I don't see that we have anything to worry about – but I'm not sure what good it will do you in court.'

'Why's that?'

'Because him being a paedophile actually makes it worse for you. It gives you a motive for wanting to kill him, the same as you have a motive for setting Formosa up. It's a big chink in our armour. We're up against a high-power defence team here. A top barrister would come at us with all guns blazing. The whole case is on a knife edge. It could go either way. What we needed was something else to sway things in our favour.'

'Well, at least we got the kids back,' said Sep.

'*You* got the kids back,' said Ibbotson, 'and you got all the glory. The police didn't come out of that part of things too well.'

'I don't feel very glorious.'

'As it happens,' said Ibbotson, 'I think we have that something else.'

The superintendent opened a drawer in his desk and took out a plastic evidence bag, inside which was what looked like a sheet of notepaper, which he pushed across to Sep.

'Don't open it. I don't want it contaminating. It's a note that was found on a body of a man discovered under a bridge in Adel Woods. I have a transcript of what it says. He took out another sheet of paper and gave it to Sep:

My name is Gilberto Battaglia, I am from Florence in Italy and I am a diamond dealer and a thief. If my dead body is found, I will have been killed by a man who is by the name of Vincent Formosa who lived in London in England but now lives in Leeds in England. He has an associate in the Leeds police called Detective Inspector Cope who also worked for Formosa when he was detective in London. Cope is the man who always gives me my instructions when I work for Formosa. I was part of the team who did the robbery at the Antwerp Diamond centre in 2003. My share was three million euros worth of diamonds. I have been selling these to Formosa over the years and I am about to sell him the last half a million euros worth but I feel my life is in danger because after this I will have nothing left to sell him and I will be of no further use to him. I am also suspicious because he has offered me a much higher price for these diamonds than he did for the others, which I think means I will not be receiving anything as I will be dead. If you know of Formosa, you will know he is a ruthless man who disposes of people who are of no further use to him. I expect he will take the diamonds and have me killed, but no matter, I am dying

anyway. It is my wish that the man who had me murdered
should be caught and punished.
    Gilberto Battaglia

'Bloody hell!' said Sep.

'Bloody hell indeed,' said Ibbotson. 'Back then the Antwerp
Diamond Centre robbery was the biggest heist ever – somewhere
between twenty and a hundred million dollars.'

'Don't they know exactly?'

Ibbotson gave a dry laugh. 'No, they don't. The people who
owned the security boxes were a bit cagey as to how much they
had in there. The people behind the robbery were connected to
the Sicilian Mafia and all but one were caught. The loot was
never found and I'm guessing our friend Gilberto was the one
who escaped scot-free.'

'Lucky for us he did. If he was connected to the mafia I doubt
if he held Formosa in too much esteem.'

'Obviously not if his dying act was to grass him up to the
police. We certainly do know what Formosa does to people who
are of no further use to him. Our people discovered the whereabouts of all of Formosa's offices in Leeds and found a bag of
diamonds in a safe in one of them. They've been valued at around
half a million euros and have been checked and confirmed as
coming from the Antwerp robbery. So, that's Mr Formosa signed,
sealed and delivered.'

'I wonder what he meant by *I am dying anyway?*'

'The post-mortem showed him to be a man with terminal pancre-
atic cancer,' said Ibbotson. 'A bullet to the brain's an easy way to
die. It saved him months of pain. We think it was a suicide note.'

'When was this body found?'

'Only a few days ago. A couple of kids with a dog found him,
although I believe it was the dog that sniffed him out. So many
people walk their dogs in those woods it's a wonder he wasn't
found weeks ago. The note was in one of his boots.'

'How long has he been dead?'

'About three or four months, apparently.'

'So, I've been taking God knows how many risks trying to
nail Cope and all the time this body was lying under a bridge,
just waiting to nail him for me.'

'Not necessarily. This letter alone wouldn't have convicted him, but it is the final nail in Formosa's coffin and, according to the CPS, along with all the other stuff, this letter really firms up the case against Cope. It'll wipe out any doubts the jury might have about the corrupt bastard.'

'I hope so.'

'Sep, Cope hasn't a prayer of getting off,' said Ibbotson, 'although he obviously thinks he has, judging from the money he's spending on a top criminal defence team he's hired from one of the Inns of Court in London. They've made him change his mind about giving Queen's Evidence and they got him out on bail – but that's as much as they'll do for him.'

'Who's doing the investigating?'

'That side of things is being investigated by the Met and the Belgian police . . . Oh, and Formosa's blown the whistle bigtime on Cope to the Met's corruption team. He's implicated in two capital charges, both of them conspiracies to commit murder down in London as well as the stuff he's done up here.' Ibbotson held up a warning finger and added, 'and, no . . . you cannot be the one to tell him about the letter.'

'So he doesn't know yet?'

'No, I'm going in to see him today with a view to tying up some loose ends with his charges up here. He'll have his brief with him.'

'And will you be telling him about the letter and the Met's charges?'

'Erm, yes. I'll be taking details of the additional charges for his solicitor to peruse.'

'And who will you be taking with you?'

Ibbotson stared at Sep with narrowed eyes as Sep added: 'If I was reinstated, it could be me.'

'Who says you're going to be reinstated?'

'Fair enough. Oh, my wife got herself tangled up with Cope as well, sir. He had her fooled, the same as he fooled a lot of people here, sir.'

'Including me, I suppose? Done up like a kipper I think you said.'

'I was indeed, sir, and I can't deny how great it is to prove you all wrong and get my life back.'

'If it's any consolation, I don't feel good about my part in all this. A lesser man than you would have sunk without trace. In view of this, is there any favour I might do for you?'

'There is, sir. Cope coerced my wife into swearing a false affidavit saying I assaulted her. I'd appreciate it if you could use your influence into not having her charged with perjury.'

'Is this because you're going back to her?'

'No, sir. It's because I promised my daughter I'd do what I can to keep her mother from going to jail. Losing her mother would damage my daughter, sir.'

'Well, I think Cope's done enough damage to children recently. I expect I can swing that.'

'And what about me being granted immunity from prosecution?'

'You might not need it. I thought it better to simply ask the CPS if they could see any value in prosecuting you under these circumstances – with the lives of two innocent children being at stake. You're officially off the hook.'

'Thank you, sir.'

'Well, is that it?'

'Sir?'

'I mean is there anything else you want me to do for you, now I'm in a good mood.'

'Reinstatement would be good.'

'I've already suggested to the CPS that you receive a severe reprimand and loss of promotion.'

'Loss of promotion to what, sir?'

'Loss of promotion to DCI. I recommended that if you come back, you come back at your old rank of detective inspector. I would normally have recommended that you come back as DCI to make up for the unfair hardship you have suffered.'

'Do you think that will work, sir?'

'It's already worked. Consider yourself severely reprimanded and fully reinstated.'

Sep was suddenly thinking back to the time when he was in his house with Phoebe and Cope – the man who had lied to make his daughter hate him; the man whose lies had turned the world against him and almost destroyed his career; the man who had threatened to arrest him; the man who Sep had promised to catch up with, and now he had, but Cope really needed to know it, and there was only one way.

'Now that I'm a copper again, sir, I will need a look at Cope's additional charges if I'm to break the bad news to him.'

'Sep, you've been a copper again for less than a minute and you're telling me what to do.'

'I imagine he'll be going down for life without parole and it'll have more impact coming from me.'

'Impact?'

'Yes, sir. These villains need a bit of impact to make them see the error of their ways.'

'You really are a cheeky sod, Sep!'

'It's what gets me through, sir.'

'Gets you through? Since you've been free of the bonds of normal police procedure you've managed to break up two major criminal gangs and the CPS are more than aware of this. I was extremely tempted to put in a request to the Home Office to employ you as a freelance criminal investigator.'

'Will I be given licence to kill, sir?'

'Don't push it . . . Detective Inspector Black.'

'But I *will* be the one to give Cope the bad news?'

'Jesus, Sep! I'll get you the bloody charge sheets.'

ghtning Source UK Ltd.
ton Keynes UK
OW05f1101200617
713UK00002B/60/P